Mars...with Venus Rising

Hope Toler Dougherty

Mars...with Venus Rising

Cover Art by *Nicola Martinez*

White Rose Publishing, a division of Pelican Ventures, LLC
www.pelicanbookgroup.com PO Box 1738 *Aztec, NM * 87410

White Rose Publishing Circle and Rosebud logo is a trademark of Pelican Ventures, LLC

Publishing History
First White Rose Edition, 2015
Paperback Edition ISBN 978-1-61116-498-5
Electronic Edition ISBN 978-1-61116-497-8
Published in the United States of America

Dedication
For my parents, Bobby and Auline Toler, who always believed.

Acknowledgments

Kevin—Thank you for your constant love, support, and encouragement. I almost always dig in my heels and kick and cry when you push me out of my safe, cozy box, but it usually results in a good thing—like this writing journey.

Anna, Hattie, Lane, and Quinn—I am blessed beyond measure to be your mother. Thank you for all your prayers for "Mom's book." Don't forget to dream big.

Lisa Carter—Thank you for your friendship, advice, encouragement, and prayers. I'm so glad I get to be your roomie at writing conferences and chat over lunch once a month. This ride is wild and way more fun with you.

Rachel Stone, Suzanne Mitchell, Emily Willard—Thank you for your faithful prayers and for not laughing when I finally admitted, "I'm writing a book."

Bible Study Fellowship ladies—You prayed for me every time I submitted an A.S.K. for my writing journey. You asked enthusiastic questions about my writing even when I wasn't forthcoming. You are always a blessing to me. Thank you.

Ken Starling—Thank you for answering all my flying questions and for mentioning Cirrus Aircraft, the plane with a parachute.

Marilyn Harding—Thank you for answering all my questions about professional counseling. Your input helped me understand Penn better and fleshed out Abby's character, too.

Ann Weaver—Thank you for sharing the story of the buried heavy equipment. Truth is, indeed, stranger than fiction.

The BRMCWC and ACFW writing fellowship—Thank you for offering the tools and friendships to make this writing dream possible.

Jim Hart—Thank you for believing in me and representing me. Thank you for believing in this story and for placing it.

Nicola Martinez and everyone at Pelican Book Group—Thank you for taking a chance on a new author.

Finally, God, thank You for giving me this desire of my heart.

1

"Come on, Peri. You're making me late. Again."

Penn Davenport wiggled the carrot in front of the escape artist horse and squeezed the halter she'd hidden behind her back.

The gray roan stretched his long neck toward the orange prize and sniffed. As tame as an old lap dog, Peri had a mind of his own. When he decided to visit the neighboring houses, he worried the lock on his corral gate until it popped and he trotted into freedom.

Fortunately, most of her neighbors on Oakland Street loved Peri, welcomed his visits and his nosey poking under their shelters or garages. Unfortunately, they encouraged his visits with sugar cubes and hugs.

If he didn't want to return home yet, she'd never be able to slide the halter over his head. She glanced at her watch. Twelve minutes until the planning meeting for the Mars Area Apple Fest began. If this crazy horse cooperated, she might have a chance to settle into a chair before the minutes were read.

"Here we go, darling. Take a bite of this delicious carrot. Come on. I know you want it." *Please, God, help me slip this halter on and get Peri back home. You know how I hate walking in late to meetings.*

Peri backed up a step, and Penn's hope for an easy capture melted like chocolate on the floor board of a locked up car in mid-July. She gritted her teeth.

Instead of retreating farther away from her,

however, the horse shook its head and stepped toward her again. His lips reached for the carrot and grabbed the orange tip. Success.

Maybe.

Peri opened his mouth, nibbled, and then crunched half the carrot with his teeth.

Penn slipped the halter over his head and captured her sociable, lovable, independent horse. She closed her eyes and nuzzled his warm neck, breathing in his musky smell. A familiar peace settled over her. Scenes from her childhood when she sought solace from this sweet creature flooded her mind. *Thank you, God. For today and for all those other times, too.*

She straightened and glided her hand down his velvety nose. "Here we go, silly boy. Time to get home." She tied the lead line to the bumper of her vintage Volkswagen and crept back to her house with Peri clomping behind her.

~*~

Careening into the Town Hall parking lot, Penn shifted down to second gear and slid to a stop beside a shiny, black motorcycle. Who in the world drove that thing? Nobody on the Apple Fest committee, for sure, but the Town Hall closed for business at five o'clock.

She gathered her Apple Fest folders from the passenger seat, slung her purse over her shoulder, and nudged the car door closed with her hip. Hugging the files to her chest, she raced up the sidewalk, grabbed the door handle, and stopped. She drew in a calming breath and said a quick prayer to find a seat without calling attention to her lateness.

As she pulled on the handle, a bell sounded,

usually announcing Town Hall customers. Today, it announced her as a late-comer to the meeting. Great. So much for arriving unnoticed. Another unanswered prayer.

Every head turned toward her as she entered the conference room and spied an empty swivel chair. Having spent her entire life in Mars, she knew all the eyes staring at her. All of them, except two black-as-night ones fringed with long, black eyelashes. Black eyes, black hair, black t-shirt. Safe bet he was the owner of the black motorcycle. Safe bet he was wearing black jeans and black shoes—or wait. Black boots, too. How original.

She slunk into the open seat. Whoa. Where did this foul mood come from? From chasing that crazy horse and walking in here late, that's where.

She laid the files on the table, willing those eyes to let her settle in peace.

Be positive. Try for a better attitude. Be glad that someone new is willing to participate. "Sorry I'm late." She mumbled her lame apology to no one in particular.

What is a guy dressed like that doing on a committee meeting for an apple festival anyway? Who strong-armed him into joining this group of retirees and stay-at-home moms?

Three years ago when she'd graduated from Duquesne University with a brand new accounting degree, her aunts had cajoled, wheedled, pleaded, and produced shimmering teardrops until she'd capitulated and signed on as the festival's treasurer.

She knew something about being strong-armed...or maybe guilted into serving described her situation better. She loved her aunts so much, she'd agreed, and would have without all the drama, even though the thought of planning Apple Fest made her eyelids droop.

"Yoo-hoo? Penny?" Clara Hough rapped her knuckles on the rectangular conference table.

Penn pulled herself back to the meeting and the interested stares from the committee members. She focused on the celery-colored wall behind Clara's head, and for the second time in thirty minutes she ground her molars. "It's Penn." She twisted the lapis ring on the third finger of her right hand.

Jacob Doran, a Korean War veteran slid his blue pen toward the stack of folders. She smiled at him, shook her head, and slid it back to his notepad.

"Hon, I thought you'd be able to be on time now softball season's over." Clara pursed her lips. "We've just finished introducing ourselves while we waited for the treasurer's report. You can chat with John Townsend," she waved a hand toward the black t-shirt and beamed, "our newest member, after the meeting. Now we need that report, Penny."

"Penn," she insisted again.

Clara ignored her again.

After dropping the Y from her name during her senior year of high school, she was Penn, not Penny. Most people abided by the change, but her aunts slipped up occasionally. She didn't mind her aunts calling her by that nickname, but she suspected that Clara used "Penny" today just to irritate her.

Once more, the pen rolled over to her place. Before she pushed it back, she caught sight of a twitch on Mr. Dressed-in-black's mouth. His eyes flickered away from her, but he was laughing. At her.

Her humiliation was complete. Chastised for being late, called by her childhood name, not once but twice, and laughed at and dismissed by the new guy. She'd been dismissed by cute guys ever since high school. Ten years ago, she'd nurse her hurt by riding Peri or retreating into books.

Instead of wallowing in her discomfort today, she straightened her spine and leaned over the cherry veneer table with her hand extended toward Mr. All-black. "I'm Penn Davenport." She willed him to look at her.

He shifted his gaze to her and waited a couple of beats before grabbing her hand. One corner of his mouth tipped up. "John Townsend. Pleased to meet you." He inclined his head, released his hold, and turned his attention back to Clara.

Another dismissal. Fine.

Clara rapped her knuckles on the table again. "Penny. The treasurer's report, please."

~*~

John grabbed his helmet and made his way toward the parking lot. A few steps ahead of him, the prickly young lady with the funny name headed in the same direction, grumbling under her breath. He felt bad for enjoying her discomfort when she'd come in late. He lengthened his stride to catch up with her.

She tugged on the door latch to a vintage Volkswagen, but it refused to move. She jiggled the handle and tapped the door with the butt of her hand. "Come on, Gretchen. Let me in."

He rubbed his jaw to cover up another smile. "Need a hand?"

Jumping, she frowned at him.

"Sorry. Didn't mean to scare you." He nodded to

the car. "Interesting ride."

Penn nodded to the motorcycle. "Safer than yours."

He grinned. "Depends on who's driving, don't you think?" He kicked the tire. "What year is it?"

"1977."

"Cool." He trailed a finger along the curved back. "Nice color."

"It's original. Called Barrier Blue."

"So teens still get to drive these old cars, huh?

Her mouth dropped open, and she blinked. "I don't know. I'll poll my students and get back with you on that."

John winced. "Ooh, sorry." *Nice. Way to win friends and influence committee members. Open mouth. Insert boot.* "I thought when Clara mentioned something about softball being over she meant...never mind. Anyway, of course, now that I look at you, you look much older than a teenager. I mean..." *Wonderful. Where's a muzzle when I need one?*

Loose brown curls framed a heart-shaped face and emphasized big, brown eyes. She did look young and a little vulnerable and a tad frustrated right now. She bumped the door with her hip and jiggled the handle again. She sagged against the stubborn door and closed her eyes. Her jaw worked.

Was she gritting her teeth?

Resignation flooded her face. She blew a loose curl away from her eyes and stuck out her hand. "I have to get going. It's good to have you on the committee. We need some fresh ideas." Walking around the car, she waved a half-hearted goodbye, then opened the passenger side door, and crawled over the gear shift to the driver's seat.

~*~

Penn steeled herself for the inevitable. Sure enough, before she turned the key, rich deep laughter spilled through the rolled-up windows. His laughs said, "Life is fun. Enjoy it." Any other time she could have appreciated the sound. It brought back rusty images of her first childhood.

Yes, any other time she might have lingered in that warm sound, but his laughter added one more cringe-worthy moment to today's list of embarrassments. She backed out of the parking space.

"Come on, Gretchen," she squeezed the steering wheel, refusing to glance in John's direction again. "Let's go home."

~*~

John watched her break lights blink off as she merged into the street and wanted to kick himself for laughing at her. He'd make it up to her somehow. This Penn person intrigued him. Interesting name. Interesting car. Cute face. Maybe volunteering with the apple festival would garner more than good feelings about helping his new community. A new friend would be a positive, but he'd have to overcome her initial impression of him first.

Did he actually tell her she looked old? He shook his head. *Way to be suave and debonair, man.* Not that he ever felt smooth around the opposite sex. Especially when innocent gestures could be misinterpreted for more than he intended. He shuddered and pushed an awkward memory out of his mind.

He slung his leg over the bike and tugged on his helmet. Yeah, he'd work on an apology, and maybe next time he'd speak without maneuvering words around a boot in his mouth.

2

The homey smells of cinnamon and chocolate wafted from the kitchen as Penn entered the family room. "Hello," she called out over the twangy sounds of blue grass music playing on the stereo. "I'm home." She dropped her purse and folders onto the couch and reached her hands above her head. Leaning to the left, then to the right, she threw herself into a full-body stretch.

Giggles sounded through the hallway. "So, how was the meeting?" Two silver heads popped, one on top of the other, beside the door jam.

"Did you meet the new member?"

"Is he handsome?"

"Is he tall?"

"Did you have a chance to talk with him?"

Their questions tumbled together and mingled with giggles. She watched her aunts sashay into the room with clasped hands and grins stretched as wide as their cheeks allowed.

Realization tiptoed across her brain and narrowed her eyes. "No wonder you were so anxious for me to get to that meeting." Penn rolled her eyes at her aunts' wide-eyed, couldn't-be-me-you're-talking-about stares. "Don't act like you two don't know what I mean. You met me at the end of the driveway, untied Peri from the bumper, and shooed me off so I wouldn't be late — which I was, by the way."

Jancie ignored Penn's chastising. "Periwinkle's such a good horse."

"Yes, he is. Yes, he is." Winnie normally agreed with her older sister except when they discussed books.

The afternoon's stress crept up her spine and clinched her shoulders. She rolled her neck. "For you, maybe. You don't have to traipse all over creation to round him up."

"You don't have to either. He always comes home when he's finished visiting." Jancie moved behind Penn and massaged her shoulders.

"He certainly does." Winnie stepped closer and stroked Penn's arm.

"The town lets us keep him because we promised to keep him corralled. Thank goodness, the mayor is sweet on you and gives us some slack." She closed her eyes and concentrated on Jancie's fingers kneading a path up her neck.

"Charles is a good man, and we're good friends." Penn heard the smile in her aunt's voice. "But that's enough about me." Jancie patted Penn's back and faced her again. "Why are you in such a bad mood? Didn't you get to meet our newest Martian?" Jancie wiggled her eyebrows.

Penn groaned. Why couldn't they live in Pittsburgh and be Pittsburghers or Philadelphia and be Philadelphians? Philadelphers? Philadelphi-ites? No matter. They lived in Mars, so they were called Martians.

"Tell us, Penny. Did you meet him? Is he handsome? Is he tall?" Excitement twinkled in Winnie's blue eyes.

Penn grimaced. She hated to extinguish that light.

"We've been down this road before."

Jancie crossed her arms and slanted her head. "We started down it, but we didn't finish our trip."

"Hilarious, Aunt Jancie." Penn combed her fingers through her hair and massaged the back of her neck. "The trip isn't very interesting."

"We'll be the judge. Spill, Penny. Oops. I mean Penn."

Penn sighed. She'd have to discuss her meeting with the new Martian. Her aunts' determination and the cinnamon-chocolaty scent had loosened her resolve to keep the meeting to herself. Surrender waited around the corner.

"First, tell me what smells so good?" As if she didn't know.

Both aunts cried in unison, "Celebration cookies!" Flanking her like armed guards, they led her toward the kitchen.

~*~

Penn dunked her warm cookie into the milk. Celebration cookies, designated for Christmas, first hyacinth of spring, last day of school, signaled high hopes for her love life.

Too bad they'd be disappointed, just like all the other times since prom when they'd raised their hopes for a beau.

Jancie dragged the blue willow ware plate toward Winnie and folded her hands on the table. "We've waited long enough, sweetie pie. Swallow that cookie and tell us the news."

Penn sipped the milk. "There is no news. Yes, John Townsend attended the meeting. Yes, I met him, but don't get any ideas about a courtship. He's not my type, and I'm certainly not his." She reached for another cookie and tried to delete the image of herself crawling over the stick shift from her mind.

"What do you mean 'you're not his type'? Anybody would be lucky to have you on his arm." Winnie patted the top of her hand. "You're beautiful, kind, smart, funny—"

"Thank you for those endorsements, but I can name just as many reasons he isn't interested." She popped up her index finger. "One, he thought I was a teenager." She added her middle finger. "Two, he thought I looked too old to be a teenager."

Winnie, ever the compassionate one, tsked tsked Penn's stubbornness. "Maybe you flustered him."

Janice frowned. "Maybe you caught him off guard or intimidated him."

"Tall, dark, and dangerous men don't get intimidated by short, goofy women."

"Oooh, sounds interesting." Winnie grinned and clapped. "I knew it. Marge Baumgartner said he was a looker. She saw him coming out of the real estate office down town a few weeks ago. She said she heard he bought that brown house over on Clay Avenue. She said—"

"Winnie, hush. Take a breath. That's gossip." Jancie turned her attention back to Penn. "What do you mean 'dangerous'?"

"He rides a motorcycle."

Jancie lowered her chin. "That doesn't necessarily mean…" She shook her head. "Honey, don't talk down about yourself. You have a fine career; you help out with the youth group at church; you're involved with your community—"

She rolled her eyes. "Mmm, thanks. I'm a great person. Hey, why am I the only one eating cookies?" Penn pushed the plate away from her.

"I'm watching my girlish figure." Winnie lifted her chin and pushed back her shoulders. Though she carried about thirty pounds over her ideal weight, she gave good, soft hugs.

"What she means is, we ate our share while we baked. Now, back to the story." Jancie never watched what she ate, but her tall frame remained as slim as it had been during her college days.

"Uh huh. Anyway, here's reason three he's not interested in me. He laughed at me." Penn pushed cookie crumbs into a pile in the middle of her napkin.

"He laughed at you? Well, personally, I think humor is the grease that keeps a marriage well-oiled. Laughter is a good thing, Penn." Jancie should know. She'd married—for the first time—at forty, a man fifteen years her senior and three inches shorter.

From the stories Penn had heard at family reunions, the two had made a striking couple for five years hosting great themed parties until he dropped dead of a stroke. The funeral had been a mix of testimonials about strong faith in God and his over-the-top pranks on loved ones.

Winnie's eyebrows shot toward her gray bangs. "Maybe you misconstrued the situation, dear. Maybe he was laughing *with* you not *at* you."

"Um. No. We finished our conversation. I grabbed the handle. The door jammed. Phooey on Gretchen, by the way, and I had to crawl in from the passenger side." Penn grimaced remembering the less-than-graceful moment.

"She wouldn't let you in?" Winnie's eyes shined

with optimism. "See, you were supposed to stay and talk."

"We had nothing else to say. So, listen up." Penn leaned toward her aunts, narrowed what she hoped were steely eyes. "Do not keep thinking about matchmaking, OK? I'm glad he's on the committee. Heaven knows we need some new blood, but we're committee members. That's it. Move on to another project, all right?" She pressed a fingertip against the pile of crumbs and licked them off.

"We love you, honey." Winnie's tone camped out just this side of whining.

She flattened her lips and used her best no-nonsense teacher voice. "I mean it. File this plan under 'Denied'."

Jancie reared back in her chair, folding her arms. "I want to meet this man before I make any broad promises. I will promise I won't embarrass you, though. How's that?"

Penn groaned, broke another cookie in two, and crunched on the cinnamon delight.

~*~

Penn followed her aunts into the choir loft and scanned the congregation. She enjoyed the peaceful feeling that settled on her every time she participated in the choir. Today she and her aunts had the special music for the call to worship. She loved singing with her aunts. They'd taught her harmony years ago, and she liked sharing their talent with the church that had always rallied around her tiny family.

After the Welcome and Announcements, Penn, Winnie, and Jancie stood with music books in hand,

and Penn searched the crowd again for the faces she knew and loved. A familiar pair of black eyes met her gaze, and John smiled at her. Her stomach seized.

She missed the opening phrase of the song, clutched her lapis ring and squeezed against the swirls of the scrollwork with her thumb.

Winnie glanced at her as she joined the aunts by the end of the first measure.

Training her vision on the group of ushers in the narthex, she concentrated on the rise and fall of her line of harmony.

What was he doing here?

In the several weeks since she'd met him, she'd never seen him in church. Why start today and make her ruin the beginning of the song? She'd been in such a happy mood this morning.

The aunts had memorized this favorite song years ago. She didn't need the music to sing her part either, but she forced her gaze back to the folder, following the black dots' trek across the staff lines.

Thankfully, her efforts in concentration resulted in a pretty good rendition of their special song. Besides the hiccup at the beginning, which still irritated her, she thought their contribution to the worship service enhanced rather than detracted from it.

As the choir joined the congregation for the sermon, her traitorous eyes spied John.

His head was bent over his bulletin. Not looking at her.

"See," she wanted to whisper to her aunts. "He's not interested."

She settled into a pew wanting to relish being right. Instead, a familiar ache, a heavy longing swelled and choked her happy attitude. She shifted on the cushion. What was wrong with her? She didn't want him to be interested. Not really.

~*~

John folded the bulletin and slipped it inside his Bible as he stood to leave the sanctuary. He'd enjoyed the service, especially the surprise from Penn. What a beautiful voice.

The tone of her voice had blended like perfectly tuned instruments with the other ladies. After the tentative start, a patch or two of goose bumps had broken out on his arms at a couple of places in the song. He stepped out into the sluggish aisle and glanced toward the front door.

People pumped the pastor's arm and patted him on the back. Everybody wanted to speak to the man.

Seeing her here with a prominent role in the service shocked him, for sure. She hadn't exactly given off any church vibes at their first meeting. Prickly, that'd been his first thought. Prickly and cute.

Hold up.

Cute, yes, but caution around cute females was his agenda these days. After the "breakup" with Stephanie. He hadn't known they were "dating." He suppressed a shudder as he remembered her tears and angry words when he'd told her he was moving to Pennsylvania. Had he been unconscious during their time together? He'd thought they were friends, good friends. When had she subscribed to *Weddings Today*?

Stephanie had been fun, just like all his friends in the apartment complex. He'd enjoyed spending time with them, but he'd thought of them as friends. Just friends.

Penn, however, intrigued him. She'd captured his attention from the time she entered the meeting the other day.

Maybe it was her good heart, the one that led her to the apple committee. Maybe it was her spunky outer shell that kept him at arm's length. Or her big, brown eyes that held a touch of humor and compassion in their depths. Maybe he just needed a friend.

No, it was more than that. Penn Davenport seemed special, and John wanted to get to know her better. As friends? For sure. As something more? Maybe.

If she'd let him.

He advanced as a group merged into the center aisle and almost crushed the pointy toe of a member of Penn's trio. "Excuse me. So sorry. I didn't get your foot, did I?"

Clear blue eyes sparkled up at him. "No harm, no foul. No worries." Then she gasped. "Oh, are you our newest Martian? Penn's told us all about you."

John glanced at Penn. If looks could kill. The red stains creeping into her cheeks heightened her cuteness. "Aunt Winnie, I—"

"I hope all good things." John grinned and noticed a movement in Penn's cheek, just like at the meeting the other day.

"John, please let me introduce my aunts to you. Aunt Winnie, Aunt Jancie, this is John Townsend, the newest member of the Apple Fest Committee."

"Happy to meet you, John." Aunt Jancie inched closer to the pastor and turned back to John. "We're glad you worshiped with us today."

"Thank you. I enjoyed your special music. You're very talented." He stole a quick peek at Penn whose mouth had leveled into a foreboding straight line.

Reaching the pastor, they couldn't continue with the small talk. When they stepped onto the front porch, John turned to Penn. "Did you get Clara's text?"

"What text?"

"Looks like you and I are on the entertainment committee."

Did she have to pop her eyes and drop her mouth so wide?

The assignment didn't thrill him either. He'd hoped to work on the construction or vendor committee or even the parking committee on the day of the event if such a committee existed. What did he know about entertainment? His idea of fun included a movie and popcorn—at home, or maybe whitewater rafting, or bungee jumping, or—

"I'm supposed to be the budget committee. I keep the books. Committee people come to me for financial requests. I don't work on other committees. Clara knows that." Penn's brow bunched up under soft-looking curls as she dug in her purse. She retrieved her cellphone and turned it on.

"Sorry. Didn't mean to bring bad news. Maybe it's just a misunderstanding."

"Now wait a minute. The entertainment committee sounds like fun. Winnie and I can give you lots of ideas." The taller woman, Jancie, grinned and cut her gaze toward her sister.

Winnie winked and nodded.

Breathing deeply, Penn closed her eyes while she waited for the phone to come to life. "I apologize, too. It's just—I'm not...I mean—I don't—"

"Hey. Me either—I think." He tunneled his fingers through his hair and shrugged. "But we're not the only ones in the group. Two or three more drew the short stick, too." John chuckled, hoping for a similar response from Penn.

She read from her palm. "Missy Parker, Al Martin, and Linda Schroeder. Is Missy back from Bucknell already?"

Winnie adjusted her Bible and her purse. "Her grandmother told me they expect her any day now."

"Al won't be much help. Isn't his wife due sometime this summer? Maybe Linda can lead the charge." She huffed out a sigh.

Jancie raised her hands as if to stop traffic. "I know. Why don't we continue this conversation over lunch? John, we'd love to have you join us." She smiled and nudged Winnie.

"That's a great idea." Winnie giggled.

Ignoring Penn's wide eyes and open mouth, John shook his head. "Thank you ladies so much, but I'm meeting someone. In fact, I need to get going. Nice to meet you both." He glanced at Penn. "See you at the meeting, I guess."

She nodded, but she didn't smile.

No warm and fuzzies for the newcomer, huh?

Maybe she was preoccupied with the committee news. Maybe she didn't need a new friend.

She moved away and helped her aunts into a car. Homesickness churned his insides, and he stuck his hands in his pockets.

"Till the next meeting, Miss Davenport."

3

Penn coasted into the parking lot of the Town Hall and noticed John, straddling his motorcycle and removing his helmet. He wore a faded crimson golf shirt and khaki shorts. What happened to his all-black look?

He limped toward her.

She zipped her eyes from his feet back to his face.

He caught her gaze and shrugged. "I got a limp."

She nodded and tried not to blush. So. He was a straight shooter. A point in his favor. "Motorcycle accident?"

He smirked. "Funny." Then he shook his head. "We had a little problem when I was born." He stretched his arms above his head and yawned. "Man. I'm tired. Just got back into town."

"You travel with work?"

"Yeah. I—"

"Hey, you two. I'm so excited about this group. Aren't you?" Linda Schroeder slid out of her minivan with ten or twelve file folders threatening to tumble out of her arms.

John lunged toward her and grabbed a handful just as they slipped over the top.

Linda racked up committee spots like Penn's students collected hall passes. She served on two PTAs in two different schools, volunteered for Meals on Wheels, served on the Arts Council and library board, chaired the town improvement committee, and taught an exercise class once a week. In her spare time, she mothered four active children.

By the looks of those folders, she had ideas, lots of them, for entertainment. Penn smiled.

Linda would be the perfect chairperson for this committee. She rattled on, leading the way to the building. "I started jotting down ideas right after last year's festival. Bands to invite, dance troupes, and I think I even have contact information for a puppet theater group." Linda thumbed through the folders, perhaps searching for the puppet group. "They performed last year for the summer reading bash at the library. Did you come, Penn? Wonderful afternoon."

Perfect.

Penn sank into a chair, her heart as light as the gauzy scarf tied around Linda's neck.

With Linda in charge, being on this committee would be a snap. Maybe they wouldn't even need Penn. Maybe she could go back to her finance reports.

Linda paused for a breath, and Penn realized she waited for an answer.

"Ahh, no. I didn't make it. I thought the bash was for children in the reading program."

"That's true, but we offered the puppet performance to the whole of Mars." Linda spread the folders on the conference table. "Now, let's see. Who're we missing?"

Al Martin burst through the front door and entered the conference room. "Sorry I'm late. I caught a speeder right before I was supposed to clock off duty." He ran his fingers over his short cropped brown hair. "Whew. Long day."

John nodded and rubbed the back of his neck.

Linda grabbed a pen and wrote the date on her yellow pad. "We need to go ahead and start. We'll catch Missy up to speed when she gets here. The first thing we should do is elect a chairperson of this subcommittee. Do we—"

Penn lurched forward, plunked her palm on the table in front of Linda. "I nominate you."

"Second!" Both men spoke at once.

Linda's eyes shined. "Well, I'd be honored if that's what you want."

Penn offered a thumbs-up. "Definitely." She relaxed against the back of her chair. "You be the leader and tell us how to help."

Linda grinned. "Great. Right off the bat, I suggest we go to Hartwood Acres. Have you ever been to the free Sunday evening concerts over there? It's a great time. In fact," she scanned her day timer, "this Sunday there's an interesting local band opening for the headliner." She focused on Penn. "How much do we have in our budget?"

"Oh, um." Penn, caught daydreaming about nominating Linda, blinked herself back to the present. "I think this committee had a little less than a thousand dollars last year. Depends on what the township allocates for the whole festival. I doubt we'll get more, but I'll check." She gritted her teeth. Why didn't she remember to bring her budget folder? One more item John could add to his Ditzy Penn list. She shouldn't care what he thought, but looking incompetent rankled.

"Less than a thousand? Hmm. OK. We might have to ask for more. Hint. Hint." She batted her eyelashes at Penn. "Anyway, we'll probably need to meet every week for a while to get our agenda set. Now. About

Sunday. Do you want to meet at the park or get together beforehand?"

~*~

Sunday afternoon after the noon dishes were dried and put away, Penn slipped outside to visit with Peri. His leathery smell soothed her. She had three months to study for the certified public accounting exam. She should have already passed it, but she hadn't. She'd taken the exam twice and passed parts of it, but she needed to pass the whole thing if she ever made her dream of working in downtown Pittsburgh a reality.

She should be studying now, but she'd set up a study schedule with Sundays off because the aunts were adamant to leave Sundays free. A heaviness settled on her chest, and she knew she needed Peri time. Tugging the brush down his neck, she nuzzled close and stroked his nose. "Hey, boy. You're sweet."

Peri tossed his head and shuffled his hooves.

"Yes, you are. I just wish you'd stay in your pen like a regular horse. I'm glad you're not visiting today. I need some hugs." She sighed. "I don't want to go to Hartwood Acres. Can't I just stay here with you, buddy?"

"Penny! You have a phone call." Aunt Winnie rang the bell mounted on the back porch. "Penny?"

Penn rubbed her forehead against Peri's neck before placing the brush back on the shelf. She jogged to the house.

Aunt Winnie leaned out the back door. "It's Linda. She sounds frazzled."

Penn accepted the kitchen phone, frantic words streaming out of the ear piece.

"Said to the doctor, absolutely not. I cannot—"

An important sounding announcement blared in the background, overriding Linda's frustrated monologue. "Linda. Hello, Linda. This is Penn. What's up?"

"What's up? Is that you, Penn? My foot, that's what's up. It's up in the air. I'm in traction, if you can believe that, over here at Passavant. The doctor will not let me go, but I'm going to speak to someone—"

"You're in the hospital? But you're supposed to come to Hartwood tonight. We're—" Penn clamped her lips, remembering her manners a few seconds too late. "I mean. What happened? How are you?"

"My heel caught in my lavender broom skirt. Do you know the one I'm talking about? Why do I insist on still wearing skirts and dresses to church when everybody else has gone to pants and shorts and anything they can pick up off their floor? Anyway, I was running late for Sunday School this morning, trying to do too much, and my heel caught my hem. I fell right out of my van door. Sprained my wrist, too." She took a breath.

"Sooo, I guess Hartwood is out for tonight?" Penn crossed her fingers.

"Unfortunately, unless I can cut myself down from this trapeze thing they've got me tied to, I won't make it to the concert. You and John will have to carry the charge for the committee."

"John? And me?" Penn swallowed. "You mean Al and Missy, too, right?"

"Al is working a lot of overtime now so that he can take some time when the baby's born. You might see him, but he'll be on crowd control and parking. Missy—who knows? I've texted her but haven't heard back."

"But, Linda—"

"Penn, the pain medication is starting to wear off." She panted like a woman in labor. "You'll be fine. Just listen. See what you think. Talk to the band members."

"Talk to the band members?" Penn bit her lip to save her molars.

"Of course. You can't get everything off their website. Try to talk with them. Let them know a little about us. See if they have a charge rate for non-profits. You can do this. John will help. He's a good guy. Gotta go. The nurse is here with my drugs. Let me know how it goes. Bye."

Excellent news.

Not.

She hugged herself, hopping to quell her rolling stomach.

Penn hadn't wanted to go when she thought she'd be able to float with the group, listen to some live music, and nod along with whatever the other committee members decided. Now the committee had become John and herself. Two people didn't make a committee. Two people made a couple.

Awkward.

Hartwood Acres attracted families and couples like malls attracted pre-teen girls. So not happening.

Aunt Winnie's eyes danced behind her glasses. "So Linda's out of commission, huh?" She tapped her lips with her fingertips.

Aunt Jancie joined them in the kitchen. The beginnings of a smile hovered over the woman's mouth.

"And am I correct in assuming that Al and Missy won't be attending?" Winnie gave up hiding the bottom half of her face and revealed a full-fledged grin.

Penn closed her eyes, concentrating on relaxing her jaw. "You are. And when I think of a valid excuse, I won't be either."

Jancie gathered Penn into a one-armed hug and jiggled her shoulders. "You can't renege on your commitment. You can't leave John to do the work of the whole committee. That poor boy is new in town. He'd probably never find the concert way over there in Allison Park."

"I'm sure he has a GPS, or he can Google it on his phone."

"If he does or if he doesn't, that's not the way Martians treat newcomers."

"Jancie, we've got to start filling the picnic basket." Winnie moved toward the pantry, rubbing her hands together and muttering. "I'm so glad I bought those lemons. Lemonade!" She disappeared for a second and brought out a closed-top basket. "I found it. Hurray."

"Great." Jancie squeezed her shoulder. "We'll need to get down the old blanket, too. Or do you want to take the folding chairs? Or you could take both, you know."

"OK, you two. Calm down. I know what you're thinking, but this will not be a date. *If* it happens." Penn's cellphone summoned her, and she stepped out of Jancie's half embrace. Grabbing her purse, she found her cellphone in the side pocket on the third ring. "It's John."

"Well, answer it." Winnie fluttered her free hand toward the phone. "Answer before he hangs up." Jancie and Winnie crowded around her to listen. Wide eyes and grins punctuated their faces as they bounced on their toes.

John's voice came out of the speaker holes clear and strong. "Hi, Penn. I guess you've heard the news about Linda."

"Hmm mmm." She rubbed her lapis ring and shrugged against the Penn sandwich her aunts were concocting.

"So I thought I could pick you up. We could ride over together if you don't mind riding on my motorcycle."

Not in this lifetime.

"Or we could just meet over there." A lame suggestion, but she had to try.

Both gray heads shook and mouthed, "No."

Penn closed her eyes to ignore their bunched eyebrows and whispered suggestions.

"Well, yeah, but Linda said parking'd be a premium. We'd save a space if we drove together and wouldn't have to try and find each other in the crowd."

She gripped the phone and pressed her hand against her galloping heart. Of course, he was right. "Hmm mmm. Sure. That makes sense, but I don't mind driving. I know the way. Where do you live?"

"I'll drive to your place. See you soon."

~*~

The afternoon flew by in a whirlwind of making sandwiches, bagging carrot sticks, filling up plastic containers with watermelon and cantaloupe balls, and baking another batch of celebration cookies. No amount of protest could sway the aunts' determination to make the picnic basket a deposit of deliciousness.

Penn inspected the contents of the basket. "Only two of us are going, remember? You have enough food in here for another whole committee. Or two."

"But you need something salty. We don't have any chips. You should stop on the way and buy a bag." Winnie wiped her hands on a dish towel.

"We'll be fine—"

The doorbell rang.

Penn's stomach flipped.

The aunts squealed and scooted into the family room. In the foyer, Penn dug in her heels and jerked her head toward the kitchen. "Give me some space, please."

She cracked the door to find John, clad in cargo shorts and a sage green golf shirt.

Nice. Her stomach fluttered and kicked up her pulse.

"Hello, John!" The aunts huddled behind Penn.

John craned his neck around her to the meddlesome aunts breathing down her neck. But when he smiled such a beautiful and sincere smile at her aunts, Penn's heart contracted almost to the point of pain. She vacillated between wanting to hug him for being sweet to them and wanting to push him back down the front steps to protect them from the inevitable disappointment.

Because if history was any indicator, disappointment waited for them if her aunts pinned any kind of romantic hopes for her and this guy. A snippet of senior prom night flashed in her mind. That night with Ronald Schmitz—whose nerdy looks equaled her own nerdy feelings and attitudes and gestures—had ended with a bloodied nose—his; and sore feet—hers, from walking a half mile home in high heels. No awkward escort to the front door. No request for a second date.

That night had been Penn's only foray into the dating world. She'd avoided it by keeping a low profile in college. Now, living with her aunts, teaching at the high school, and volunteering with the youth group didn't exactly put her in the line of many eligible bachelors.

"Come in, John. Penny, dear, let the man in. We've got a lovely basket for you." Jancie led the group back into the kitchen.

John glanced at Penn, a question in his eyes. "It smells fantastic in here."

Penn found her tongue. "Cookies."

"Celebration cookies." Winnie winked. "We baked them this afternoon so that you'd have a treat at the concert. You'll have a great picnic, if I do say so myself."

John lifted the basket from the wooden table. "Wow. This weighs a ton. I guess you're coming, too, right? To help eat all this food?"

Penn rubbed her arms.

John didn't want this sham of a committee activity to be a date either.

"Thanks so much for asking, dear, but my back's acting up again." Jancie massaged the small of her back.

"Oh, no. No, we can't go. I need to put my feet up. I don't want my ankles to swell." Winnie wiggled her right foot.

Interesting. Penn drummed her fingers against her elbow. First time she'd heard of these ailments. No matter. She and John could concentrate on evaluating the band and not worry about swatting down matchmaking attempts by her lovable but misguided aunts.

"You two better get going to claim a good spot." Jancie shooed them back to the front door. "Here's the blanket, Penn. Don't forget to grab the chairs from the porch."

"I'll get them. You better go rest and feel better." Penn arched a brow. "We'll be back in a little while."

"Do not hurry one bit. Enjoy the evening. *Enjoy*, Penny." Winnie reached up with a peck for her cheek and a quick whisper. "He's a nice one, honey."

Penn's withering glower died on the back of Winnie's head as she retreated up the steps to the porch.

John had maneuvered the basket onto the backseat and placed the camp chairs on the floor.

Penn tossed the blanket into the back and slid into the driver's seat.

John climbed in beside her. "So, you got your door fixed." He flashed a tentative smile.

Not a trace of mockery or even teasing in his eyes. Still, the memory of crawling over the stick shift the first time she'd met him humiliated her all over again. She gritted her molars. "The door isn't broken. Gretchen—she—it just sticks sometimes. There's no rhyme or reason." Penn shifted into reverse and scanned the rear window, avoiding his eyes. "I've had it checked out. Tony, the mechanic in town, has greased and jiggled and poked—everything's good. She's just..."

"Temperamental?"

"Exactly."

~*~

Why did he have to bring up the sticky door?

30

Way to bring up a fun memory for her, Don Juan. His mouth curved at the picture of her crawling through the passenger side door. He turned toward his window to hide the smile from her.

So cute.

So prickly, too.

He'd have to try harder to make friends with her. In town for a couple of months, he'd met a handful of people. Penn won the prize as most intriguing person so far with her mixture of quirkiness and prickliness, not to mention those big, brown eyes.

Glancing at her profile, he slid his hands over his shorts.

For sure, he'd try harder.

4

"If you take the basket, I can carry the chairs and blanket." Penn put the key in her shorts pocket and pushed up her seat to grab the blanket.

"Wow. This looks great. And it's free?" John held the basket in front of him and surveyed the growing crowd.

Penn nodded.

He loved it. Who wouldn't?

She and her aunts came most Sunday evenings during her childhood summers to enjoy the free concerts. Part of her loved listening to the music under the stars, raiding the picnic basket filled with goodies. The other part of her dreaded Sundays at the park when jealousy gnawed at the tender places in her chest.

She'd watch the other children walking by her holding hands with a parent or running through the crowd with siblings, and the longing for an intact family pervaded her chest and choked her breathing.

As an adult, she recognized the sacrifice her aunts had made for her, grateful beyond words for the women who loved her unconditionally. As a child, she wanted to be like everyone else.

"Yeah. It's cool." She hitched the straps for the camp chairs over her shoulder. "We should pick a spot to sit, I guess."

"Linda suggested sitting near one of the

sculptures. Al can find us while he's patrolling the crowd. She mentioned Missy might be around, too. I think her text said Large Escargot?" John scrunched his nose.

Penn forgot herself for a moment and chuckled. She pointed toward a large, steel sculpture on the left side of the sitting area in front of the stage. "There. It's a David Hayes piece, if you're interested in modern art."

"Interested, maybe. Knowledgeable, definitely not." He switched the basket to his left hand, gesturing toward the sculpture with the other. "After you."

~*~

A lime green Frisbee sailed into the middle of the blanket. John grabbed it and swished it back to a waiting little boy who looked to be about six years old.

Penn admired the expert flick of his wrist. "You've done that before."

"I played Ultimate Frisbee in college. It's like riding a bike." He stretched out on his side beside the basket and raised the lid. "I can't believe all this food. It looks great."

She reclined in one of the chairs, her bare feet resting near her abandoned sandals on the blanket. "It tastes even better, but don't take my word for it. Have a sandwich. My aunts are great cooks."

"I'm going for the cookies first. Haven't had a homemade one in a while." He popped opened the bag's plastic zipper. "What did they call them—party cookies?"

"Celebration cookies."

"What are they celebrating? It's not your birthday,

is it?"

Penn winced. If John knew the aunts were celebrating the fact that she was out on their idea of a date at Hartwood Acres—with him, he'd probably laugh his head off. "No. It's not my birthday. They're just celebrating Hartwood Acres." She crossed her fingers in a childlike fashion to negate the half lie that slid so quickly out of her mouth. "We used to come here every summer."

He swallowed and grabbed another cookie. "These are fantastic. Do you think they'd give me the recipe?"

"Sure." She dug her toes into the nubby softness of the blanket.

A microphone squealed as a band member did a sound check.

"You like to cook?"

"Not sure exactly. I'm learning. Been told I make a mean omelet, though."

Who told him that? An old girlfriend, perhaps? Against all good reason that thought rankled. She ignored it. "Good job." She smiled. "Scrambling eggs is a good start."

"You haven't ever made one if you think an omelet is scrambling eggs." He brushed the crumbs off his hands and rolled onto his stomach. Leaning on his elbows, he focused on her. "I'll make one for you sometime, and you can judge. You'll find out—I speak truth and only truth."

Penn lost herself in his black eyes for a few seconds. A dreamy, make-believe scenario floated through her mind—ringing his doorbell, being invited into his apartment, offering her cheek for a welcoming kiss...

She gripped the canvas arms and squared her

shoulders to derail those thoughts. She refused to be sucked into the aunts' line of thinking that wouldn't lead anywhere but frustration and disappointment.

Remember Ronald Schmitz? The memory of his bloodied nose, administered by her own right hook after trying to take advantage of her on prom night, was a strong deterrent to runaway silly thoughts.

Not wanting her to miss any high school rite of passage, her poor aunts had engineered a pity date with Ronald, the son of a neighbor of a friend. After that night, she could check Senior Prom and Date Rape Near Miss off her bucket list.

John's invitation, probably him just being polite, still quickened her heartbeat and diminished the breath in her lungs. She shook her head to empty it of any residual daydreams of spending time with John besides, of course, in connection with the committee.

"You don't like omelets?" He rested his chin in his palm.

"I do, but—"

"Great, then. We need to—"

"Hi, Penny. Sweet! You're right where Linda said you'd be—at the big snail." Missy Parker, fresh from a graduation trip to Cancun and with a deep tan to prove it, stood with her cellphone in one hand and her other on her hip. "Perfect timing." She nodded to the stage.

Band members found their places with their instruments. Excited applause and cheers greeted the musicians who waved back at the audience.

Perfect timing, indeed.

~*~

Penn studied Missy as she flirted with John. Fascinated, she regretted that she didn't have a notepad to jot down tips. Not that she'd need the tips, but Penn liked collecting information.

A master at flirting, Missy trained her attention on John, touched his wrist more than once, shoved him on his shoulder when she thought he was teasing her.

"No, really." John shrugged. "I'd never heard of Bucknell until the basketball team played in March Madness a few years ago." He tented his knees and leaned back on his arms.

Missy's eyes, emphasized with a heavy black line, stretched wide. "Well, it's a great school. I'm proud to be a graduate." She flipped her hair and loose, blonde curls tumbled down her back. The light breeze that had set in at dusk ruffled wispy tendrils around her face.

They'd make a striking couple. Both were tall with glossy-page features. Those characteristics guaranteed stares in a crowd, but their coloring, the exact opposite of each other, tipped the scales into the stunning category.

Missy's flaxen hair, still as light as it was in elementary school, shouted, "Look at me," especially cuddled up close to John's raven locks.

She pictured Missy, just inches shorter than John, staring up into his dark eyes and batting her blue ones over one of his omelets.

That familiar Sunday-in-the-park pang squeezed Penn's heart. She glanced at her arms to reassure herself she wasn't turning green.

"Isn't that right, Penny?" Missy extended her from-here-to-there legs in front of her and wiggled purple-tipped toes. "Penn?"

"What? I'm sorry. I—" Penn winced. Caught not

paying attention again, just like at the committee meeting.

"John should talk to Joe Zimmerman."

"Talk to Joe?" Penn had missed most of the conversation. What in the world did John need Joe for? "I didn't know Joe knew anything about bands."

Missy laughed. "No, silly. For his house. He needs some help refurbishing it."

Penn's head jerked back. Her mouth fell open. "You've got a house?"

Why was she so surprised by that revelation? Because he drove a motorcycle. That's why. And he wore black clothes…at least sometimes.

"Yeah." Sitting up straight, he reached his long arms over his head, dropped them onto his knees. "I closed a few weeks ago. It needs some work, and I'm not exactly handy with a hammer yet." He glanced toward Missy and nodded. "Having somebody I could shoot questions to would be great."

Penn narrowed her eyes. "You bought a fixer-upper, but you don't know how to fix it up?" Her mind raced with the pitfalls of this kind of major investment. Her chest tightened. She tilted her head and pursed her lips. "You bought a house that needs work, but you don't know how—"

John held up his hand. "Hey, now. I didn't say it's a hopeless cause. It needs work, but it's not a complete dump. And…" He winked at them. "I watch the DIY channel every chance I get."

Penn raked her fingers through her hair and held the ends for a second before releasing. She shook her head. "You watch Do It Yourself programs? But you've never actually done anything like this before?" Her voice rose with each word.

She forced her breathing to slow and released her grip on the arms of the chair. His actions meant nothing to her. She flexed her hands and smoothed her Capri pants. She had nothing at stake in what could turn out to be a serious catastrophe, but she didn't want a catastrophe to happen to him.

John leaned toward her. "Would it make you feel any better to know that I made a pretty sweet birdhouse when I was about twelve?"

Penn gaped at him. She noticed the twinkling in his eyes just before he burst into the same uninhibited laughter she'd heard when she climbed over her stick shift.

Missy joined in. "Oh, girl, your expression is priceless."

Wonderful.

Both of them were laughing at her. They enjoyed the same kind of humor, too. She twisted her ring to the inside of her hand, drawing comfort from the cool, smooth surface of the blue stone.

Penn calculated the minutes left in the concert, how many for travel time, and, if she could park the car without the aunts realizing they were back home, she could dispense the goodbyes in a flat eleven seconds.

John tapped her knee. "Just teasing you a little."

She gathered her wits that had scattered when his hand touched her. "So. You never built a birdhouse."

"No, no," he laughed. "That's true. I built one. Earned a badge for it, too." His smile, warm and open, signaled joy and anticipation about what was happening next. His twinkling eyes promised fun and a not-too-serious approach to life.

Penn took a serious approach to everything.

"My granddad helped me nail it up in my backyard. A bluebird moved in and raised a nice family. So I'd say my first house was a success." He grinned at Penn.

"Building a birdhouse doesn't exactly equate with refurbishing a people house."

"You're right, but I'm willing to learn. Plus, I figure I can write a few how-to articles in the process."

Missy gasped and grabbed his hand. "Ooh, you're a writer. That's fabulous. I wish I'd known you last year. You could have helped me with my senior paper." She made quotation marks with her fingers when she said, "helped," and giggled.

He liked words.

She liked numbers. More ammunition to blast through the aunts' plan for matchmaking.

John stood and stretched. "I guess we ought to make our way down to the band. We're supposed to try and meet them, right? Anybody got any ideas on how we do that?"

Missy jumped up beside him, but Penn remained seated. "I'll stay here and keep an eye on our stuff. You two go ahead."

Missy bounced on her toes. "Come on, John. This'll be fun. Meeting bands isn't that hard. Leave it to me." She slid her phone into the back pocket of her pink shorts and linked her arm in his.

He'd be in capable hands, no doubt, with Missy.

Penn blew out a slow breath and dropped her shoulders.

By the time they returned, they'd probably have all the musicians' email addresses, cell numbers, and a commitment to play the festival.

Missy was nothing if not determined.

Penn had known Missy since she was a toddler and remembered her as a freshman when she was a senior in high school. People noticed her and followed her even then.

They'd probably have their first date scheduled when they returned. She pressed her hands against her abdomen and swallowed hard.

When the aunts learned of the date, they'd be disappointed for a few days. She could deal with their disenchantment, especially if it meant they'd leave her alone and stop asking questions about John. She could focus again on studying for the CPA exam.

Good plan.

~*~

Penn cruised Gretchen into the gravel driveway and set the parking break. Just a couple more minutes, and she'd be inside and halfway to her pajamas.

John shifted in his seat. "So—when am I cooking for you?"

"What?" Penn's heart jerked in her chest and beat out a frantic rhythm. Why was he bringing up omelets again? Didn't he have a dinner planned with Missy? Wait. If he did, he'd be a player. He'd—

"Omelets. Remember? I'm going to prove to you that my omelets are to die for. When works for you?"

The front porch light left on by the aunts illuminated his hopeful eyes and raised eyebrows. This guy wasn't a player. He had the looks but not the swagger.

"Whaddaya say? Are you free sometime this week?"

Penn's mind raced through her calendar. Pretty

much open book except for her study sessions. Why couldn't she think of conflicts, places she had to be? Because she lived a boring, non-eventful life which is what she preferred except when the empty slots left her without an excuse in times like this.

She ran her fingers around the leather-covered steering wheel and lost herself in the soothing, pebbled texture. How many times did she hide herself in this car, her dad's car, when she needed a timeout from her world? If the aunts didn't find her in the stable with Peri, they knew she'd either be behind the wheel or asleep in the backseat.

A short laugh brought her out of her reverie.

"I guess your silence is my answer? Trying to find a way to let me down easy, huh?" He ducked his head and reached for the door handle.

"What? Wait. No. I was just...I was thinking about something else. Sorry." She gripped the steering wheel. "You're serious about the omelets?"

"Of course, I'm serious. I wouldn't have mentioned it otherwise. I feel I need to prove my worth as an egg chef."

"But I thought you were refurbishing your house?"

"It's a fixer-upper, mostly out-dated stuff. You know. Green kitchen. Shaggy carpet. Wood paneling. Not uninhabitable. I haven't started yet so you won't have to worry about eating sawdust." He raised his eyebrows. "What'll it be? You up for the best omelet in the world or not?"

She couldn't help but laugh. "You're so sure of yourself."

He shrugged. "If I don't believe in myself, who will? Yes or no?"

"Um, OK, I guess."

He grinned. "Not exactly enthusiastic, but I'll take it. Earlier in the week works better for me. What about Tuesday night?" He tipped his head to the right, waiting for her answer.

What in the world would the aunts say? Plenty, no doubt.

"Sure. Tuesday works." Tuesday. Two days from now. How would she navigate the questions, the comments, the shining eyes as Jancie and Winnie contemplated the evening?

"Great. And you'll get to meet my new roommate, too."

"Your roommate?" Ah, not exactly a date.

"Yea. He's the cousin of a friend from college. Don't know him too well. I just met him a few Sundays ago, but he seems cool. His cousin pointed me to Mars in the first place."

~*~

From behind the front door window, Penn watched the motorcycle until it disappeared beyond the street light, and a heavy sigh whispered in her heart.

He wasn't interested in her at all. It wasn't a date. It was only a...a what? A kind gesture?

Yes, a gesture she should've offered to him. He was, after all, the newcomer in town. She'd let the aunts take care of hospitality acts. They believed in reciprocal invitations.

A tiny smile hovered around her mouth. The aunts could write a manual on the art of intervening. They'd raised their skills of intervening into others' lives to the master level.

John didn't know what he was getting himself into.

5

Penn hesitated at the front door of the two-story brown house on Clay Avenue. She held a pan of homemade cinnamon rolls that still needed a few minutes of rising time. Her aunts had assured her the rolls were the perfect ending to a breakfast-for-dinner kind of evening.

Thrilled to the point of nervousness when she told them—at noon—that she wouldn't be home for dinner, they'd bustled through the kitchen slinging flour and brown sugar on every flat surface. They'd insisted she call John to tell him she'd bring the rolls for dessert.

They'd refused to listen to her protests of why it was simply an evening with a fellow volunteer. They chose to sing, "A date. A date. A very important date" instead, their nod to Lewis Carroll's white rabbit.

Why did she agree to come tonight? She closed her eyes and remembered her aunts' sweet pep talk.

"Go" they'd said.

"Have fun," they'd said. "Get to know him. Praise his omelet. You'll have a fabulous time."

Unfortunately, these sweet, sweet women had a completely wrong idea of the upcoming evening, but she loved how they always championed her no matter what.

Sucking in a fortifying breath, she raised her finger to the doorbell, but the door burst open.

John draped a dish towel over his shoulder.

"Welcome, welcome. I saw…Gretchen, right? I saw Gretchen parked out front. I was kinda worried you'd changed your mind when I didn't hear the doorbell. Wait a minute. Does it work?" He pushed the button, and the bell sounded right on cue. He grinned and reached for the pan of rolls.

"Homemade cinnamon rolls. I can't wait. Come on in. So what do we do with these?"

Penn still searched for how he knew Gretchen's name. When could she have let that slip? Only a handful of people knew she'd named her car. Three to be exact.

"What do we set the oven on?" John moved back toward the kitchen.

She followed him. "Not yet." Penn recovered her memory of the aunts' instructions. "They need to rise for about fifteen more minutes, then bake them at 375 degrees." As she reached the threshold, her sandal caught the rolled edge of the linoleum. Before she could catch herself, her cheek bounced off the rounded corner of the counter top, and she braced herself for the floor.

~*~

As John set the pan down near the stove, he heard a cry. Whirling toward the sound, he grabbed her just before she hit the floor.

"Oh, man. Are you all right?" He lowered her into a sitting position and knelt beside her. "That stupid floor. I forgot to get a throw rug." He winced. "I'm so sorry." Not pausing to think about the intimacy of his next move, he pushed soft curls back away from her face.

Eyes squeezed shut, she held her cheek and bit her lip, pulling in long, slow breaths.

"You hurt your cheek?"

Her head moved an infinitesimal bit. A nod?

"Can I see?"

A full minute passed. He chewed his lip. Why had he procrastinated in buying a rug? A head injury. Way to begin an evening meant to impress. First thing tomorrow morning...

"Penn, please, I won't touch it, but I need to see how it looks so we know what to do."

She lowered her hand and raised her lids, slowly as if movement might increase the pain. Tears glistened.

Please, please, please don't cry. I can help you if you just don't cry.

He dragged his eyes away from hers and focused on the injury. "No cut. No blood. Looks like it's already swelling, though. Let's get some ice on it." He grabbed a plastic bag out of a drawer, threw some ice cubes into it and wrapped it up in a dish towel. "This should help."

She'd leaned against a cabinet, covering her cheek again as if protecting it from any more damage. He sat down opposite her and offered the ice pack. "Here's the ice. Please take it, Penn."

She opened her eyes, and the tears were gone.

Thank You, Lord.

"Take this, and I'll get some ibuprofen for you. You're not allergic, are you? That'll reduce swelling and maybe hold off a headache. Oh, man, I'm so sorry." He dragged his hand through his hair.

Still nothing from Penn.

He tried for levity. "What'll people think when

they hear my house whacks my dinner guests?"

A tiny chuckle escaped from her mouth. She winced. "Stop. Don't make me laugh." She licked her lip. "Don't make me speak either." She reached for the ice pack and held it a hair's breadth away from her cheek.

"It works better if it actually touches the skin."

"Just give me a minute, will you? I'll get it there. I have to prepare myself first." She touched the pack to her cheek and bit her lip again. "It's cold."

"Perfect. It'll work then." He worried the pocket flap on his cargo shorts. "Is it taking away any of the pain yet?"

She spoke with miniscule movements of her lips. "If you mean is it easing the excruciating throbbing and burning on the left side of my head, then yes. If you mean the excruciating humiliation cloaking my whole body, then no." She sighed.

"Humiliation?"

She closed her eyes. "Yep."

"Not following you." He searched her face.

She shifted the pack. "I always seem to show off the most graceful points of my character when we're together. It's a wonder you don't call me Miss Grace."

"First, you tripped over something I should have fixed before you got here. That's on me, not you. Second, what're you talking about? You've felt humiliated before?"

Penn rested the pack on her lap. "My cheek is frozen. I've got to give it a break."

"Fine. You can put it back in a minute." He rested his elbows on his bent knees. "You were saying?"

"Oh, you want me to recount my humiliation? Fine. How about the first and probably the worst time?" She stared at him.

He flipped back through their few meetings. "Which is ...?"

She blinked. "You seriously don't remember the first apple meeting? When I had to crawl over the stick shift...because Gretchen wouldn't let me in?"

He couldn't hide the smile that crept across his face. "Yeah. I remember that, but don't be embarrassed. Stuff like that happens all the time."

"Oh, really?" She traced the linoleum pattern with her index finger. "I can't imagine stuff like that happening to you."

"Why not?" He stretched his long legs beside her.

"Because...because you dress in black and ride a motorcycle."

He looked down at his khaki shorts. "My clothes aren't black." He cocked his head. "Are you colorblind?"

"No. I've seen you in black several times."

He paused and rubbed his chin. "You're right. I guess I do wear black sometimes. When I'm at the end of my clean clothes stash. But that doesn't have anything to do with embarrassing moments."

"Cool people don't have embarrassing moments."

His eyebrows shot up. "You think I'm cool?" He'd never considered himself cool. Loved, of course. Fun to be around, uh huh. Cool? Not a bit. His older brother pressed that point whenever possible.

She closed her eyes and replaced the ice pack.

"I'll take that for a 'yes.'" He grinned. "Are you ready to stand? This floor isn't just dangerous. It's not very comfortable either." He arched his back.

Instead of answering, she positioned her free hand to push herself up. He moved to his knees and grabbed her elbow to help.

"Take it easy at first. You might be a little woozy." He led her to the stool beside the butcher block in the center of the kitchen. "Sit here—the perfect viewing spot to view the master."

~*~

Penn's whole left side of her face ached. Eating was the last thing she wanted to do, but she didn't want to disappoint John either.

He watched her with little boy excitement lighting his eyes.

"It's a good thing we're having omelets. I can make yours as soft as you like. You won't even have to chew." He gestured at the island covered with small mismatched bowls of diced tomatoes, onions, mushrooms, green peppers, and a jar of jalapeno peppers. "I've got just about anything you could ask for, but just cheese works fine."

"Just cheese."

He tapped a slender jar with a whisk. "These bacon bits are really tender."

"Cheese."

"One cheese omelet coming up." He turned to a cabinet. "But first let me get you some ibuprofen."

Something rattled at the front of the house, and the door swung open.

John swiveled from the sink with a glass in hand. "David, what's up, buddy? Come meet the friend I told you about."

She twisted her ring and squeezed the smooth stone into her palm. In the haze of searing pain, she'd forgotten that tonight's guest list included someone else. She peaked at the door and did a double take. That would probably be the last time she'd forget him.

David stood at least six-feet-three or -four inches. By the size of his shoulders, he must have played football at some point in his life. He carried a gym bag but looked as though he'd just showered. His damp blond hair perfectly accompanied bright blue eyes. He made a presence in a room, for sure.

Both men reached her at the same time. One held a glass of water and two capsules; the other reached to shake her hand.

"Hey." David's eyes widened when he noticed the pack. "Wow. What happened?" He glanced at John and back at Penn. "Looks like you got the worst end of the deal. Are you OK? I'm David, by the way." His hand dwarfed hers, but his grip felt firm, not bone-crushing.

"I'm Penn. I'm fine." She popped the capsules in her mouth and pushed them down with a big gulp of water.

"Penn had a run-in with the linoleum." John pointed to the floor covering curling at the threshold. "Remind me to get a throw rug tomorrow." He grabbed three eggs out of the carton. "Are you hungry? Because I'm ready to create."

~*~

The omelet was probably the most perfect scrambled egg dish she'd ever had. The edges, tinted with a touch of golden brown, cradled a fluffy, light center that pocketed three different cheeses cooked to just this side of bliss.

John was right. He was a master at making an

omelet. He was right, too, about not having to chew.

Thank goodness. Her cheek throbbed with a new fierceness.

"So what do you think?" He leaned on his elbows and grinned. "Tell me how much you loved it."

At his hopeful expression, her heart melted like the gooey cheeses in her omelet. "Delicious scrambled eggs." She smiled, at least as far as her aching cheek would let her.

"I'll say." David reached for another bacon strip and crunched a bite. "Fantastic. This looks like the beginning of a great relationship. What else do you cook?"

"We've got cinnamon rolls for dessert thanks to Penn's aunts."

"Cool!" David wiped his mouth and craned his neck to see the rolls cooling on the counter.

"But omelets are the only menu choice right now. Maybe I can add a few other dishes before too long. What about you?" John retrieved the pan and set it between them.

"I can work a microwave." David wiggled the small spatula under a plump roll and pulled it away from the others, dripping liquid cinnamon all the way to his plate.

"All right, then. I guess I better crack open that cookbook sooner rather than later." John glanced at Penn. "You look like you're ready to call it a day. You want a roll, and then I'll drive you home?"

"You're right." She dabbed at the corner of her mouth with a napkin from a local fast food restaurant. "I am ready to go home, but I drove, remember?"

"I remember, but I don't think it's a good idea for you to go by yourself. I know you don't want to ride my bike, so I'll follow you."

"John, honestly, you don't have to do that. I'll be fine." She pushed back from the kitchen table.

"I know I don't, but I'm going to." He separated a roll from the others and dropped it onto his plate. "I'll just take one before we leave."

Penn heard the determination in his voice and wanted to argue the point, but she didn't have the energy. Nursing her cheek, trying to keep up with the banter between the two men, even eating had sapped her reserves. "I'll pass on the rolls. You two can share all of them. Bring the pan to the next apple meeting."

John, already chewing half a roll, nodded. He swallowed and pointed to the pan. "Twelve rolls, man. That means six apiece. I'll have another one when I get back." He tossed the rest of the sticky bread into his mouth and licked his fingers.

David wiggled his eyebrows and reached for another one.

~*~

Penn climbed out of the Volkswagen and turned to wave goodbye to John, but his attention centered on pushing down his kickstand. She closed her eyes and squeezed the keys in her palm. She needed a relaxing, hot bath, not more conversation with John who stood by his bike, unbuckling his helmet.

"John, thanks for seeing me home, but I'm good now. Goodnight."

He hung the helmet on the handlebar. "Nice try. I'm walking you to the door. I want to get my side of the story in." He grinned.

"You think I—"

The front door burst open.

"John, what a special surprise. Come in and have some lemonade." Aunt Winnie stepped out onto the front porch followed by Aunt Jancie close behind.

"Hello, ladies. I'd love to, but I think Penn needs to call it a day." He nodded his head in her direction.

Both aunts frowned and glanced at Penn.

"What's the matter, sweetie?" Aunt Jancie adjusted her glasses high on the bridge of her nose.

"Nothing. I—"

"We had a little accident back at the house. It's my fault, and I hope you'll forgive me for not taking care of her better. She's got a nasty bump on her cheek." He pressed his lips together, hands shoved into his back pockets.

The aunts turned to her so they could see better. They sucked in a gasp and covered their mouths.

"That looks painful, Penny."

With the aunts fawning over her and John acting like she was his responsibility, Penn felt five years old. "It wasn't his fault. I didn't look where I was stepping and tripped."

"Tripped over old, curled up linoleum that I should have at least covered with a rug. My first re-do project is the kitchen which I plan to start on next week when I get back in town."

"You're going out of town again?" How many trips had he made since she met him?

"Yeah. I've got a—"

"Oh, my stars!" Winnie, usually a stickler for good manners, broke in so fast Penn blinked. "I've got the best idea. A paper bag floor!"

"What?" John and Penn answered together this time.

"A paper bag floor. It's all the rage on the craft sites." Jancie joined in with her sister. "You tear pieces of brown paper and glue them to your floor, then paint over it with polyurethane."

"We've seen pictures." Winnie stepped more closely to John. "The floors look gorgeous. I'm sure your kitchen would look great with one."

John eyed both women but, to his credit, didn't laugh at them. "A paper bag floor, huh?"

"Yes. Eye catching and economical, too." Jancie add a practical point.

"Sounds interesting." John shrugged. "I'd be up for it."

"We can help." Winnie's eyes shined. "We know exactly what to do."

The aunts folded their arms across their chests in unison.

Discussion over.

~*~

Penn grabbed the hot water handle with her toes and released more water into the bathtub. The liquid warmth swaddled her, pulling tension from her muscles as she envisioned herself bobbing down a babbling brook that flowed by a meadow full of daisies and bachelor buttons. Usually this relaxation technique combined with lavender bath salts worked to settle her nerves.

Tonight, however, her rebellious mind kept playing the last scene on the front porch. A paper bag floor? And the aunts volunteered to help create it? What about those ailments that kept them from Hartwood Acres on Sunday?

She had a pretty good idea that she'd be the one crawling on the floor amid the scraps of paper. Not a flattering image. *I can't help him do that floor. I don't have a crafty bone in my body.*

She closed her eyes as she remembered the wonky hot pads she'd tried to weave on her plastic loom, the burned edges of salt dough Christmas ornaments, the crooked Nativity barn fashioned with Popsicle sticks. She'd learned to leave the crafts to the aunts. Why wouldn't they leave her out of the crafts?

Because they're still plotting. Still trying to get John to be interested in me. She and John would be the only people in history wooed into a relationship by way of a paper bag floor.

Poor John.

She smiled, and her cheek protested. She touched it with the tips of her dripping fingers. The dull ache reminded her of the fiasco earlier in the evening. How could she be so clumsy? Why did she always look so foolish in front of John?

He'd been gentle with her throughout the whole ordeal, calm and in charge, too. His dark eyes brimmed with concern for her pain and regret over neglecting the potential hazard. He went above and beyond with the escort back to her house.

Penn's initial impression of him couldn't be more incorrect. Instead of being arrogant or too-cool-for-school, he was compassionate and patient.

He clearly enjoyed Jancie and Winnie, too. He'd accepted their invitation to dinner for next Friday night—contingent on his schedule, of course.

What was he doing this Friday night? How busy is his schedule? She tapped her forehead, water droplets sprinkling her eyelashes and cheeks. *Quit thinking about his schedule, Penn. Not your business.*

Maybe she wouldn't have to worry about redoing a floor either. Maybe he'd find a sale on linoleum he couldn't pass up. Maybe her aunts would forget about the floor when they remembered her craft disasters.

Not.

They'd never forget the dinner. They'd already dragged out their go-to recipe books and created a list of several grocery items before she'd had a chance to draw her bath. The giggles from the kitchen table drifted up the stairs and teased her.

Shaking her head, she stretched her toes to the handle again and welcomed fresh hot water to her bath. She forced herself to focus on relaxing and refused to entertain the question that knocked on her brain, demanding attention—what new fiascos awaited her at the dinner party?

6

Penn yawned and her cheek pinched with a reminder of John's kitchen counter top. She sipped her cappuccino and waited for the rest of the Apple committee to appear. An early morning meeting was a good idea. Catch people before they got involved at work, before their minds filled with other responsibilities. Plus, she could get it behind her and focus on studying for her exam.

Jacob Duran cleaned his glasses with a blue and white handkerchief. Clara pored over papers in several folders. A few more people and the meeting could start.

The front door of the Town Hall dinged, and John held the door for Missy Parker. She looked gorgeous in white denim shorts and a navy polka dotted blouse. A messy blonde bun allowed several wisps to float around her face, upturned to John.

A burning sensation curled in Penn's stomach. It spread and squeezed her heart when Missy's laugh tinkled and produced a smile from John. *Jealous?* That thought caught her attention.

Could she really be jealous? She'd tried so hard not to get caught up in the aunts' romantic talk. She thought she was immune, but now here she was wishing she were the one walking in with John.

His attention left Missy and settled on Penn. He smiled a hello and moved to the seat beside her although Missy had chosen a seat across the table.

"How do you feel today?"

Again with the concern in those dark brown eyes.

"Fine. Thanks." She hoped he didn't see the frantic blood vessel tapping on the side of her neck. She twisted her ring and held the lapis against her palm.

He craned his neck to inspect her cheek. Close enough for her to smell his woodsy aftershave.

"It still looks pink. Hasn't turned purple yet. Looks like the ice kept the swelling down." He pulled his gaze back to hers. "Still sore, I guess." Sympathy furrowed his brow.

"Yeah, but it's fine. I'll live."

He grinned. "Good."

"Hello, everyone. Thanks for getting here bright and early this morning." Clara called the meeting to order. "Linda is still struggling with her broken leg, but she assures me the entertainment committee is in capable hands." She arched a look at Penn.

Penn made a mental note to thank Clara for her encouraging smirk.

The front door chimed and Al Martin yawned his way to the seat opposite John. "Sorry, guys. Just finishing the graveyard shift." He rubbed his temple. "Been up all night trying to catch whoever is stealing the heavy equipment over near Valencia."

Jacob's eyes lit up. "I heard about that. Talk is that the stuff is buried somewhere."

"Buried? Heavy equipment?" John frowned. "But why? And how?"

Jacob tapped the table with his pen. "Revenge is what I heard."

"I heard that, too. If it's true, we'll find out. Bank on it." Al pressed his fingertips into his closed eyes.

"Can't keep something that wild secret for long."

"Well, we're glad you could get here, Al." Clara paper clipped a note card to a folder. "Let's keep this short so you can get on home to bed." She handed the folder to Penn. "Linda wanted me to give you this file. Her notes from last year. Now, we need an update on our budget. Penn, that's you. "

~*~

John held his helmet in one hand, the door with the other. Missy gestured for Penn to go ahead of her. Penn received the message she sent and walked through, leaving Missy to walk with John.

He didn't pick up the message, however. "Good to see you, Missy. Bye. Hey, Penn. Wait up."

A seed of joy split open in Penn's heart. She turned to see him limp to catch up with her. A grin escaped from teeth that had clamped down on her bottom lip.

"I've got the cinnamon roll pan in my saddle bag." He stopped at his bike to unhook the silver buckles.

Her shoulders slumped. He didn't want to see her. He wanted to return Winnie's pan. The joy evaporated, leaving an emptiness in the region of her heart.

He joined her by the car and offered the pan. "So I guess we're still on for Saturday night?"

She nodded. "They've already planned the menu, made the shopping list. They're buying groceries tomorrow." She hesitated. "They can't wait."

"Me, either." He rubbed his stomach. "They won't let me bring dessert or anything, but would it be OK if I brought flowers?"

"You don't have to bring anything, but flowers would be great. They love anything floral." She reached for the door, but he grabbed the handle first.

The door swung open. Easy as pie. No sticky door. No temperamental Volkswagen.

Traitor.

She sat in the driver's seat, dumping her folders and the pan in the passenger's side.

"Sweet. Sounds like a plan." He shut the door and waved.

From her rearview mirror, she watched him climb onto his bike and slip the helmet over his head.

Sounds like a sweet plan.

~*~

"So let me get this straight. You financed your trip across America by selling socks at flea markets. Is that right?" John tilted his head and leaned back in his chair.

"No, no, no." Aunt Winnie pushed her plate away from her. "The trip was paid for lock, stock, and barrel before we left. We just brought the socks along for running around money, just-in-casey money."

"Justin Casey? I think I went to school with him." He grinned at Penn, and her breath caught in her throat.

The aunts howled. "Oh, John. You're a hoot." Aunt Jancie slapped the table.

It was a silly joke, but she laughed, too, and it felt good. The whole dinner had been fun, hearing John's stories, sharing theirs.

"OK. So I guess that sounds like a pretty good idea."

"Not really." Penn couldn't resist prodding the rest of the story.

Jancie clucked her tongue. "We don't have a happy ending. About the socks, anyway." She peered at Winnie. "Where were we, sister? Somewhere west of Chicago?"

Winnie nodded. "I think so. Some little Illinois town. A charming place to begin with." She sighed. "We'd just set up shop and, I think, sold a couple of pairs, when the local deputy stopped by our booth and asked for our permit."

John leaned forward, cupping his chin in his hand. "That was a problem?"

"We didn't have a permit." Remorse crept into Winnie's voice.

Penn remembered how rattled the aunts were at their first run-in with law enforcement.

"Did anybody tell us we had to have a permit?" Jancie raised her hands, palms turned toward the ceiling.

"No."

"Did we need one in Ohio?"

"No. Had not one problem in the Buckeye State."

"Right, but he closed us down in Illinois." Jancie folded her arms across her chest with an exaggerated sigh.

"What'd you do with the socks?"

"Lugged them all the way to the Pacific Ocean—"

"And all the way back to Mars, P.A."

"So... you didn't try to sell in any other states?"

"No." Winnie shook her head. "We didn't think it was worth the hassle."

"And the socks?"

Penn pounced. "You need a pair?"

John reared back his head and roared. "Seriously. You've still got them?"

"Not all five hundred pairs, but I think we have a few left. They've donated socks to worthy causes for years." She leaned toward him and whispered, "If you hear anyone refer to them as the sock ladies, now you know why."

Jancie pursed her lips. "They do not."

"Great story." He plucked another sourdough knot from the basket. "I really shouldn't have another, but these rolls are fantastic."

Aunt Jancie inclined her head. "Thank you. Have as many as you want, but save room for dessert. Chocolate cake."

"Chocolate cake? I feel like I just won a contest, and the prize is this fantastic meal." John sipped his water and rested against the slats in the chair. "Thank you again, ladies."

Aunt Jancie giggled. "My word, hon, but you do go on." She dabbed her mouth with her napkin, but Penn saw the satisfied grin she tried to hide with the cloth.

Aunt Winnie brought the cake to the table and served the first slice to John.

"Mmm." He swallowed a bite. "Chocolate chips inside?"

"Yep. Chocolate icing, chocolate cake, and chocolate chips. It's probably the best cake they make." Penn savored the tip of her slice. "My favorite, for sure."

Puffed up by the compliments, the aunts smiled, swished their shoulders, and batted their eyelashes.

Aunt Jancie cut the edge of her piece with her fork. "John, my late husband used to drink milk with this cake. Would you like a glass?"

With his mouth full of chocolate, John widened his

eyes and nodded.

Aunt Winnie glided back to the kitchen.

"You know, I've had chocolate cake in…I don't know… maybe nine or ten different states. In fact, my boss invited me to eat with him the other day in this four-star restaurant in Georgia. Chocolate cake for dessert, too, and I'm telling you this cake right here," he pointed his fork to the half slice left on his saucer, "this tremendous piece of chocolate bliss beats that impostor hands down."

Penn grimaced. "You travel a lot. Your boss lives in Georgia?"

"No, he's from Wexford." He sliced off another bite. "We were down there because he wanted to golf with some buddies for the day. Nice life, huh?" He slid the chocolate morsel into his mouth.

She knitted her eyebrows. "So were you writing about golf? I'm sorry. I'm not following. You were in Georgia for the day with your writing boss?"

Aunt Jancie stiffened in her chair. "Penn, sweetie, could you hand me another napkin, please? John, have some more cake." Her voice rose and cracked. She grabbed for a random bowl and dragged it toward her plate.

John turned his dessert plate. "Still working on this piece. Thank you." He smiled at Jancie and turned his attention back to Penn. "Sorry, Penn. My flying boss. Next week he's got a meeting in Ohio, so I'm flying him over there for the day." He smiled. "Somewhere west of Cleveland."

Penn gripped her fork until her knuckles turned white. "Flying?" Her voice was barely audible.

Aunt Winnie, returning from the kitchen, froze in the doorway, the milk sloshing over her fingers.

"Yeah." John glanced at Penn and his gaze fell on her knuckles. He narrowed his eyes. "I'm an on-call pilot."

Penn's fork dropped and clattered on top of her knife. She crossed her arms in front of her, grabbed her sides, and fought to pull in air. "Pilot?" She forced the word through tight lips.

"Yeah. Penn, are you all right?" John leaned toward her, but she pushed her chair away from the table.

"I'm sorry, but...ah...I need...I need to..." She shook her head. "Sorry." She sprinted out of the dining room and mounted the stairs two at a time.

~*~

What just happened? Something upset Penn, but what? Was she sick? They'd been talking about flying. Was she afraid to fly?

John looked for help from the aunts.

Jancie leaned against the table with her elbows, face in her hands and shaking her head.

Winnie had placed the half empty glass of milk on the table and now stood with her eyes closed, wringing a napkin and chewing on her bottom lip.

"Ladies?" He shifted toward the stairs. "Should I go after her?"

"No!" Two pairs of eyes flew open and pinned him to his chair.

"Sorry, John, dear."

"Sorry, it's just—"

Both spoke in short bursts before taking a slow breath.

Winnie returned to her chair and rolled the corner

of her napkin into a tight point. She kept her gaze on Jancie who, after several moments of what seemed to be silent communication between them, shut her eyes and nodded.

Jancie pushed her unused spoon back and forth beside her plate. "We knew this was going to happen."

"Yes. Yes, we did." More turns on the napkin point curled it into a spiral in Winnie's fingers.

"We should have told her about your job, but we thought waiting was the best idea." Jancie clasped her iced tea glass and wiped a swath of condensation with her index finger. "We wanted Penny to get to know you…"

"We wanted to welcome you to Mars, help you get to know the community. We hoped Penny and you could become friends and maybe in time your job wouldn't…she wouldn't…"

"Yes, we should have mentioned it to her before now, but the reason we didn't is Penn's story. It's up to her to tell you." Jancie rubbed her forehead.

"Exactly. Yes, it certainly is." Winnie fretted with the napkin, attacking another corner.

"She looked so…" Jancie glanced toward the staircase, her chin trembling. "Oh, my girl. My dear girl."

"Ladies, please." He leaned toward them. "I'm lost here. I get that Penn's upset…or sick. What is it? Tell me, please. I want to help."

Silence from the aunts. Silence and more shaking heads.

Winnie couldn't stop wringing her hands.

"Ladies, I kinda figured out that flying isn't her thing, but lots of people don't like to fly. There's more to the story." He waited. "Am I right?"

Jancie nodded. "We'll give you the bare bones, but you'll have to get details from Penny." She sighed. "Oh, it's hard, John. We don't normally talk about this. Haven't in years."

"My sister's right. It's hard, too hard, but you need to know."

Jancie drooped in her chair. "Haven't you ever wondered why Penny lives with us, two old aunts?"

"Instead of with her parents or even in an apartment by herself?" Winnie rolled the spiral into the center of the wrinkled napkin.

"I suppose so, but I've never really mentioned too much about my parents either."

Jancie reached across the table, seized Winnie's hand, and pressed her lips together. "When Penny was six years old, her parents and her little brother went for a flight in her dad's Cessna, and it crashed."

Winnie kneaded Jancie's white knuckles. "All three were gone in one afternoon."

John's stomach clenched. No wonder she had to leave the table. She'd lost her family in a plane crash. "What about Penn? She wasn't with them?"

Jancie shook her head, "No, at the last minute, a friend called with an invitation to play. Melody let her go. She never saw her parents or baby brother again."

"Melody and Thomas died instantly from the impact. Little Jasper died at the hospital."

Both women stared at the table in front of them, lost in their tragic thoughts. Their eyes shone with tears.

John, careful of their feelings, needed to hear the rest of the story. "And you took her in."

Jancie gasped and blinked. "Yes, we did." She patted Winnie's hand then rubbed wrinkles from the tablecloth. "I'd been retired from teaching for about a year or so. My husband was dead. Nothing was keeping me in Oxford. Winnie had retired from the Department of Social Services about six months earlier."

"Our brother, Graham, Penny's grandfather, still ran his company. He served on the school board and was a deacon in the church." Winnie shrugged. "Melody's grandmother, who raised her, lived in Florida. Everybody else was either too busy or too old. We had time on our hands." She lifted her chin. "We were the perfect choice."

Jancie pressed a napkin under her nose. "Penny knew us. They visited Oxford twice a year. We'd come up here a time or two. She loved us."

He needed all the details. "But you live here, not Oxford."

"Right. She'd been through enough." Jancie folded her arms against her chest. "We wanted her to have stability, so we moved." She shrugged. "Stability for her. Adventure for us."

"Exactly." Winnie nodded and smiled at her sister. "An adventure for sure."

The pieces of Penn's story clicked in John's brain. He understood her refusal to ride his motorcycle, her distrust of new or different things, her subdued, fragile air hiding underneath a prickly shell.

He wanted to understand more. "Who was the friend she visited that day?"

"John, we've said enough. Penn can tell you anything else you want to know—or at least what she'll let you know."

Winnie ignored Jancie. "Abby Parker. Missy's older sister."

7

Penn ascended the stairs two at a time but didn't slam her bedroom door. She didn't want to give them anything else to think about—or talk about. Heart pounding, she closed it with a soft click as she turned the lock. In the sanctity of her room, she dove onto her bed, tears and sobs captured within the soft puffs of her pillow.

She sobbed for the parents she had trouble remembering and the brother she missed even now. She cried for the friendship forever fractured because of her survivor's guilt.

She cried, too, for the guilt that came close to smothering her whenever she'd let herself mourn for what might have been. She cried because the aunts tried so hard to make her happy.

They loved her unconditionally. They contended with her quiet spells and prickly moods. They'd carted her to church and Girl Scouts and sports events. They bought Peri for her and gave her every material advantage.

If pink shirts were the rage in elementary school, they dressed her in pink shirts like every other girl in third grade. If everyone learned to ice skate, they signed her up for lessons. They gave her everything they could, except what she wanted most of all—her parents and brother back.

Penn crushed her pillow harder to her face and

cried for John. She'd tried not to enjoy his company, tried not to fall victim to her aunts' matchmaking ploys, but she'd let herself because it felt good. He was fun and funny. He was kind to her and to her crazy aunts. He didn't let his limp sideline him. Brave and strong, he did whatever he wanted.

She should have known. No. She *had* known. How many times had she told her aunts he wasn't for her? But she hadn't listened to her own words.

He rode a motorcycle. He met life head on and didn't worry about what ifs. Who bought a fixer-upper without skill or knowledge? John did because he wasn't strangled by potential problems or what ifs.

She wanted to be like that.

When the emotional storm passed and the last shudders subsided in her exhausted body, she rolled over onto her back. She heard the old grandfather clock chime the half hour. Slanting her aching eyes took effort as she glanced at her alarm clock.

Eight thirty. She pushed herself to sitting and leaned against the bed board. A headache beat a persistent rhythm between her temples.

She didn't have to look in a mirror to know she was a sight. She blinked grainy, raw eyes. Stuck in place, her contacts made any eye movement uncomfortable. Her nose, swollen from the tears, glowed with red that showed in her peripheral vision.

Her face needed a rinse. She should try to rectify the damage, but the crying had depleted every ounce of her energy. No worries about moving, however. She had no plans of returning to the dinner party.

Muffled voices floated up the stairs from the foyer. Subdued sounds. Had they told John her story? Probably—even though they'd always honored an unwritten rule. They never talked about it. They didn't need to. They knew the story inside and out.

She'd lived it.

Well, if he did know, fine. It wasn't as if they were a couple or anything. They'd never been alone together unless one counted the few minutes in the car driving back and forth to Hartwood and the few minutes in his apartment before David returned.

Again—fine. No harm, no foul.

Her studying needed attention. She'd have plenty of time now without the distraction of reciprocating dinner dates with the aunts and John. She'd study, study, study, pass the CPA test, get a fabulous job in Pittsburgh, and move to an apartment there where no one knew her as Penny-the-girl-who-lost-her-parents.

A shiver skipped up her spine, and she hugged herself, her ring pushed into her side.

The plan didn't seem as tempting as usual tonight.

~*~

John struggled to keep his mind on the instruments in front of him. Thank goodness, the weather cooperated with this trip. Clear, calm days made flying easy. Easier, at least. No thermals to thump the Cessna and jolt the pilot into stress mode.

Smooth flying—one reason his mind kept backtracking to Penn. His heart ached for her. No wonder she seemed a little closed off, a little timid.

No, not timid. He'd seen a bit of her back-bone show up at the apple meetings. More like cautious. Yes, cautious about new experiences.

He couldn't imagine losing his parents—and one of his brothers. He shook his head. He wished she pick up her phone or at least return one of the four calls he'd left since last Saturday night.

Winnie and Jancie told him to be patient, commiserating with him when he'd called the land line, but they held on tight to their gate-keeper roles, not giving the phone to Penn, simply reiterating, "She'll be fine. Don't worry."

Butler Airport came into view, and he radioed to ask for clearance. "Butler traffic, Cessna 46722, fifteen miles southeast at two thousand five hundred, landing, requesting airport advisory."

The voice from the airport crackled over the intercom. "Cessna 46722, Butler traffic, runway zero two in use, wind calm, altimeter 30.02, enter left downwind, report turning left base."

"Cessna 46722, roger."

Several miles outside the traffic pattern, John scanned the horizon for other planes. When a silver flash grabbed his attention from the left window, he glanced toward the ground. He noticed a pile of brown dirt, reminiscent of a grave. No, it looked exactly like a grave right after the casket was lowered and covered with fresh dirt.

For him to notice this grave-like mound from his vantage point, it had to be huge. The pile protruded from the earth with an enormous reach, partially obscured at one end by a…what? A weeping willow tree?

Interesting. What would fit in a hole that big?

Just before entering the traffic pattern, he noticed a rectangular hole. A big, rectangular hole. Parked beside it, an empty pickup truck waited. The hole edged beyond the front and back sides of the truck. At one end of the hole, a backhoe worked on what looked to be a ramp.

John dragged his gaze back to the front windshield as snippets of conversation flashed in his mind. "Stolen equipment. Buried. Revenge."

Who had been talking? Where had he heard this crazy talk? He squinted and concentrated on the instrument panel, but those words fluttered in the back of his mind.

He grabbed the microphone. "Butler traffic, Cessna 46722 turning left base runway zero two."

"Cessna 46722 cleared to land."

He turned the plane onto the left base of the landing pattern, and the memory of the conversation returned with clarity. Al and Jacob. They'd discussed the buried equipment at the last Apple Fest meeting.

Had he really seen what he thought he saw? Or had that truck been parked beside the hole to carry off the dirt pile? But why would anyone dump the dirt on the ground instead of dumping it straight into the truck? Waste of time and energy.

His heart thumped, escalating the adrenaline that normally accompanied every landing. He forced his attention back to his main task, promising himself to call Al as soon as he finished this flight.

Buried equipment? Seriously? He'd thought Jacob had been joking at the meeting.

Apparently not.

~*~

John sent up a quick thank you prayer for a safe landing. Just before touchdown, a rogue crosswind had required a crab angle set up on the final approach, and he transitioned into a side slip during the flare. A couple of bumps later, he taxied to his parking spot near the hangar.

Not a text book landing, but he subscribed to the tenet he'd heard from almost every pilot he'd ever known. Any landing one walked away from was a good landing.

Unfolding himself from the cockpit, he stretched and turned on his phone. He wanted to talk with Al before doubts mushroomed about what he saw. Hearing Al's voice mail kick in, he frowned and pressed his fingers to his temple. He left a quick message with just enough details to create interest without confusion. He didn't want to leave a crazy message about buried equipment.

His phone indicated a message.

Andy Duffy, youth pastor at Love Community Church, invited him to be one of the chaperones with the youth group to the amusement park on Saturday.

He'd hoped that maybe Penn would have come around by then, and he could visit with her, but the way things were going, that hope probably wouldn't happen. He pulled up his calendar. No flights scheduled.

He rubbed his chin. A day at an amusement park would be fun. He loved roller coasters. He also wanted to get to know Andy better.

They'd had a couple of lunches since the first time John had visited the church. Besides the fact that Andy was married with a baby on the way, this acquaintance might be the beginning of a good friendship.

Yeah. He'd go on Saturday. Maybe Andy would have some advice about Penn.

8

Penn threw her head back against the church bus seat and laughed at the antics of Grace and Trudy, rising freshmen. Teaching junior and senior classes, she hadn't taught them in school yet, but she'd known them since they were born.

Embodying the definition of giggly teenage girls, they whispered secrets, pealed with laughter, and whispered something new. They loved singing in the youth choir, but almost every time the group sang, either Grace or Trudy would elbow the other one. The struggle to control themselves would ensue—biting the bottom lip, refusing to make eye contact with each other. Giggles usually erupted before the song ended.

Their enthusiasm spilled onto everyone near them. At present, both faced her over the back of their seat, singing an impromptu song about going to the amusement park with a youth group.

"*Dear ole Pe-enn. Dear ole Pe-enn.*
Fun chaperone. Fun chaperone.
She-ee likes to crochet. She-ee likes to crochet.
Covers for phones. Covers for phones."

Their lyrics sent them into hysterical laughter bending them double. They clutched each other.

"You silly girls, I'm crocheting baby booties, not a phone cover. And that's 'Ms. Davenport' to you, by the way."

A movement at the front of the bus caught her eye,

and she looked straight into the dark brown eyes of John. The smile froze on her lips. She sucked in air and managed to nod in his direction.

He smiled back before dropping his gaze to the floor and following Andy down the aisle.

At her gasp, Trudy and Grace jerked their attention to the front, slid to their seats, and giggled.

"Hi, Penn. Thanks again for coming today." Andy gestured behind him. "Do you know John Townsend? He's agreed to help out today, too."

"Yeah."

"Uh huh."

Penn's eyes flickered toward the window. Was there any way to escape spending the day with John?

More giggles from the seat in front of her.

"Joh-nn Townsend. Joh-nn Townsend.

Coming, too. Coming, too.

La la la la la la. La la la la la la.

La la la. La la la."

John rewarded the young teens with a grin that highlighted the dimple in his right cheek.

Andy shook his head. "You girls already starting? Rare form, today, huh?"

Giggles.

Krista, Andy's wife, appeared at the top of the bus's steps. "Andy, everyone's out of the fellowship hall. I think we're ready."

"Great. Thanks, hon." He clapped his hands. "Let's get this show on the road. John, if you want to sit up front, you can help me navigate." Andy nodded to the empty seat behind the driver.

John glanced at the backpack occupying the place beside Penn and the shoulder bag in the seat across the aisle. "Sounds good." He caught Penn's gaze. "See ya when we get there."

The two of them moved back up the aisle and jockeyed for position with Krista. She laughed and kissed her husband on the cheek to cheers from the teenagers.

Krista plopped down across from Penn. "Now I should be able to make it until the park bathrooms. I hope, that is!" She laughed and adjusted the maternity top covering her expanding mid-section.

Determined to settle the chaos racking her insides, Penn focused on her companion. "How're you feeling?"

"Terrific. I won't be able to ride most of the rides, but I don't mind holding the belongings for everybody else. I'm just happy for a fun day with Andy—even if he is technically working. This is a good group. Not any troublemakers, you know?"

Penn agreed. These teenagers were good. She knew most of them from church. Others she'd taught or seen at school. The teenagers didn't worry her, but the tall, dark, and handsome chaperone chatting with Andy stole her breath, raced her heart, and caused her to bite her lip. *John Townsend, the P-I-L-O-T.*

He'd want to talk about last Saturday's dinner. She wanted to avoid that conversation.

And him, too.

She'd envisioned this day differently, for sure. She'd planned to sit with Krista, teaching her to crochet booties, watching the teens' paraphernalia, maybe riding a tame ride or two if Trudy or Grace asked her.

Now add to that list: steering clear of John. More than likely, she wouldn't have to worry too much about him.

The boys already peppered him with questions

about his motorcycle. They found his daredevil lifestyle fascinating.

Good.

He could ride all the rides with the new members of his fan club, and she could spend the day with Krista as planned.

~*~

Or not.

The teens jostled each other with all the anticipation of puppies waiting for kibble as Andy finished his youth pastor speech about applying sunscreen, staying together in groups of at least three, and meeting back at the picnic tables for lunch. As soon as he said, "Have fun," they burst into the park in every direction.

Andy grabbed Krista's hand and called, "See ya in a few," over his shoulder.

John stood beside the bus with his thumbs hooked in his belt loops.

Penn blinked. What had just happened?

She and John were now a group? If her aunts had been anywhere near the park or if they'd known John was chaperoning, too, she'd believe those two were matchmaking again.

Trudy and Grace, with two other girls, skipped toward the section of the park with most of the big rides.

Her stomach clenched with a longing ache for their silly giggles to buffer the awkward silence settling on them.

John ran his hand through his hair before shoving both in the pockets of his khaki shorts and rocked on his heels. "So, Penn. Looks like it's you and me."

"Looks like it." She adjusted her sunglasses. She tried not to notice the way his hair feathered around his face, accenting his eyes. A scent of cotton candy drifted by her nose, and she focused on that instead. She'd buy some this afternoon.

John nodded toward the coolers and grocery bags dotting four picnic tables. "We really leave all our stuff on these tables and no one bothers them? Seriously?"

She grinned. "Yep. That's one of the special quirks about this park. We claim our tables now and use them at lunch."

"Cool."

More awkward silence.

She took in a deep breath and exhaled. "Listen, I'm not much for the rides, so if you want to catch up with some of those boys, no problem."

Eyebrows shot above his aviators. "And leave you by yourself? What kind of friend would I be? Come on. We'll find a ride that suits you or die trying." He unfolded a glossy map of the park and studied it.

She pushed her shoulders back. "I really wasn't planning to ride today. I thought I'd squirt sunscreen, hold cellphones so they didn't drop out of pockets, count heads, that kind of thing."

He peeked over the edge of the map. "That sounds like a really big time." John's grin softened the sarcasm and tugged at her heart. "You know, chaperones can have some fun, too."

"I'm completely aware of that, thank you. I've chaperoned before. It's just...our idea of fun is probably poles apart."

He closed the map, not taking time to refold it by the original creases. "Penn." His voice dropped a notch. "I'm not one for ignoring a pink elephant. I'm sorry about the other night. I thought you knew I'm a pilot. I didn't know how you feel about flying."

Rats. She didn't want to have this conversation. Another difference between the two of them. She could've gone all day ignoring the pink elephant lumbering between them. She latched onto the part of the conversation that didn't hurt too much. "I thought you were a writer. You told me you'd write an article about refurbishing your house."

"Right. I do plan to. I'm just sorry that you felt...maybe ambushed or something."

Ambushed? Because she'd stumbled from the table and hidden in her room the rest of the night? Because she'd left her aunts to answer his inevitable questions? Because she'd acted like some kind of head case?

She chewed on her bottom lip trying to think of something to say. "No problem. Don't worry about it."

He shook his head, squinting at her. "You didn't answer your phone all week. Or return my messages."

"My phone's been off. I've been studying." She looked at the baskets on the tables, ignoring his eyes.

"You're telling me a twenty-something kept her phone off all week?"

She shrugged, and her gaze wandered to a dad pushing a double stroller. "I needed to concentrate. We have a land line at home."

"Yeah. I tried that, too. Your aunts are great gate keepers, by the way. They protect you very well."

Her head jerked back to him. "You think I need to be protected?"

"No. Especially not from me."

She couldn't think of a response.

Shrieks, laughter, and music from the rides filled the silence between them.

He stepped closer to her. "Penn, I just moved here. I'm trying to make friends. I'm not going to hurt you. I'm not that kind of person."

Friend. That word again? Fine. He wanted a friend, not a girlfriend. The question was—could she be friends with a pilot?

~*~

As soon as the words left John's mouth, a vision of Stephanie floated through his mind. He was that kind of person. Although he hadn't meant to, he'd hurt Stephanie, a friend from the local ski club. She'd read much more into their time exploring the slopes and drinking peppermint hot chocolates than he'd intended.

He'd been forthright about applying for piloting jobs. He dropped details about various airports into their study sessions for her real estate license exam, but when he announced his move to Mars, she'd offered a position in her father's real estate office. She'd convinced herself he was a natural for selling houses.

Stephanie's error in assessing his personality proved she didn't know him. He hated selling, would fail at selling ice at the equator.

After respectfully declining the offer, he'd left for his apartment. She'd called before he could unlock his door.

Her words burned into his brain. "I need to be clear. You're really moving? To...to...that place in Pennsylvania? That Moon place?"

"Mars."

"Whatever. So what does that mean? I mean...where does that leave us?"

"Us?"

Her quick intact of breath should have been a red flag for him, but it confused him rather than warned him.

"John?" She whined the question in his ear. "We've been seeing each other for six and a half months. Doesn't that count for anything?"

John's heart tightened with the words reverberating in his mind.

"Stephanie, I..." He shook his head at the memory.

How could she have misinterpreted their friendship, painted them as a couple? They'd never kissed, never even held hands. Most of the time their activities had included three or four other friends. "Stephanie, I'm sorry, but..."

"Are you breaking up with me over the phone? Seriously, John?" He'd heard the catch in her voice. "I never thought you'd treat me like this." Then the phone had clicked off.

He cringed. It'd be a while before he'd stroll down the couples' path again.

"John?"

He dragged his attention back to Penn, an interesting mix of vulnerability and steely resolve. She came across as fragile sometimes, but she'd shown backbone at the Apple meetings. He wouldn't have to worry about her misunderstanding his intentions. He smiled at her. "What?"

A shyness shaded her eyes. "I said, 'Are you ready for this experience?'"

He rubbed his hands together. "Absolutely. I was born ready. Which way to the roller coasters?"

She shook her head. "I don't do roller coasters. Remember?"

"Didn't do." His smile turned mischievous. "Come on. Let's go have fun." He placed his hand at the small of her back and gave her a tiny nudge toward the old part of the park.

Penn pushed down a feeling of panic. That section held the big rides—the roller coaster, and all the rides that made people shriek in terror. All the rides that she'd like to avoid.

But John wasn't headed to the roller coaster, thank goodness. He joined the not-so-long line for the Tilt-a-Whirl.

"Let's start with this one. One of my all-time favorites." He pulled her hand. "Come on. The cars don't even leave the platform. They just spin. And not too fast either."

His enthusiasm was endearing.

So she ignored him and considered the ride. The cars spun and rocked and rolled up and down like a carousel. The spins looked fast sometimes. Other times the cars only rocked back and forth. Most of the riders howled with excitement, their heads tipped back and their mouths wide open. Laughing, not screaming.

Maybe she could do it. She'd try at least for the handsome man chuckling at the spinning cars full of people having fun. The line moved ahead, and it was their turn to have fun. The ride attendant gave them a car to themselves. Nice.

John took her hand to help her inside the car. Very nice.

He gave her a pep talk as other cars filled and the seat bar clicked into place. "You're going to love this."

The platform creaked and began its slow rotation

over the rollers, creating an up and down motion. She stole a glance at John with a this-isn't-so-bad look.

He grinned.

Picking up speed, the ride pushed the car into a few partial spins. Feeling the centrifugal force pull her to the left then the right, Penn gripped the bar and planted herself in the middle of the seat, willing herself not to sling into him.

A giggle tickled her throat. She bit her lip to stifle it. With the constant barrage of swinging back and forth and up and down, she gave up trying to corral her laughs. A steady stream of her chortles mingled with John's chuckles.

Suddenly, the car twirled with a quick whipping motion sending her right into the whole length of him. He didn't seem to mind. Instead, he grinned again, threw his arm around her shoulders, and pulled her tighter against him. "This way we can fight the force together."

Oh, yeah. She liked the Tilt-a-Whirl.

~*~

Two hours later, she led him back to the picnic tables filled with coolers and grocery bags.

John scratched his jaw. "Our stuff is still here."

"You doubted?"

"Well, you have to admit, not many places have this leave-your-stuff-wide-open nobody-will-touch-it policy." He slid the top off a cooler and popped a green grape into his mouth.

Penn accepted a sprig of grapes he offered her. "True. This is a special place. Its tradition and family atmosphere, I guess."

She relaxed on the bench opposite John and scanned the entrances to the park. "Every other summer the youth group goes to a bigger park with bigger rides but no picnic policy."

Trudy and her gang emerged from the trees to her right. "Get your chaperone on. Here they come."

John stopped his investigation of the baskets and coolers to crane his neck toward the still giggling teens. He chuckled. "They remind me of my cousins."

Andy and Krista stepped into the picnic area, Andy's arm draped across her shoulders. Krista's arm hugged his waist. Andy plopped down beside Krista on the opposite side of the picnic table. "We got a great day at the park. Light crowd. Slightly overcast sky. Seventy-five degrees. Perfect."

Krista handed him a sandwich and fished another one from the cooler. "Penn, this one has your name on it. You got a special one?"

Penn shrugged. "You know the Lovely Ladies." She tugged the sandwich from Krista's fingers, a little embarrassed the ladies circle always singled her out.

Krista let go but eyed Penn with scrunched eyebrows. "No one else has a sandwich with a name on it."

"Just special, I guess."

Let it alone, Krista. It's only a sandwich.

"Hey, you guys," Andy called to the other tables. "I better see you at church tomorrow giving hugs to the Lovely Ladies. They're the 'hands that prepared the food' for you this morning at five AM."

Trudy sang out, "'This morning at five AM' is redundant." Giggles from the girls' table.

Andy snorted, "Good vocab word. Now eat."

John unwrapped a turkey and cheese. "Lovely

Ladies?"

Andy smiled and nodded. "The Lovely Ladies of Love Community—a group of retired women. I don't think there's one of 'em younger than seventy-five. Always makes sure the youth group, or any church group really, is fully stocked with food—all homemade by the way—before leaving on a trip. A terrific bunch."

"Impressive. I figured their moms made the lunches. You've got a great church. Feels like a big, extended family."

Krista leaned away from the table and arched her back. "Feels so good to sit down. I'll chaperone the SoakZone this afternoon. Putting my feet up while the kids splash down the water slides sounds like a plan. Hey, Penn." She peered from across the table. "What kind of sandwich is that anyway?"

Penn popped the corner she'd just torn from her bread into her mouth and shielded rest of the sandwich which her hands. How to get out of this conversation with her dignity intact? The glob of bread and peanut butter expanded on her tongue. Was it twice as big as the original morsel? She rubbed her lapis ring with her thumb.

Andy leaned toward her, taking exaggerated sniffs. "PB and J? Not exactly." He grimaced." I don't think it's jelly. Can you tell, John?"

Penn managed to push down the swelling wad and twisted off the top of her water bottle. "Cut it out, you guys. It's just my sandwich." She pulled the cold liquid into her gummy mouth. *Leave it alone. Please leave it alone.* She swallowed. "I'll sit with you at the water park."

"Oh, no, you don't." John reached for a carrot stick, keeping his eyes on Penn. "We've got a date with a roller coaster."

A date.

But with a roller coaster? Not in this lifetime.

Before she could answer, Krista grabbed the plastic bag containing the second triangle and examined the contents. "Is that...mayonnaise in there?" Her jaw dropped. "Looks like mayonnaise and peanut butter. Penn?"

Andy grimaced. "Mayonnaise?"

"So what if it is? It's my sandwich." She cocked her head, arched her eyebrow and waited, palm open, for Krista to return her lunch.

Andy shuddered. "Mayonnaise."

John chuckled and shook his head. "To each her own."

"Especially if she's expecting. Sounds kinda interesting to me." Krista waved her baggy of ham and cheese at Penn. "Wanna trade halves?"

9

John crossed his arms against his chest. A determined smile lit his face. "It's time, Penn. You know it. Come on. Let's get in line."

"I don't know it." Penn clamped her teeth on her bottom lip. She skimmed over the crowd, hoping to find a familiar face that might distract John from his aim of getting her on that roller coaster.

"My turn to choose the ride." He pointed to the track partially hidden in tall trees. "I choose that one."

"I rode the Ferris wheel and the Paratrooper. I think I deserve some credit, for Pete's sake." She pivoted from the dips, twists, and hills of the coaster just in time to catch a whiff of pizzas that roiled her stomach.

He snapped his fingers. "Snaps to you for having fun at an amusement park. You did have fun, right? You didn't scream, cry, or throw up."

"Is that your idea of a compliment?" She twisted her ring around her finger and squeezed the smooth, round stone. Penn couldn't remember much about those rides.

Once John gathered her close on the Ferris wheel and left his arm draped across her shoulders, she had trouble appreciating the gorgeous scenery of the Laurel Highlands.

Except for her racing heartbeat brought on by the height of the wheel and John's thumb tapping the beat of a carnival song on her collarbone, the experience wasn't so bad. She'd rank the anxiety level somewhere between taking a final exam and bungee jumping.

With its ten umbrella-covered benches that rose and fell as the ride slowly rotated, the ride looked scarier than it turned out to be. In fact, the breeze stirred by the ride refreshed and calmed her.

Or was that John's hand on top of her fingers clenched around the safety bar?

"And, although I still can't believe it,' he shook his head, "I rode the trolley and the carousel."

She clutched her left elbow. "We weren't the only adults on those rides."

"True, but the other adults were accompanied by toddlers and preschoolers."

She tugged at the hem of her shirt, refusing to acknowledge the truth in his statement. "It's tradition. I ride those rides every time I'm here."

"Come on. Let's have this conversation in line." Placing his hand on her shoulder, he led her to the long line for the roller coaster.

"Wait a minute. I haven't agreed to get on that thing." She wanted to resist his argument, stand her ground, but her willful body took its place beside him.

"Not yet, but I have at least thirty minutes to convince you you'll love it. If you still want to wimp out when we get to the front, I'll say, 'go in peace.'" He patted her shoulder. "You'll be fine, Penn. You loved the other rides."

"Says you." Her heart had risen up into her throat making real conversation a trial. Tears threatened to surface.

"You giggled and sighed the whole time we were swinging through the air." His eyes twinkled as he slanted a look at her. "I wondered if you'd turned into Trudy for a minute."

"Cute. You know how to talk to the ladies, huh?" Desperate for an idea to change his mind, Penn scanned the nearby booths. She pointed behind his back. "Look, there's an ice cream kiosk. Let's get some of that ice cream of the future." She loved those little pearls of frozen mint chocolate. The cookies and cream was pretty good, too.

"Great idea—after the 'coaster. I'll treat for accomplishing our goal."

The line moved up.

Her lungs forgot how to process oxygen. "Our goal? To scare me to death? To humiliate me when I scream bloody murder?" She sucked in more air, counted to ten, and released it to another count of ten.

He shrugged. "Sometimes it's important to shake things up a bit. Stepping outside the box you've erected around yourself helps you grow."

"Again—says you, Mr. Daredevil."

The light in his brown eyes extinguished. Furrows lined his forehead. "I'm not a daredevil, Penn. I just enjoy the life God's given me. I want that for you, too." He held her gaze for a moment and turned around. "Come on. Let's go get a treat."

Penn's stomach clenched. She grabbed his arm and squeezed. "Wait, John." She did not want to ride that stupid roller coaster. She didn't want to disappoint him, either. She wanted to soar with the eagles, like the verse in Psalms said, but years of standing on the sidelines weighed her down.

Maybe John could be the person to help her break loose some of those chains.

He shook his head. "We don't have to do this. I'm

sorry I pushed you, Penn."

She held up her hand. "Don't talk me out of it now." She closed her eyes. Live the life God gave her. She wanted to live that life, not hang back as usual. Penn studied the man half turned away from her, ready to help her take a baby step outside her box. "I really don't want to do this, but...I think I have to." Fluttery sensations filled her chest. "I know I have to."

"You don't have to. You—"

"Stop." She pinned him with her I'm-serious-don't-mess-with-me teacher eyes. "I've made up my mind, but you have to promise some things under the threat of excruciating pain if you ever break the promise."

The corner of his mouth lifted. He arched a brow. "Oh? And what do I have to promise?" John stepped forward again.

She swiped her hand over her mouth. "That you won't laugh at me. That what happens in that car stays in that car. That you never mention how many times or how loud I scream—to anyone else—or to me."

"Is that all?" The twinkle reappeared in those dark eyes.

"Maybe." She wiped her clammy hands on her shorts. "If I think of anything else, I'll let you know."

"I'm sure you will."

~*~

Penn sagged on the picnic table bench with Krista and waited for the stragglers to appear from the outer reaches of the park. Exhausted, mentally and physically, she looked forward to the ride back home. Maybe she'd catch a nap on the way. Fortify herself before facing her aunts and their questions about her day.

Wouldn't they be thrilled with her foray into amusement park rides? As much as she loved them, on earlier trips to the park, their pleas for the exciting rides had yielded nothing but more orbits on the carousel.

She stretched her legs and smiled, remembering the roller coaster experience.

At the front of the line, John had seen the fear emanating from every pore in her body. He'd changed his mind. "You're trembling, and you're white as a sheet." He'd grabbed her arm. "Come on. Let's go."

John had shuffled backward two steps when she'd bellowed, "No."

Jumping to attention, the teenage ride attendant raised his eyebrows and asked if she needed help. A knock-out drug might have been helpful. Though her breathing came in short puffs, she squeaked out a few words. "No. I'm doing this. You have to help me."

She hadn't seen a thing during the ride. She'd closed her eyes as tight as a bank on Sunday.

The couple who shared the car with them screamed behind her, but their screams mixed with giggles.

Her screams never relented, bouncing off the trees and echoing through the park.

When the eternity ended, the car bumped and lurched along the tracks to the exit shoot.

John's deep laughter rewarded her bravery. "You did it, Penn! Wow. Was that great, or what?" He hugged her to him and rested his chin on top of her head.

She'd opened her eyes to his searching gaze inches

from her face.

"How are you? How do you feel?" Concern hovered on his countenance, but something else accompanied it. Was it pride? Delight?

She couldn't figure it out. She couldn't think. She couldn't speak. Her bones had departed from her body. She drank in huge calming breaths to battle the exhilaration of the ride. And the intensity in his eyes. Her fingers ached from her death grip on the safety bar locked in front of them. She still trembled, but lightness surrounded her heart. She'd smiled at him.

His eyes dropped to her mouth. He leaned toward her and...

Would he really have kissed her?

She'd never know. Trudy and her pals had spied them, screaming their names from the path near the ride's entrance. The spell broke, and she crawled out of her seat, a difficult feat for someone without bones.

Andy's voice brought her back to the present as he led the count off to make sure everyone was present. Number ten didn't answer. "Hey, who's number ten?"

"Jack." A voice called from the back of the group.

Jack Williams, a rising senior.

Penn had taught him Algebra II two years ago. Good student. Not a bad kid.

Andy huffed and slapped his hands on his waist. "Somebody call him and tell him, 'This bus is leaving, and he better get here. Pronto.' He knew the departure time."

"His phone is off. It went straight to voicemail." Amy Hinnant, the probable class valedictorian, pushed her phone back into her shorts pocket.

Andy pointed a finger at a boy hiding behind Amy. "Daniel, you two were supposed to be a group.

Why are you here without him? Where is he? Spill."

Daniel Wooten shuffled around Amy and shrugged. "We were together till about two or so."

Andy's mouth tightened. "What happened at two?"

Daniel cleared his throat. "We were standing in line at the Potato Shack to buy some fries. We saw some guys from the Pine-Richland football team. We know 'em from camp. Their youth group came today, too. Jack started talking with one of the girls from that group. He decided to ride the Ferris wheel with her." He peeked at Andy through his long, side swept bangs.

Andy rubbed the back of his neck. "And?"

"And I didn't want to ride the lame Ferris wheel again. So..." Hunching his shoulders, Daniel stuffed his hands into his pockets.

Lame? The Ferris wheel had turned into one of her favorite rides, especially with John beside her. With his arm around her.

"So, what...?" Andy kept a lid on his growing frustration. "He went with the girl, and you...?"

Daniel hung his head and starred at his leather flip-flops. "I started hanging with Amy and her group."

Andy grunted and rubbed his face. "I've got a bus load of exhausted people ready to hit the road and one AWOL Romeo."

"Come on." John thumped him on his back. "Let's go look for Don Juan. The ladies can keep the troops in line."

Easy for him to say. Her legs felt like pudding.

"Fine." Andy pointed to the two oldest boys. "But Daniel, you and James are going with us. That way we can split up and cover more territory." His voice didn't invite questions or complaints. "The rest of you stay right here at these tables. Do not make any trouble." He reached for Krista and kissed her temple. "Sorry, babe. We'll try to find him as quick as we can. We'll call when we've got him."

John smiled at Penn. "You OK?"

She nodded.

He glanced at the teens, several of whom had already stretched out on the grass. "I don't think you'll have a problem with these guys. They're ready for the bus. See ya in a few."

~*~

Forty-five minutes and one half-hearted, teenage apology later, Penn leaned back in her seat. She would have been asleep by now, but John's leg brushed against her every time the bus swerved or ran over a bump in the road. The zings that sailed through her body acted like a double shot of caffeine.

John didn't seem affected by her presence. His eyes closed, he sat with his hands folded in his lap, the picture of relaxation.

She shifted to study his profile. Her gaze traveled down his long, straight nose and skipped to his cheek where she knew a dimple crinkled when he smiled. She discovered a faint scar running along his high cheekbone perpendicular to his jaw line. What happened to mar his otherwise perfect face?

Eyes popped open and rotated toward her.

She jumped in her seat and stifled a scream.

He faced her with a grin. "I think I'm supposed to say, 'Like what you see? Take a picture. It lasts longer.'

If I was fifteen, that is."

And you're definitely not fifteen.

But I would love a picture of you. I'd set it on my dresser and look at you every morning and…no. Won't work. She pushed a curl behind her ear, wrapped her arms around her stomach. *Stop the runaway thoughts about this pilot.* Penn shook her head. "I don't think you'd say that when you were fifteen."

"Then you'd be surprised. I grew up with two other rough and tumble boys. We could be pretty sassy when we wanted to, and, believe me, we wanted to most of the time." Stretching his right leg into the aisle, he grinned at her like the rogue she'd imagined him to be the first time she met him. "So. You were staring at me?"

The rapid change in conversation caught the breath in her throat. Penn scrambled for words. "Um. I noticed your scar." *Way to point out his flaws, Penn.* She frowned. "Sorry. I…"

"No worries." He skimmed the scar with the tip of his middle finger. "My brothers and I were horsing around in our family room. I was about six or seven. Mom had just yelled that somebody was gonna get hurt when Jake dive bombed me. My head crashed into a glass-topped table. Shattered like snow all over the carpet." He tapped the scar.

"A shard cut me right here. While we waited in the ER, my mom confessed she hated that table—a leftover from my dad's bachelor pad. I think she appreciated my sacrifice for her sense of decor so much that she never said, 'I told you so.' She's good like that." John rolled his shoulders. "I think it gives me character—kinda like my limp." He tilted his head. "What do you think?"

Her heart clenched at the way his dark brown eyes crinkled at the corners. "I think you like making lemonade out of lemons."

"Absolutely." He flattened his hands in front of him like a scale holding imaginary weights. "Lemons or lemonade. Which would you choose?"

You. Heat flooded her cheeks. Did she say that out loud?

John slumped in his seat and closed his eyes. No teasing.

She hadn't spoken aloud. Tension evaporated leaving a pleasant exhaustion in her muscles. She glanced out the window at the fading light.

I'd choose you, John Townsend.

10

Penn clomped down the stairs for an overdue study break. She needed some Peri time. As her foot touched the parquet floor at the bottom of the stairs, a red canvas shoe burst open the front door. A brown bag of groceries hid the identity of which aunt wore red today. Jancie called to her from the front door. "Penny. Penn. Yoo-hoo? Are you busy on Saturday?"

"I'm right here." Penn met Jancie at the door and freed the bag from her. "This Saturday? I'm studying."

"Good. We just saw John at the grocery store. He mentioned he'd refinished his kitchen cabinets and repainted the appliances, so of course he's ready for a new kitchen floor. A paper bag floor. I told him we could put one in for him this Saturday. I knew you were free."

"I'm studying. The exam's in fourteen weeks." Her heartbeat accelerated at the reminder of the CPA exam, not the idea of being with John again. Or so she told herself. For the umpteenth time this week.

Winnie entered the foyer with another bag and the car keys dangling from her thumb. Purple adorned her body as well as her feet. "Two more sacks are out in the car."

"Set that down and come help me with the other two, please." Jancie glided out the door with Penn behind her. "Hon, you've been studying so much your head's gonna fall right off your neck. You can take a morning break on Saturday, surely. The floor won't take long."

Penn lifted the smaller bag out of the back seat. Handing it to her aunt, she grabbed the larger one for herself. "It won't take long?" She bumped the door closed with her hip. "When have you ever made a paper bag floor? What about your back? A few weeks ago it wouldn't let you ride over to Hartwood. And now you're going to crawl on a floor all day?"

Jancie frowned and skipped up the stone steps to prove a point. "I'm not decrepit."

"And I guess Winnie's swollen ankles have magically deflated?" Penn followed her aunt to the kitchen where Winnie filled the refrigerator drawers with produce.

"Oh, I feel fine now. Didn't I tell you?" Winnie wiggled her left foot to prove her dexterity.

"Great." She set the bag onto the counter and slapped her hands on her hips. "But don't you think crawling on the floor might start swelling your ankles again?"

"Absolutely not. Besides, you'll be the crawler, dear. You and John, that is. Jancie and I are the brains behind the job. You two will be the hands and feet." She opened a new bag of pretzel rods, crunched off the end of one, and offered the snack to Penn.

"The brains? That implies you know what you're doing." Penn selected a rod and punched the air with it, emphasizing her argument. "Let me repeat my question—when have you ever laid a paper bag floor?"

Winnie shrugged. "That's beside the point." She dusted salt crumbs from her iris-colored blouse.

Penn leaned against the counter and, still clutching the pretzel, crossed her arms in front of her chest.

"That *is* my point."

Jancie slid a rod from the bag and joined in. "Penn, honey, we know all about it. We looked it up on the Internet."

Penn rolled her eyes. "You looked it up? On the Internet?"

Jancie waved her pretzel. "We know about stuff like that."

She bit the tip of the rod. "Anyway, Francine's cousin over in Gibsonia put one in her powder room a couple of years ago. She loves hers. It's easy. You'll see. John's excited about it."

Winnie bobbed from one purple tennis shoe to the other. "We're bringing breakfast, and then he's taking us out for lunch at Uncle Bob's. He said he's been wanting to try out that place for weeks."

Uncle Bob's? Penn hadn't eaten at Good Ole Uncle Bob's since at least fifth or sixth grade. Uncle Bob's used to be the only place for Saturday lunches after youth soccer games. The aunts ordered the fish sandwich every time.

She folded her arms over her stomach. "I'm sure he suggested Uncle Bob's." Her chest tightened. Saturday would be a lost day of studying. "Do I have to remind you that I'm all thumbs when it comes to crafts and DIY projects?" Her stomach churning, she laid her pretzel on the counter, untouched. "And I'm sure I don't have to remind you that he's…he's a…well, you know how I feel about flying. So quit your little matchmaking schemes."

Winnie blinked wide, innocent eyes. "We're helping a friend spruce up his kitchen. Don't worry about your thumbs, sweetheart. Just do what we tell you to do, and everything will be fine."

Famous last words.

~*~

The wafting aroma of cinnamon rolls woke Penn on Saturday morning. She smiled at the decadent scent and rolled to her back, extending her toes toward the edge of the mattress. A knock accompanied the sweet scent.

"Good morning. Good morning. Good morning to you. Good morning. Good morning. I'm fine. How are you?"

For as long as she could remember, Winnie had greeted her with the same little song.

Her aunt stepped halfway into the room. "Time to rise and shine, sleepyhead. The rolls are almost done, and we need to get over to John's."

Penn's eyes flew open. The morning ritual definitely did not include mentioning John Townsend. She peeked at her clock. The hands pointed to seven o'clock. A groan rumbled at the back of her throat.

Winnie jiggled the mattress. "Come on, now. John's waiting. We don't want to disappoint him." She bustled back out the door.

Penn pulled a pillow over her head. Fifteen minutes later, wearing a pair of ancient shorts and a vintage Pittsburgh Pirates t-shirt, Penn joined her aunts in the kitchen.

The rolls cooled on a trivet.

Jancie and Winnie bent over a board propped up on the table.

Winnie pointed to the board. "See this one is definitely upside down. Good thing we tried it out first."

Jancie lifted her glasses and bent to the table. "I see what you mean. We'll have to be careful."

Penn poured herself a glass of orange juice. "What's up?" She dreaded the answer but dreaded the surprise of learning the answer later in the morning more.

"Good morning, sweet pea." Jancie greeted her with a smile. "We're just looking over the template we made for the floor."

"A template?" Penn grabbed a banana and broke the top of the peel.

"We wanted to try out our ideas before we got to John's. We practiced on this board last night while you were studying." Jancie gestured to Penn to observe their handiwork.

Penn snorted. "So you're a little skeptical about this paper bag thing, too, huh?"

Winnie jabbed a finger at Penn. "Absolutely not. We just want to be prepared to the fullest extent. Good thing, too." She studied the board again. "We found out that there's a right side and a wrong side to paper."

"A right side?" Sleepiness fled from her widened eyes. "Seriously?"

"Seriously, Penny. We'll show you how to tell the difference."

Penn swallowed the last of the banana and carried the peel over to the compost canister. "Two more bags of trash already? I emptied the can Thursday. How can three people create this much garbage?" She nudged a white garbage bag leaning against the cabinet with her canvas docksider.

"Wait." Jancie lunged for the bag. "That's not garbage. They're full of paper balls. We started last night so we could get a jump on things for this morning."

Bags of paper? Get a jump on things? Penn unwound the bread tie on one of the bags and peered inside. "It's full of crumpled up paper." She removed a handful of paper balls from the bag.

Jancie nodded. "Exactly. We tore and crumpled last night so that you and John could start gluing first thing this morning. Winnie and I will tear and crush to keep you supplied with pieces to glue." Fiddling with her scarlet collar, she wiggled her eyebrows. "Teamwork."

Penn closed her eyes and sighed. "You have this all worked out, huh?"

Both gray heads nodded this time.

"And we have to crumple the paper to make it work?" She dropped the balls back inside the bag.

"Yes, dear. The wrinkles add texture and depth to the floor." Jancie covered the cinnamon rolls with aluminum foil and draped a dish towel around the pan for carrying.

Penn arched a brow. "Depth and texture. To a paper bag." She retied the bag. "If you say, 'the floor will make the kitchen *pop*,' I'm handing in my resignation. And meaning it."

"Grab the rolls, hon. Winnie, don't forget the glue and mixing bowl. We don't want to keep John waiting. He's making some special coffee for us." Jancie collected the roll of contractor's paper and the bags.

Let's do keep him waiting. In fact, let's not do this. She dragged her palms over the soft denim of her shorts.

Another morning with him plus that whole day at the park equaled too much time with him. How many times could she look foolish in front of John? The orange juice and banana warred in her stomach.

She pushed the warm pan against her midsection to quell the butterflies shivering inside. She hadn't seen him in almost two weeks, yet she still had to force him from her mind so that she could study. She didn't want him filling up her thoughts every day.

Didn't want to ride that disaster-bound train.

~*~

John stirred his coffee. "So you don't really use paper bags?" He lifted his mug sporting a team emblem and hid a smile.

Jancie shook her head. "I guess it's...what do you call it? Poetic license to call it a paper bag floor, but contractor's paper is more durable." She poured more water into the chipped enamelware bowl and stirred the glue mixture with a paint stick. She waved to John and Penn. "Could you two fetch the trash bags, and I left the rubber gloves in the car, too."

John licked his forefinger and thumb before wiping his hands on a napkin. "Mmm. These rolls are the best."

Penn fixed her aunt with an I-know-what-you're-doing glance before following John out of the kitchen.

He held the door open for her. "Nice shirt. Number twenty-one. That's...Clemente, right?"

"Yeah, my dad's all-time favorite player." She chided herself for donning this shirt. She should have dug deeper into her drawer. Maybe John didn't know anything about Clemente. Maybe it was a lucky guess when he knew whose number she wore.

"Interesting." He descended the front steps two at a time.

OK...he wants to go there. She'd learned that John

always chose to dive in, not ignore sticky subjects. "Don't you mean 'ironic'?"

He frowned. "Ironic?"

"He died in a plane crash." Her tone implied the "duh" at the end of the sentence. She glanced down the street, hoping to see a runaway dog, or a siren-blasting police cruiser, or maybe even Peri trotting down Clay Avenue. Anything that might distract John from this conversation.

"You're right. He died in a plane crash, just like your parents." His voice dropped. "But do you remember why he chartered that plane?"

"Of course. He took a humanitarian trip." She caught a whiff of a late-blooming peony, her mother's favorite flower. Her thumb groped for her lapis ring. Empty. The ring remained at home, safe from floor renovation. Her arms hugged her middle instead.

"Exactly." John slid his hands into his back pockets. "He died taking emergency aid packages to victims of an earthquake. People might not remember that he had a lifetime batting average of .317. Or that he won the Worlds Series Most Valuable Player award. Or that he was awarded the Presidential Medal of Freedom."

He cocked his head. "But, if people know Roberto Clemente, they know he died helping people." He reached into the car, grabbed the box of rubber gloves, and handed them to Penn. "That says a lot about your dad. His favorite player was Clemente?" He collected the bags. "Cool."

Tears burned behind Penn's eyes. She cleared her throat and searched for something else to say. "You seriously know his batting average?"

He chuckled. "I don't play the game." He glanced

at his leg, "but I love it." He tapped his temple with his forefinger. "The thinking man's game."

She swiveled toward the house.

"Penn." He touched her elbow.

She stopped with one foot on the front step, turning back to him. She dropped her gaze to the white letters on his faded green t-shirt, resisting eye contact until he lifted her chin with his knuckles.

"Are you OK?" His thumb stroked her jaw, spiraling tingles all the way to her stomach.

Her heart melted at the genuine concern in his brown eyes, but she couldn't tell if the emotion generated from friendship or from something more. Did she want it to be something more? She squared her shoulders. "Sure. I'm good."

"Well, then. Let's get this party started. I need a paper bag floor."

~*~

John pushed his empty plate away and reclined in the booth. "Delicious fish sandwich. Tremendous, but delicious. I'm stuffed." He patted his stomach. "If I continue eating like I have today, I may have to change the way I calculate weight and balance on my next flight." He held his breath when he realized he'd mentioned flying, but let it go when Penn didn't wince.

"Oh, you worked hard this morning. You need sustenance." Jancie dredged her last fry through the ketchup puddle on her plate.

"All of us worked hard. Thanks so much again. The floor looks great." He dipped his head. "I have to admit. I had my doubts." He raised his hand when Penn started to protest. "At first. The idea intrigued me, though, and I'm glad we went ahead with it. I'm the only guy I know with a paper bag floor."

"You're likely the only person in a one-hundred mile radius with one." Smirking, Penn swiped the condensation on her glass of iced tea.

Winnie dismissed Penn's statement with a wave of her hand. "Now once the glue's dried—check it tonight—probably tomorrow morning, for sure–you can apply the first coat of polyurethane. You'll need at least five or six. Usually takes about a day to dry between coats."

"I'll check tonight, but tomorrow I'm out bright and early for a trip down to Florida." He tossed his napkin beside his plate.

"Ooh, nice trip." Winnie glanced at her sister, who agreed with her. "No problem. We can stop by and put on some coats while you're gone."

The color that rose in Penn's cheeks heightened her cuteness.

"I'd never put you to that much trouble. David can apply the coats while I'm gone. I'll explain the schedule tonight."

"Well, if you're sure. We wouldn't mind a bit."

His smile softened his refusal. "I'm sure. Thanks, though."

"And since your kitchen is out of commission for at least a week, please let us cook for you and David."

'Thank you, but I'm gone the whole week. I'm sure he'll enjoy an invitation." A burning sensation zapped John's chest. He clenched his teeth. The idea of David accepting a dinner invitation from Winnie and Jancie felt wrong.

Especially if the invitation included Penn.

11

The numbers blurred before Penn's weary eyes. She'd been studying account balances for two hours, and at this point in the day, the column of assets looked too much like liabilities. She pushed her chair from her desk just as a squeal came from downstairs.

"Penny. Guess what? Penny." Winnie's twittering voice skidded up the stairs. "Our John's a hero. A real hero. Penny, come down and see the paper."

Penn opened her door.

Newspaper crackled along with giggles and sighs.

The aunts were hunched over the kitchen table with the weekly *Mars Trumpet* spread on top.

Winnie pointed to the corner of a page. "Look at that picture. Very photogenic, don't you think?"

Jancie fanned herself with a circular. "Of course. Handsome, smart, community-minded, good citizen — the whole package."

Penn hesitated, prayed for strength, crossed the kitchen threshold, and braced herself for another onslaught of matchmaking entreaties. She hadn't seen John in almost two weeks, but that hadn't stopped her mind from entertaining thoughts of him several times every day. She'd hoped that the old adage — out of sight, out of mind — would hold true for her. The opposite one — absence makes the heart grow fonder — played out instead.

Forcing the image of his face from her page of

numbers became a daily habit. Instead of accrued interest totals, she saw his mahogany eyes smiling at her. Instead of debenture stock and lending securities, she saw the dimple in his chin.

Old conversations replayed in her mind until she was sick of them. She fantasized new ones. She had to stop. Penn scrubbed a hand over her face and joined her aunts at the table. "What's up?"

"It's fantastic. John helped nab the burglar. The one stealing heavy equipment all over Butler County. Look." Winnie pointed to the paper again. "See him standing beside his plane? Is that Al Martin?"

Winnie sighed. "This is so exciting." She clasped her hands in front of her multicolored, beaded necklace.

Penn's eyebrows scrunched as she bent over the table to get a good look. Her breath caught in her throat at the sight of the plane. "He did what?"

Jancie slid into the wooden chair with the blue gingham pad covering the seat. "John played an important role in apprehending the thieves. I guess it happened sometime Tuesday. Just in time for Mary to write up the story."

Penn twisted her ring and held on to the stone. A shiver skipped up her spine as she surveyed the picture. She'd daydreamed of John for two weeks, remembering his jokes and gentle observations about Clemente.

She'd managed to block out any thought of flying or planes or heights, but the weekly paper chronicled that part of his life in black and white. The plane filled the background of the picture and commanded Penn's attention.

John's plane? In the image, he leaned toward Al

with a victory smile in mid-pump of a handshake.

The picture taunted her.

This is what John did for a living. This was why there'd be no happy ending to matchmaking attempts.

She squeezed her ring again. "He caught the thieves? How?"

Lifting her glasses, Winnie peered under the lenses to see the words better. "It says here John saw some large holes on his way back to the Butler Airport. He called Al with his suspicions after he remembered a conversation about missing equipment."

She skimmed her finger over the paragraphs. "It mentions the Apple Committee." She peeked at Penn. "Did you hear the conversation?"

A vague recollection about buried equipment flitted through her mind. What she'd assumed to be small-town gossip turned out to be real news.

Winnie grabbed a pair of scissors from the junk drawer and snipped the article from the paper. "Here, dear. Don't you have another meeting today? Give this to John."

"No, Aunt Winnie," Penn declined the offered picture. "He won't want..."

"Oh, pish posh. Of course, he'll want copies." She waved the paper in front of Penn. "Everybody wants extra copies when they're in the paper. He can send one to his mother and grandmother and..."

"Winnie's right, but if you don't want to give it to him, we'll save it until we see him. No problem." Jancie accepted the article from her sister, folded it, and slipped it into an envelope.

Penn groaned. She could take him the article. Especially now that it was closed inside the envelope, and she wouldn't have to look at the plane again. "It's just...I wasn't exactly planning to go to the meeting."

"Not planning to go?" Headed to the sink with an apple in her hand, Winnie stopped mid-stride to focus on her niece. "Why not? You have to go. You made a commitment. People are—"

"I know. I know, but I have to study."

"You need to take a break. Numbers are going to start falling out of your ears." Winnie rinsed the apple and chose a paring knife

"I'm taking a break now." Penn stretched her neck to her left and rolled it to the other side.

Jancie folded the remaining paper. "I agree. You need a balance of studying and time off." She pegged Penn with a quick once-over. "You look to me like you've lost some weight."

"Well, you need to up-grade your glasses." Penn groaned again, admitting defeat. "All right. I'll go to the meeting and take the article for John, but I'm not staying more than an hour. I'm not hanging out all night."

Winnie smiled, quartering her apple. "I'm sure you'll be your usual gracious self."

~*~

Penn's tension headache drummed a dirge behind her eyebrows as she counted the squares in the dated wallpaper behind Clara's head.

Clara droned about deadlines and budgets weaving her pen over her candy cotton-colored fingertips.

The envelope with the newspaper article sat in her purse, untouched because John was a no show. She glanced at her watch. Thirty minutes into the meeting.

Pretty safe bet she wouldn't see him tonight. Thirty more minutes and then she'd excuse herself—politely, of course.

Despite loathing his job, Penn couldn't help herself. She wanted to see John again. Although his absence tonight weighted her heart and closed her throat, she could see the end of this train ride—a great, big wreck.

Her strong-willed heart refused to listen to her arguments regarding John's vocation. Her imaginative mind created various scenarios of his quitting flying to write full time or becoming an English teacher at Mars High or opening a construction company—any job that didn't include a plane.

The door chimed and startled her back to the present.

Jacob shouted, "Woo-hoo. Here he is. Mars's own hero. Good job, buddy."

Tingles raced around her heart and pushed up the corners of her mouth. She shouldn't be so happy to see John.

Surprise melted into embarrassment as John rubbed the five o'clock shadow covering his jaw. "Sorry I'm late. I—"

Clara lifted her hand to stop him. "No need to apologize one bit, John. We're proud to have you as a member of our committee. Congratulations on helping to rid our town of miscreants." She led the group in applause and a couple of whistles from Jacob.

John caught Penn's eye and winked at her.

She pushed her fist into her stomach in a vain attempt to quash its fluttering.

He sat opposite her beside Jacob and shrugged. "I just made a call. The sheriff's department did the rest."

Jacob slapped him on the back. "Proud of you, son."

Missy reached across the table and squeezed his hand. She held contact for six seconds.

Penn counted.

Al chimed in from the end of the table. "You did more than make a call. You took me up, at no charge to the department, by the way, and I was able to radio the exact location of the 'graves.'" He made air quotation marks with his fingers. "Craziest thing I've ever seen. That Nolan is certifiable." He massaged his forehead and stared at his notepad in front of him.

Jacob leaned forward, ready for every detail. "I heard he buried a dump truck, a front loader, and some antiques. Is that true, Al?"

"He buried a zero-turn lawn mower." Al counted on his fingers. "He buried a John Deere front loader tractor, a huge box of antiques, and get this, a brand new Ford F-150. Do you know how big a hole has to be to bury an F-150?"

Jacob's eyes widened.

"B-I-G. That's how big." Al rubbed his crew cut and frowned. "I don't understand it."

Jacob clasped his gnarled hands above the table. "Why in the world did he do it?"

Al sighed. "Before he clammed up at the sheriff's office, he carried on about getting even. Seems his girlfriend broke up with him. Started talking to another fella. That guy and Nolan supposedly had a tussle a few years ago over some unpaid work. Nolan bided his time, and the girlfriend thing tipped the balance."

Clara frowned. "I get the stealing part. Revenge. But the burying part? Why not sell the stuff and pocket the money? That's a lot of work just for revenge."

Jacob settled back in his chair. "Revenge is sweet. So I'm told."

Al shrugged. "Why does Nolan do anything? He's crazy. He's been in and out of jail since he went to juvenile hall in high school. It's a shame."

Penn caught a look of compassion on John's face before he turned his attention to his hands. Did he feel sorry for this Nolan character?

"But we can be grateful to concerned citizens like John who help our men and women in uniform keep our streets safe for us." Clara offered a thumbs-up to John.

"Here. Here." Jacob led another round of clapping.

John held up flattened palms. "Thanks, everybody, but I think we need to get back to the meeting."

"Indeed we do." Clara grabbed her pen and perused her note pad. "We need some people checking out the Three Rivers Arts Festival in Pittsburgh before it ends Sunday. Everything's down there—music, food, arts and crafts. Missy, John, Penny? How about it?"

"I'm in a wedding this weekend." Missy smiled at John.

The hopeful glint in the younger girl's eyes summoned another sense of heaviness in Penn's chest. Thinking of Missy and John together heated her cheeks.

Clara persevered. "Penny?"

"Um, probably not. I'm studying all weekend."

Clara snorted. "Well, I'm going. Wouldn't think of missing it. If some of you could get down there, you'd help out this committee tremendously. Let me know if you need a ride." She shuffled several pages. "OK. Let's move on to the Fourth of July parade. We need to have a presence there." She slid a sign-up sheet to her right. "If everyone takes a block, two people per slot, no one will have to man our booth more than thirty minutes."

John raised his hand. "So we've got two festivals, huh?"

Clara shook her head. "The parade isn't a festival, but it's a big deal here. A few churches have bake sales, and the high school booster club will sell t-shirts and season passes, but we don't have any real food vendors or music. We always have a booth to advertise the Apple Fest. Sign up volunteers, that sort of thing."

John nodded. "Gotcha."

Penn marked the Fourth on her calendar and subtracted hours from her study time. Added more of watching Missy flirt with John.

~*~

Penn inserted her key into the driver's side door lock. She'd waved goodbye to John as Missy grabbed his arm on his way out. Her ribs pinched together again, but she told herself it was for the best. The mantra, "He's a pilot. He's a pilot," played in her head.

"Penn. Wait up." John breezed up to her with a grin. "We've got to stop meeting like this."

Was he kidding or did he mean it?

"You got a problem with parking lots?"

"No, silly. I was teasing." He dropped his grin, his dark eyes serious. "I'd meet you anywhere."

She squeezed her folder against her tap dancing heart, a shield against John's nearness. "You would?"

His smile appeared again as he leaned on Clara's green sedan, propping his helmet under the crook of his arm. "I chased you out here, remember?"

He chased her?

The tap dancing in her heart sped up a notch. Time to change the subject. "Congratulations on your police work, by the way. The streets of Mars are safer today because of you. Good job." She retrieved the envelope containing the newspaper article and offered it to him. "You made the paper. We saved you a copy."

He chuckled, peeking inside. "Safer streets, huh? I don't know about that, but thanks." He scratched his throat. "Craziest thing. Never been a part of catching thieves before. For sure, never heard of burying trucks and lawn mowers before either."

"You've never lived in Mars before."

"Oh, is that it?"

"Absolutely. Mars, the motherland of crazy."

"You know that begs the question, 'what do you mean—motherland of crazy?'"

Penn glanced at her watch. "Trust me. We don't have time to get into all that."

"I know a segue when I hear one." He shoved his free hand into his pocket. "Do you really have to study this weekend? The arts festival sounds cool. We could scout out stuff for Clara, have some fun while we do that, and you could explain the Mars penchant towards crazy. Want to go?"

She blinked and tipped her head. How did they get to this point? They were talking about crazy Mars. Now he invited her to the festival.

Her heart thumped against her chest.

Of course, she wanted to go.

Of course, she couldn't go.

Forget about studying. She couldn't go because she was pretty sure the forecast promised future pain.

She'd suffered through the agony of losing loved ones in a plane crash. She refused to put herself in line for more tragedy.

~*~

John could see "No" forming on her lips, her brain scanning for reasons to decline his offer. He had to make his offer one that she couldn't refuse. "If your aunts are up for it, I'd like to take them, too, as a proper thank you for my floor. I haven't had a chance yet." He couldn't read the emotion that skirted across her face before she lowered her head.

Disappointment, maybe? What she thought was a date turned out to be an invitation for the whole family.

"You paid for our lunch at Uncle Bob's, remember? That was a proper thank you."

"Paying for a couple of fish sandwiches doesn't compensate for a morning of manual labor." He raised his eyebrows. "Do you think they'd like to go?"

"Are you kidding? They love it. They go every year. The rain kept them home last weekend, but they've already checked the weather for Saturday."

"Sweet. So they're on board." He dipped his head to match her gaze. "What about their niece? Can you spare a few hours to show a transplant another part of the area he's moved to?" He saw the struggle in her eyes. He couldn't relent now. "Come on. Help a poor newcomer out. I hear Pittsburgh's a beautiful city, but I haven't had a chance to see it yet."

She rubbed the blue stone turned toward her palm.

"Please?"

She bit her lip.

"Pretty please?"

She closed her eyes and let out a breath. "OK, but I really do have to study."

"No problem. How about you study in the morning, and I pick you up after lunch? We can spend the afternoon touring the festival."

"You're picking us up? Do you have a side-car with your motorcycle?" She grimaced. "Wait. It doesn't matter. I'm not riding in a side car-even if you do have one. We can take their car. It's bigger than Gretch— than mine."

He covered his heart, feigning hurt. "Hey now. I asked you. I can come up with a ride that works."

"Oh, really?" She arched a brow.

"Yes, really." A puff of wind ruffled the curls around her temples. He gripped his helmet to keep his hand from smoothing those curls. He remembered how soft they were when he'd brushed them off her temple the night she'd tripped in his kitchen. "I'll be by about 12:30 Saturday, OK?"

She nodded.

"Will you tell your aunts, or should I call with the invitation?"

"I'll tell them. See you Saturday." She turned toward the car door and reached for the handle at the same time he did. She drew back her hand as soon as his brushed against hers. Not exactly a good sign. He opened the door for her. "See you Saturday."

~*~

Penn sank behind the steering wheel, thankful to be away from the scrutiny of John's eyes. Another

Saturday with him, but not a date. A man in the twenty-first century does not ask chaperones on dates with a woman he's pursuing.

Therefore, John is not pursuing me.

Help a newcomer out. Therefore, he wants to see Pittsburgh. *A thank you for the floor.* Therefore, he's still paying for help with his remodeling. *Therefore, therefore, therefore, he is not interested in me.*

Good.

She should be relieved. She wouldn't have to decline offers for dates. She wouldn't have to explain why, even though he was a perfectly wonderful man, she couldn't become involved with him unless he promised never to set foot in a plane again.

And signed the promise. And notarized it.

She should be relieved. Instead, a familiar weight settled around her heart, making changing from first to second gear a monumental effort.

"Gretchen, let's go home."

12

Penn surveyed the crowd milling by artisan booths. It was a great day for a festival.

Winnie licked her waffle cone. "Mmm. This butter pecan ice cream hits the spot. Thanks again, John."

John, working on a scoop of mint chocolate chip, saluted her with a flick of his fingers.

"That blues band could play. I'm so glad we got here in time to hear the last set. Now when does Ralph Stanley play?" Jancie crunched her cone.

"We don't want to miss him. He's our favorite." Winnie dabbed at the corner of her mouth with a napkin. "Remember when we saw him at Hartwood Acres?"

Ralph Stanley, a bluegrass music legend, was the aunts' favorite performer. *Man of Constant Sorrow* always generated either tears or goose bumps for both of them.

During the Hartwood concert, his grandson, maybe ten or twelve years old and sporting a black cowboy hat, joined Dr. Stanley on stage, accompanying him on several songs.

The aunts, nursing a minor crush on their musical hero, swooned at the joy shining from the grandfather's face as he sang.

John retrieved a program from his back pocket and managed to unfold it without losing his cone. "Ralph Stanley. Seven o'clock. He's supposed to be at the Point Park stage." He glanced at Penn. "Do you know where that is?"

She swallowed a bit of her moose tracks ice cream. "I have an idea. It's not too far from here."

They cruised along a section of booths showcasing handmade jewelry.

Winnie stopped at one displaying hand dyed scarves and fabric purses. "I know someone who's having a birthday soon." She sang the words and giggled. "You haven't given us any ideas for your present this year, Penny. What do you want? Besides a Jell-O cake, that is."

"A Jell-O cake?"

Winnie chuckled. "When she was about eight or nine, she loved strawberry Jell-O and asked for a Jell-O cake for her birthday. Making the layers was no big deal, but assembling them..."

Jancie squeezed her eyes shut and bit her knuckle. "The wobbly top layer was too heavy for the whipped cream frosting. It just squished the white fluff out of the sides. Sat flat on top of the bottom layer-until it slid right off onto the counter." She shuddered.

"Winnie came close to losing her Love Community membership card that day." Jancie laughed at her own joke.

Jancie pursed her lips. "Wrong, sister. I kept my cool. Barely, but that was my first and last Jell-O cake."

"It still tasted good." Penn still felt the need to defend her choice.

John smiled at Penn. "So your birthday's coming up? When?"

Penn closed her eyes against the heat rising in her cheeks. First the Jell-O story and now her birthday story which would inevitably reveal her real name. She peeked at the booths for an escape route.

Jancie gave Penn a one-armed hug. "Penny's our patriotic baby."

"You were born on July fourth."

"Not exactly. I missed it by one day."

"July fifth. Her birthday's July fifth, but she still got a great name out of the deal." Winnie wiggled her eyebrows and licked another swath of ice cream before it dripped onto her thumb.

"Her name?" John's eyebrows bunched together. "Penelope?"

"Independence." Both aunts grinned and raised their cones in tribute.

"Independence?" Lines creased John's brow.

Penn pinched her nose and dragged her hand through her hair. She nodded, but kept her eyes on a basket of scarves.

"Independence." He stepped toward her. "Penn, that's a great name."

Penn grimaced. "Yeah, right. Tell that to all the elementary boys who had a field day once they learned my real name." She led the group from the table to make room for other shoppers.

He waved the imaginary tormentors away. "Elementary boys. What do they know?" He popped the tip of the cone into his mouth.

"John's right. It's a great name." Winnie grabbed her hand. "Your parents loved you so much, honey. They gave you a special name."

He rescued her. "You know, come to think of it, all of you have interesting names. I've heard of Winnie before, but I've never heard of Jancie." He tossed his napkin into a nearby garbage can. "Winnie's short for Winifred, right? Is Jancie short for something?"

Penn sent up a quick thank you prayer for the turn in the conversation.

"Winifred's a good guess, but wrong, and Jancie stands alone. It's not a nickname."

"I'll explain my name, Winnie. You explain yours." Jancie, as the oldest sister, took charge. "My name was originally Janice. Janice Joan Davenport—then Johnson when I married, giving me luscious alliteration. But I digress."

Jancie cleared her throat. "Someone made a type-o on my birth certificate and didn't proof the information. My mother saw the name, thought it fit me better, and never called me Janice again." She arched her neck with a flourish. "I'm Jancie." She curtsied. "Pleased to meet you."

"Now me. Jancie was enamored by—" Winnie slanted a glance at Jancie, who trilled her tongue for a drum roll. "Winnie the Pooh. I am not Winifred. I am Winnie Robyn Davenport and proud of it."

Penn rolled her eyes. "My grandparents allowed their one-and-a-half-year-old to name the new baby."

"And I love it. Thanks, big sis." Winnie planted a kiss on her sister's cheek.

"That's a great story."

Winnie finished her cone and dusted her hands. "Tell us the story of your name."

John raised his palm toward the next craft table, and the group moved forward. "Not much to tell. It's a cliché. Named after my grandfather. Like two other boys in my class. John T, John D, and John K. To this day, I have old friends who call me John T."

"A good, solid, normal name." Penn's breath jammed in her throat when John smiled at her. She'd spoken out loud. She skirted her attention to a tray of bracelets at the next table.

"In other words, boring." John laughed. "But thank you."

"A fine name indeed." Jancie moved farther down the table. "We have a few Johns in our family, too."

"I think she's made my point." John's voice, right beside her ear, surprised her.

Her hand fluttered into an earring stand. She grabbed for the earrings. "Miss Grace, that's me."

"No. Miss Penn. That's you." His fingers brushed hers as he helped right the stand, raising the hair on her arm.

Winnie selected a cardboard square. "Penny, look at these earrings." Lapis beads adorned silver drop earrings. "Aren't they beautiful?"

"That's the same kind of stone as your ring. What's that stone?" John grabbed her hand. "Can I see your ring?"

Penn rubbed the stone once more to still the shivers zinging through her body. His warm fingers stole her breath. She pushed the stone to the top of her finger with her thumb.

He leaned closer and lifted her hand toward him. For a swift second, Penn expected him to kiss her hand, but, no. He was interested only in the ring.

She shook off an oppressive feeling that resembled disappointment and focused on her ring. She loved it, an oval lapis stone cradled in elaborate antiqued gold scroll work that extended down the sides of the ring. Beautiful in its own right, the ring meant more to her than just an interesting piece of jewelry.

"It's stunning. Is it an antique?" John met her gaze but kept her hand in his.

His eyes, so close to hers, mesmerized her. She

couldn't think of a word to say.

"Another great story. Tell him, Penny." Winnie nudged Penn's arm. "Tell him about your ring."

Penn cleared her throat. "It's..." She hesitated. Did she want to tell this man, this pilot, anything else about herself? About her life? About her family?

He ran his thumb over her knuckles and smiled a soft smile that made her feel safe and special. Her heart shifted. "It was my mother's." She licked her lips. "Her engagement ring."

"And—" Jancie prompted her.

"My parents found it in an antique shop on one of their dates."

"And we wrapped it up for Penn's seventeenth birthday—"

"With the key to the car, don't forget."

"Along with the key to Gretchen, her father's Volkswagen, and she's worn the ring ever since."

John squeezed her hand. "Cool story. Thanks for telling me." He let go.

She stuffed her hand into her pocket and moved forward to the next booth, grateful for the chance to restore her breathing to normal.

~*~

A soft breeze blew in from the Monongahela River and ruffled John's long bangs into his eyes. He fingered them away from his forehead.

Penn fisted her hand before she could brush them back herself. Not a productive way to think. She had to stop those kind of ideas. They wouldn't lead anywhere but trouble.

They rested, eating sandwiches on a thin blanket

John had pulled out of his backpack. Jancie and Winnie, chattering about Ralph Stanley, had dropped onto the blanket without one complaint of hurting backs or aching legs or swollen ankles or any other kind of body ailment. Did the remedy come from anticipation of live bluegrass or their crush on John?

Winnie swallowed a bite of her Reuben sandwich. "I haven't had one of these in years. I'd forgotten how good they are."

John turned his mammoth Italian sandwich to the left and to the right. "Mine smells great, but do I know how to eat this thing?"

"Mash it with both hands. Don't worry if some of the fries fall out. It's part of the experience." Jancie tugged a fry from between her turkey and cheese.

He clamped the ciabatta roll and pressed. "I've seen cole slaw on sandwiches before but never fries." He glanced at Penn. "You seem pretty happy with yourself. A piece of pita bread is a lot easier to handle than this." He held up his sandwich.

"OK, here goes." He stretched his mouth as wide as he could and chomped down on the crusty bread. Three fries dropped onto the napkin in his lap. Sandwich sauce dripped down his chin.

Penn laughed and handed him another napkin. She swirled a corner of the pita bread through a dollop of hummus. "I've had those before. I didn't want to miss my hummus and grape leaves."

Two musicians stepped on stage to inspect the stringed instruments and do a sound check. Whoops and whistles skittered across the audience. Jancie and Winnie joined in with loud claps.

"It won't be long now." Winnie sipped her lemonade.

"You know, this isn't bad. I don't think I would've come up with this concoction, but I think I like it. And you said fries on top is the only way the sandwiches come?" John asked.

Jancie adjusted her straw. "I believe so. I heard a rumor that someone asked a waitress once for the fries on the side, and she said something like, 'here, the fries come on the sandwich. Take it or leave it.'"

Winnie frowned. "Surely that's not true. It's not very nice."

"I said it was a rumor. Who knows?" Jancie folded the wax paper around her sandwich and set it on the blanket. "I need a break. I'm stuffed."

John studied Penn's plastic carton of food. "How're your grape leaves?"

"Delicious. As usual."

He wrinkled his nose. "I've never had them."

"Seriously?" This tidbit didn't ring with Penn's idea of John.

"That surprises you?"

"Of course."

He cocked his head. "Why 'of course?'"

"I thought you liked trying new things. You seem to be up for anything." She shrugged. "It's hard to believe you've never tried them."

"It's kinda hard to believe you have."

She drew her legs up and hugged her knees. "Why do you say that?"

He opened his mouth but hesitated.

"What?"

He licked his lips. "I didn't think you liked new things."

Ouch.

"I like new things." The words sounded a little

suspect to her own ears.

Is that the way he saw her? A boring, stuck-in-a-rut person who ate vanilla ice cream and sat in a corner while the world turned in front of her? Not a fascinating picture. And for the record, she ate moose tracks ice cream this afternoon, not vanilla.

"Hey," He smiled at her over his sandwich. "I didn't mean that as an insult. Just an observation."

"It's not a new thing or an old thing. I just enjoy Greek food." A lump rose in her throat.

"We all do. We go to the Greek Food Festival down in Oakland every year. Fun and scrumptious." Winnie patted Penn's knee. "That baklava this year was to die for."

Penn peered at the bowl of grape leaves and swallowed against the tightness threatening to cut off her speech. "Do you want to try one, John?"

He raised his sandwich. "I'm still working on this monstrosity. You enjoy them."

Penn offered again. "I'm getting full. Try one. See if you like it."

He wrinkled his nose again. "I'm good. But thanks."

She nudged her aunt. "Aunt Jancie, I think he's scared to try a grape leaf."

"Go ahead, John." Jancie jiggled the ice in her cup. "They're good. The grape leaves have an interesting, tangy flavor. Not bad, just interesting. You'll like the mint and lemon mixed in with the lamb."

"It's got lamb in it?" He cringed with an exaggerated shudder. "You're eating Bambi?"

"Bambi was a deer, John," Winnie whispered.

"Right. You're eating Lamb Chop?" Mischief played around his mouth.

"Seriously? Are you a girl or what?" Penn extracted a plastic fork from a wrapper and speared a grape leaf. She waved it in front of him. "Try one. I dare you."

He blinked at her and grinned. "OK. But not a whole one. Cut it in half, please. No, in fourths."

Penn sliced off the end of a grape leaf with a plastic knife. Grains of rice fell from the rolled delicacy. She handed the fork to John.

"My hands are full." He opened his mouth, waiting for her to feed him the food. His eyes challenged her.

Her mouth fell open. He'd set her up for this deed. Part of her wanted to meet the challenge. Part of her wanted to drop the fork and run.

She bent toward him, holding the fork just in front of his mouth. He leaned forward and closed his mouth around it. She allowed eye contact for a second and dropped her gaze to his lips as she pulled the fork free. He leaned back.

"Mmm" He chewed the morsel and swallowed. "You're right. Very interesting." He spoke to Jancie but focused on Penn.

She dipped her head away from his scrutiny and stabbed the remaining grape leaf with her fork. Her racing heartbeat supplanted her appetite.

~*~

Winnie and Jancie sang a Ralph Stanley song complete with harmony as they mounted the front porch steps.

Winnie jingled the keys out of her waist pack and unlocked the front door. She turned to John at the bottom of the steps. "We had such a fun time today."

"Yes, we did. Thank you for thinking of two old ladies." Jancie transferred her sole purchase, a watercolor of the old Three Rivers Stadium, under her left arm and patted John's shoulder with her right hand.

"I don't know who you're talking about." John rested a foot on the bottom step.

The aunts giggled, and Penn expected a blush colored their cheeks.

"Come in and have some cookies with us." Winnie covered a yawn with the back of her hand.

"As much as I love your cooking, I'll pass this time. We had a big afternoon." He stuck his hand in his back pocket. "How about a rain check?"

Jancie rubbed her eyes under her glasses. "A good idea. We have to sing tomorrow, and I need my beauty sleep." She glanced at Penn, sand then back at John. "But, you know, that swing over there is a good way to wind down after a long afternoon. You might want to try it."

Penn blushed. She opened her mouth to protest, but John spoke first.

"Fantastic idea. Penn, let's wind down for a few minutes." He ascended the remaining two steps with one long stride and sauntered to the swing at the end of the porch, not giving her a chance to decline.

Winnie elbowed her side and gestured toward the swing. "We'll say 'good night' then and thank you again, John."

Penn's foot begged to stomp at the maneuvering of her aunts.

Why wouldn't they stop matchmaking?

Her traitor heart pumped hard at the prospect of

alone time with John. It refused to listen to her brain repeating, "Do not like this man. Do not like this man."

Too late. She liked him a lot.

He grinned from the swing.

"Good night, sweetie." Jancie kissed her cheek and nudged her toward John.

She moved along the porch, dragging her feet, steeling her heart.

13

Penn joined John, and he pushed against the slatted porch floor with his toe, creating a gentle swaying movement. His presence, broad shoulders and all, filled the swing. His upper arm brushed against hers.

She slid closer to the side of the swing to give him room. To stop the tingling where his arm touched hers.

He reached over her head, extended his arm behind her. "There. That's better."

Not better for her racing heart. Not better for her struggling lungs. What could they talk about? She needed a good, safe, quick topic. *Think. Eureka. Jancie and Winnie.* "You made them really happy today. Thanks."

"They're sweet ladies. Being with all of you made me happy, too." He leaned back and closed his eyes.

So. They come in a package. No news there.

Hearing it from his own mouth should have relieved her. Instead, that familiar feeling of disappointment knotted her chest. The sweet fragrance of a potted gardenia tickled her senses but failed to work its usual calming magic. She rubbed her ring. *God, help me out here, please. I need peace. I need wisdom. I need a road map.*

~*~

John drummed his fingers on the back of the swing. He wanted to rest his hand on Penn's shoulder, but he sensed he had to move slowly with her.

Fiddling with her ring again, she was as skittish as the colts his little brother trained. No problem. She intrigued him enough to take his time.

"Yeah. I'm glad ya'll could go downtown today." He stretched his legs out and crossed his weaker foot over his stronger one.

"Ya'll?" She raised her eyebrows.

"A perfectly good word. Especially where I'm from."

"Where's that?"

"Virginia. Born and raised."

"You don't have much of an accent."

"My mother taught English for years. Made us enunciate with perfection but couldn't extricate 'ya'll' from my vocabulary."

"Jancie and Winnie think it's infinitely superior to the 'yinz' you hear around here."

"Oh, yeah?" He shrugged. "Different words. Pretty much same definition. It's probably what you get used to." *Good job. Silly conversation.* He needed another one to keep her relaxed. "They were good sports with the Jeep today. I worried they might balk at our ride."

A laugh bubbled across her lips, kindled a warmth in the pit of his stomach.

"Are you kidding? They loved it. Didn't you hear them giggling in the back seat? They like to play the old card with all their aches and pains when it serves them well, but they're fairly agile. They usually do whatever they want. In fact," She angled toward him. "They walked in the Apple 5k last year."

"No way."

"Yes, way. Took them an hour to walk and the afternoon to recover, but they did it." Her raised chin revealed sparkling, black-as-ink eyes. Her smile tipped the corners of those eyes. Nice. How could he keep that smile coming?

"Wow. Good for them." He bent to swat at a mosquito feasting on a tender spot below his ankle. "As much as you act as if they exasperate you sometimes, you really do love them." He settled back in the swing, closer to her this time by millimeters. His arm rested partially on the back of the swing, partially across her shoulders. Very nice.

She frowned. "Of course I do."

"Because they raised you."

"Because they sacrificed for me. They uprooted their whole lives for me. They sacrificed then and still do, just like any—" She pressed her lips together and studied the chipped paint on the arm of the swing.

He waited for her to finish. When she remained silent, he answered for her. "Just like any parent?"

"Just like anyone who loves someone else."

"They for sure love you."

"I know." She chipped off a paint flake. "Anyway, you made their week with that red Jeep."

He plucked at his shorts and let her change the subject. He'd ask more questions another time. "I'll let David know. He'll be glad they enjoyed it. I'm sure he got a kick out of my motorcycle." He scratched his ankle with his opposite foot. "I'm sorry about my comment tonight."

"What comment?" Her words were soft, but a wariness cloaked the inquiry.

"The one about you not liking new things."

A cool front invaded the porch, and the weather had nothing to do with the temperature.

She dipped her head, too late to hide her lips that straightened into a tight line. "No problem."

"I'm serious. I didn't mean it as a critique." How could he resurrect that enchanting smile? "It was really just an observation."

"An observation?" Her gaze darted to his face and back to the wooden arm. "You've been studying me?"

"Not like a science project. I just notice things."

Penn narrowed her eyes. "Like what?"

Should he continue this conversation? Would it pull her back into herself? She was just beginning to relax.

Working on another paint chip, she waited.

"Like you rub your ring when you're nervous or upset."

Her right hand immediately flexed and flattened against her thigh.

"You don't have to stop. It's not a bad thing."

His hand covered hers. She didn't rebuff him.

"I've just seen you do it sometimes...like at the meetings when Clara is badgering you about the budget or when your aunts are exasperating you."

She shifted, fiddling with the hem of her shorts with her free hand.

"That's not a bad thing."

She continued staring in the direction of the yellow rose bushes flanking the front steps.

John released her hand and touched her chin, rotating her face toward him. The street lamp didn't illuminate the expression on her countenance, but he had no trouble reading the teeth biting her bottom lip. His thumb prickled, aching to rub against her mouth and banish the tension from her jaw. He probably shouldn't. She'd probably bolt upstairs or slap him or...curiosity strong armed him and pushed his thumb across her lips.

She stiffened. Not promising. But her gaze zeroed in on his lips. Ahh. A positive sign. Maybe she was interested despite her initial reaction.

He corralled a smile ready to spread across his face. He'd like to explore that idea, but tonight wasn't the night. "It's something I noticed. Like you noticing my limp. No big deal." He cupped her cheek, tucked a springy curl behind her ear.

The swing crackled when he leaned against it. Reaching up, he grabbed the chain and motioned to the bay window on the other side of the front door. "This is a great porch. So peaceful."

A floral fragrance reminded him of his grandmother's farm. "I'd love to add a wraparound like this one to my house, but I don't have the funds or the know-how. Yet."

He hoped she'd light into him again about refurbishing his house with no real experience, but she didn't take the bait. She'd closed into herself again. He sighed and checked the time.

The swing bounced behind him when he rose. "It's getting close to midnight, and I've fed the mosquitoes long enough." He lifted his foot behind him and rubbed his ankle. "I better shove off. Don't want to be your excuse for sleeping late tomorrow morning."

At her rounded mouth, his suggestive words dawned on him.

"Wait. Hold up. I'm sorry. I didn't mean..."

Her fingers fluttered away his apology. "Don't worry. I knew what you meant."

John winced. "Open mouth. Insert foot." He caught her hand and squeezed it. "I really did have fun today, Penn. Thanks for showing me the festival."

"Anytime."

He smiled. "I think I'll hold you to that." He descended the stairs two at a time and jogged with his lopsided gait to the Jeep. As his hand reached for the silver door handle, he glanced back at the porch.

She swayed in the swing, watching him.

Yep. He'd take that as a positive sign, too. He waved and slipped into the driver's seat. "I certainly will hold you to it, Penny."

~*~

Penn watched the taillights until the Jeep turned right at the corner of Stanton Street. The swing wobbled without John's weight balancing the bench. She didn't like her speeding pulse or the heat rushing around her heart that his touches produced. She especially didn't like the lump in her throat his departure created. Her shoulders sagged against the swing, and she hugged herself.

What if he turned around and drove back to her? What if he waved and walked up the steps and said, "Sorry, Penn. I forgot something."

She'd say, "What?"

He'd say, "This." And he'd pull her up from the swing, into his arms and lower his mouth and—

Penn jerked out of the swing, leaving it bouncing and the extra chain at the top clanking in protest. Yanking the door open, she restrained herself from slamming it. She didn't want to face the aunts right now. She turned the key and rested her forehead against the varnished oak.

Why wasn't locking her heart as easy as locking the front door?

14

A few days later, Penn strolled down town to take her place at the Apple Fest booth.

The aunts had left before her to take three gift boxes full of celebration cookies to sell at the church's booth.

She headed for the flying saucer planted, for now, in the town square.

Someone or really several someones, in keeping with tradition, would have to move it to another location in town on the eve of Apple Fest.

She spotted Clara wrestling with a card table, and John appeared from behind the saucer to help.

Penn's heart sped up several beats.

Dressed in black, must be time for his laundry.

John's presence surprised her. She hadn't checked the volunteer sheet at the meeting, didn't know who'd signed up to partner with her. Happy tingles zig-zagged through her insides at the prospect of spending her shift with him.

"Good morning. How can I help?" Penn grabbed a folding chair and opened it beside the table. She glanced at John, the black t-shirt coordinating with his dark hair and deepening his eyes. Oh, he was cute.

"Hey, Penn." His smile crinkled the corners of his eyes.

"Penn, good you're here." Clara hauled a stack of fliers out of a monogrammed canvas tote bag. "These are for anyone interested in volunteering for us. They get a sheet, and we get their name and e-mail or cell number." She tapped a yellow pad with a marker. "Don't let them leave without that info. Got it?"

"No problem."

"It looks like you and John have the first time slot. I'll be back to help Missy at 9:30." She wiped her forehead. "I need more coffee right now."

John waved at Clara. "Later." He sank onto a second chair beside Penn. "She's a good leader."

"Yeah. Better her than me."

He stretched his long legs in front of him. "So all we have to do is sit here and take names?"

"Pretty much." She stacked the fliers to look busy.

"So tell me about this flying saucer." He cocked his head to the silver disk behind him. "What's the deal?"

"Not much to tell. It's been here for years. Somebody's idea of the perfect landmark for a town called Mars. Only it's a floating landmark."

"Floating?" He locked his hands behind his head.

"You'll see. A few days before Apple Fest, somebody comes by and moves it."

"Ah." John nodded. "Kind of like stealing the opposing team's mascot before a big game?"

"Except it's more a change of scenery than stealing."

Clara clipped back to the table, clutching a medium-sized cardboard cup of coffee. "How many volunteers so far?"

Penn swept the page with her index finger to make sure she didn't miss any names. "None. So far."

"Are you kidding me?" Clara turned the page toward her. "Not one? Penny, volunteers help make our festival a success. We need them. Are you calling people over to our table? Talk it up. We need some signatures." She tapped her chin with her fingers. "I thought locating beside the saucer would be perfect."

"Clara, people aren't thinking about apples today. They're thinking about the parade."

"We've got to make them think of apples." She glanced down the street. "I'll be back."

"I'm sure." Penn hadn't meant to speak out loud, but John's chuckle confirmed she had.

He scanned the street. "I guess we can try."

She crossed her arms. "I'm not a salesperson. If people don't want to do something, I don't want to talk them into it."

"Even if it's for a good cause? Even if it's good for them?"

Penn made a face and adjusted the already neat pile of papers.

The next fifteen minutes yielded one volunteer.

John had charmed a mother pushing a double stroller with two toddlers. He held his hand high for a celebratory slap. "I got one. Now it's your turn."

Penn high-fived him. "She was easy. She just wants to get out of the house."

"John, some help, please." Clara's voice carried from down the street, but they didn't see her in the crowd. A bunch of helium balloons bounced toward them.

John grabbed the attached ribbons and took them from Clara.

She pushed the hair back from her face. "Whew. They're harder to handle than they look." She dangled her arms beside her, flexed her fingers. "Let's tie these to the table and chairs. Brings attention to our booth, don't you think?"

"Absolutely." Penn accepted a balloon John had freed from the knot holding the bunch and tied it to the back of her chair.

"Hi, Penn." She whirled at the sound of a voice she hadn't heard in years.

"Abby." Her heart jolted so much she flattened her palm against her chest, ready to recite the Pledge of Allegiance except she couldn't say a word.

"It's good to see you." Abby smiled at her, a tentative, questioning smile. "How are you? It's been a while."

"See. I told you she looks cute." Missy looked cute as usual in gray shorts and a pink cami.

Abby slid her wristlet from her shoulder, twisting the long strap around her hand. "I like your haircut."

Penn pushed curls from her temple. She'd kept her hair long until midway through college. In an effort to look older, she'd lopped off ten inches and donated the locks to a charity that made wigs for children undergoing chemotherapy. Without the weight pulling it straight, soft, loose curls had sprouted all over her head. "Thanks. You're visiting for the Fourth?"

"No. I'm back at home, starting my internship through Pitt in a few weeks."

Missy grabbed John's arm. "John, this is my sister, Abby."

Squeals from across the street signaled the aunts' approach. "Abby, you're a sight for sore eyes. How are you, dear?"

Both aunts squished Abby between them and settled in for a mini reunion.

Several minutes later, with all the news from the Parkers and a promise for Penn and Abby to have lunch sometime soon, the aunts, Penn, and John found themselves at the church's booth and nibbled still-warm cinnamon rolls.

"See. I told you we had the perfect spot to watch the parade." Winnie licked white icing off her finger.

John swallowed. "Glad you invited me to tag along."

Penn gave thanks not only for the sweet treats but also for the reprieve from Abby and Missy. Her heart needed time to recover from the shock of seeing her childhood friend.

From the time they were old enough for play dates, the two had been inseparable until tragedy destroyed her family and severed the friendship.

Although she knew it was a wrong idea, Penn linked the plane crash with the Parkers and kept her distance, especially from Abby.

A trumpet cadence snapped her back to the future. She startled, knocking into John's chest. "Sorry. I wasn't ready for that sound." His arms rushed to settle her, speeding her heart again.

John let her go. "No need to apologize. Caught me off guard, too."

"Here it comes. The ROTC color guard is always first in line. Look. The youth group's float is next." Winnie waved a miniature flag at the float. "Hello, Trudy." The teenager lobbed a handful of candy toward them.

A piece of peppermint pinged Penn on the shin. "Owww. Toss the candy. Don't throw it." She bent to protect her smarting leg and another piece bounced off her head. "Cut it out!"

"Sorry. Sorry. We love you, Miss Davenport. We'll see you at the game." The girls shouted their apology, but their attention had moved to the next group of unsuspecting targets.

John laughed. "They really do love you, you know."

"I'm feeling their love all right." She rubbed the top of her head.

"Sounds like you're going to the game." He unwrapped a piece of chocolate caramel candy.

"Yeah. We'll go to the softball game then eat at the cookout at church." She glanced at him. "Are you going?"

"Andy mentioned it the other day. Sounds like a fun time."

Jancie wheedled into the conversation. "The church softball game? What a good time we have. You have to come, John. Penn always—"

"We always go. A lot of fun." *No need to give away all our secrets at once, Aunt Jancie.* "Look. Here comes the band."

~*~

Penn stepped up to the plate and bent her knees, readying for the first pitch of the third inning. John hadn't showed. Just as well. She had a feeling his being in the crowd would make her nervous.

Stupid, but doing her normal thing of hitting the ball and running around the bases without worrying about what he thought relieved her.

Deborah, the pitcher for Mt. Lebanon Faith Church, served an arced ball toward her and—bam. Sweet spot.

She'd hit a single in the first inning, a double in the second. Now she got her homer. She knew it when the ball hit the bat. She jogged around the bases, listening to the aunts chant her name. Two paces from home plate, she rewarded them with a grin.

John clapped along with them.

Her tennis shoe caught the edge of the base and propelled her toward the catcher.

The catcher, an English teacher she recognized from North Allegheny, broke her fall with her mitt, but the centrifugal force sent them both into a spin.

Someone in the crowd cheered. "A homer and a dance for the price of one!"

Penn gritted her teeth. How would she ever live this down? She thanked the catcher, curtsied to the bleachers, but refused to make eye contact with the aunts, and especially John. She'd pretend she hadn't seen him.

If he could distract her to the point of making a fool of herself during an easy jog home, no telling what would happen during a fly to right field. She needed to concentrate on the game, not on the handsome man sitting between her aunts.

The concentrating helped her hit another double in the next inning and shag a pop up in the sixth, but the ladies from Mt. Lebanon prevailed, edging out Love Community by two runs.

The aunts and John met her after the traditional "good game" line up on the middle of the field with their own pats of congratulations.

Jancie hugged her. "Good game, sweetie. What a way to put the cherry on top of that homer, too."

"Thanks for the reminder. You know me, Miss Grace." She stuck her glove under her arm.

"Miss Softball, too." John's hand felt warm on her shoulder. "Who knew you could play like that?"

"We did." Winnie reached up and planted a kiss on her cheek. "We'll have to show you all her trophies sometime."

Penn rolled her eyes. "No, we don't." She dusted off her shorts.

John grinned. "I'd love to see them."

She removed her ball cap and shook out her curls. "I think it's time for the hotdogs. Anybody hungry?"

John accompanied them to the picnic tables near the pavilion and handed each one a paper plate.

"This food is compliments of Mt. Lebanon. They lost last year, so they pay with the cookout." Jancie surveyed the table clustered with dishes and bowls. "Take notes, girls, because supper'll be on us next year."

Penn accepted a roll but declined a hotdog.

John pointed to her plate. "Did you forget something?"

"Penny doesn't like hotdogs. She eats the bun with all the trimmings." Winnie scooped potato salad onto her plate.

He jerked his head back. "Seriously?"

"True. I like all the other stuff." She wrinkled her nose. "Just not the main ingredient."

"Cool. To each his own." He stacked two on his plate.

Winnie grabbed a plastic cup of lemonade. "I've spied a great place to sit for the fireworks. Follow me." She headed toward her picnic site.

"She knew where to stand for the parade. I'm a believer." John waited for Penn to fall in behind the aunts.

~*~

Winnie led them to a spot with camp chairs and a blanket spread between them. "See. Isn't this nice? We set our place up before the game."

Jancie shook out her napkin. "Always thinking, sister. Great place to watch the fireworks. I'm glad you could join us, John. Sorry we have only the two chairs."

"We're not too far from the food either. If you want more." Winnie settled into the second chair.

John tipped his plate revealing the food mounded on it. "I think this'll do. Thanks for inviting me. David's vacationing with his family this week."

Talk turned to the softball game, and Penn, sitting with her legs crossed on the blanket, endured some good natured teasing about tripping over home plate.

Penn set her plate on the blanket. "My shoe caught the edge. I couldn't help it."

Jancie swallowed the last bite of her hot dog. "At least you managed to touch the plate so the run counted."

Penn fiddled with her napkin. "Not that it mattered in the long run."

"Too bad you couldn't have points for style. Because if that were the case..." John wiggled his eyebrows.

"Thanks so much for your two cents." Penn threw her balled up napkin toward him, but he swerved out of the way.

"Ooh, looks like your aim could use some work."

She sucked in a breath and reared her hand to give him a friendly smack.

His fingers closed over her wrist before she could blink.

She tugged against his grip, but the clench

remained firm. His strength surprised her, and showed on her face before she could hide it.

A slow grin cut into his five o'clock shadow. "Years of riding a motorcycle." He flexed his other hand. "And exercising with hand grips."

His hand, warm around her wrist, felt strong and solid, not confining or smothering. She liked his touch. She liked looking at his face. His dimples emphasized his grin. The scar above his cheek added interest, and her fingers itched to trace the mark. And his eyes...why had she never noticed how long his eye lashes were? She parted her lips.

"Miss Davenport. Miss Davenport." Grace and Trudy skipped toward them breaking in on her thoughts. Good thing, too. What was she doing, thinking things like that?

What was he thinking?

"Oh, those silly girls." Winnie flattened her mouth like she did when she was exasperated with Penn.

Penn startled at her aunt's reaction...and the fact that her aunts were seated with them. In that wacky few minutes when she'd taken leave of her senses, she'd forgotten they were there. She'd forgotten everything except John.

"We've been looking for you."

"You found me."

"Good job today at the game. That home run was awesome!"

"Thanks."

"And especially the little dance afterward." The girls giggled. "We've never seen you do that before."

John chortled.

She ignored him.

He'd let go of her wrist when the girls called her

name, and now he stacked the empty plates. The absence of his fingers left her feeling bereft. She massaged her wrist to lose that feeling. She didn't like it. She didn't want to like him.

John rose with the plates and left for the garbage cans.

"And you won't see it again either."

"Oh, we might. One of the boys took a video of it with his phone, I think."

"What?"

"Enjoy the fireworks. Won't be long." And they were off.

She didn't have time to consider the consequences of her not-so-proud moment showing up on social media. The hairs on the back of her neck signaled John's return from the garbage cans. She could worry about the video later. Now, she had other things to concentrate on. Like keeping her gaze turned toward the sky, waiting for the show. She didn't want to get lost in his eyes again. She didn't want to wonder about his thoughts or stare at his dimple.

He stretched out on the blanket, his hands bent behind his head. "It's a beautiful night."

"Especially for fireworks." Penn's excitement colored her words. She checked her watch. "It's almost time."

Jancie chuckled, settling back in her chair. "A few more minutes, sweetie. Cool your jets."

He shifted his head to peer at her. "You like them that much?"

"She loves them!" Winnie reached over and patted Penn's knee.

"You hate roller coasters but love fireworks?"

"What's wrong with that?"

"Nothing. Just surprising."

Penn frowned. "Why is it surprising? How are the two related?" Did he consider her a science project to be observed and analyzed?

"Surprising isn't a bad thing, Penn. Just something else to know about you. Like the way you can knock a softball out of the park."

Her throat constricted. Was he keeping a list? Was that a good thing? She opened her mouth to ask, but a boom jerked her upright on the blanket. The corresponding light fastened her attention to the sky.

Cheers sounded as the shimmering colors of red and blue sprayed above them.

"That one looks like a chrysanthemum. I think those are my favorite." Jancie likened all the types to her favorite flowers.

They discussed each new image that appeared, commenting on the colors or how some lights lingered longer than others or the stars that glittered across the sky.

Penn clapped with her aunts a few times if the effect was particularly stunning.

Twenty minutes later, the last light of the finale burned out, and the crowd applauded the celebration.

John helped pack up the chairs and offered to carry them home.

Penn declined before Winnie could nod her head. "We're just a couple blocks that way." She pointed east. "You're that way." She pointed west. "Thanks, but we'll manage." She didn't want another porch scene like the other night, and she could guarantee the aunts would maneuver it. She still needed to understand what had happened between them when he'd held her wrist.

He made a face. "I don't mind the walk." He reached for the chairs she had slung on her back.

"No." At her aunts' quick glance, she tempered her sharp refusal. "We appreciate it. Really, but we're good."

He dipped his head, and guilt niggled in her mind, but she stood her ground. After that...that unsettling connection earlier in the evening, she needed some time by herself. As much as she wanted to explore what it had meant, she had to stop thinking about it until later.

She caught the glance between the two sisters folding the blanket. She knew her words and actions disappointed them, seemed strange and ungrateful. She knew they wanted John to be a suitor, as they called it, but she wasn't ready.

"OK. If you sure." John's brow wrinkled.

I know I'm being weird, but I can't help it. "I'm sure."

"Hey, happy birthday tomorrow." His mouth turned up in a slow, warm smile.

He remembered. Her heart clenched. She schooled her features to remain calm and not betray the joy bubbling inside her chest. "Thank you."

Winnie clasped her hands. "John, have dinner with us. Just a little celebration."

"Thanks. I wish I could. I'm going out of town tomorrow."

A deflated feeling pressed against Penn's insides. Melancholy? No. For sure, not melancholy. Fatigue, probably. Definitely not melancholy. What was wrong with her? One minute she pushed him away. The other, she wanted to pout because he'd miss her birthday. Was she six years old?

"You take good care then." Jancie draped the

folded blanket over her arm. "'Bout ready to head home, Winnie?"

"Yes, indeed-y. Bye, John." They stepped away from Penn.

John touched her elbow. "Sorry about dinner tomorrow night. I hope you have a special day anyway."

"Thanks. The aunts always plan a good time."

"I'm sure." He cocked his head. "You were fantastic at the game today."

Heat crept up her neck. Her breath stuck and hovered just above her lungs. All she could manage was a whispered, "Thanks."

"OK, then. See ya." He stuffed his hands in his pockets and headed toward the pavilion.

15

Penn tightened the reins, and Periwinkle stopped at the edge of the road. She checked for cars and tapped her heels into Peri's flanks to urge him across. With traversing the backyards of kind neighbors, they'd have to maneuver only Stanton Avenue before arriving at the open farmland north of town.

She'd studied for three hours straight this morning and longed for a change of scenery. Exhausted from numbers and definitions and from forcing John from her mind every six or seven minutes, she needed Peri time.

The horse strained against the reins, revealing his desire for the ride as well.

Penn looked forward to the ride but also to the treat she'd promised herself every time John's face appeared in her mind. *Not yet, Penn. Accounting now. John later.*

Peri recognized the farm and broke into a trot.

She laughed. "All right, boy. You want this ride as much as I do. Well, have at it." She snapped the reins and nudged the flanks again. Peri's gait quickened to a canter.

Squinting against the wind whipping off Peri's head, she let him run where he wanted. He knew what to do.

Twenty minutes later, she lounged in front of a sugar maple, and Peri grazed a few feet from her. She broke off a piece of a granola bar she'd stuffed into her knapsack. She chewed the chocolaty oats and nuts, allowing the flavors to work with the scenery to soothe her.

She loved this place. Timothy Martindale, a friend from church, allowed her access to his farm. During high school, she rode here at least once a week, usually twice. Now her visits came less often.

Hidden from the road, the pasture lent much needed privacy to a hurting teen. A few cows occupied the area but never complained about sharing their domain. In the past, they ignored the horse and his rider.

Today was no different. Penn didn't want to be bothered. She'd earned her free time with Peri, and she allowed her thoughts to wander to the topic that filled her mind every day.

John.

He confused her so. What was going on with him? He was attentive and kind to her. He seemed interested to a point. Then he'd group her together with the aunts. He invited all of them to the festival. He'd said he'd enjoyed being with them at the festival, not with her.

But then, for just a split second the other night, she was certain he'd intended to kiss her. He'd brushed his thumb over her lips. He'd cupped her cheek. He'd begun to lean toward her but stopped and tucked her hair behind her ears. Started talking about the porch, of all things.

What if he'd done it? What if he'd kissed her? Would she have let him?

Part of her wanted him to as much as she wanted anything. Part of her was scared to the point that her fingers trembled now at the thought.

She dug inside her backpack and found her go-to thinking candy. She popped a nugget into her mouth and added another. Two was better than one. She held them in her mouth, letting the chocolate melt away to the caramel center.

What about at the picnic? When he'd held her wrist, she'd seen a question in his eyes. What did he wonder when he searched her face? Did he see her as a timid loser, living at home with her aunts?

He was surprised she liked fireworks. What did that mean? Did he see her as boring, a fuddy-duddy who wouldn't try new things? That revelation from the arts festival still smarted a little bit.

The first time they met, he'd grouped her as a teenager. Did he think she was too young? Was that the cause of his hesitation? How did he really feel about her?

More to the point, how did she feel about him?

She closed her eyes and pictured him, tall and dark. His strong hands tapered into long fingers. She could still feel them around her wrist.

She smiled remembering the way his black hair parted and fell away from his temples, curling below his ear lobes. Longer than what she usually found attractive but perfect for a free spirit like John. A free spirit? A free spirit who flies planes? She pressed her hand against her chest hoping to slow its beating.

She fished another candy from the box.

Could she fall for a pilot? Someone who flew planes for a living?

Peri nudged her shoulder.

She startled. "You ready to go home, buddy?" She rubbed his nose. "What do you think? Could I handle waiting for John to come back from a flight? Checking the weather? Listening to news reports?"

Images from her childhood flooded her mind. Images she hadn't thought about in years, not since Dr. Suzie had helped her work through that awful time after the accident when Abby's mom had set her on her lap and explained that her parents' plane had crashed.

Mrs. Parker hadn't relayed the entire story at that point. She'd hugged Penn and told her they'd find out the answers to all her questions the next day. Until then, she could stay with Abby for a sleepover.

Penn could still see Abby's wide, blue eyes and the scared look Mrs. Parker tried to hide.

Abby. Her best friend until…

Now Abby had returned for her Licensed Professional Counselor internship.

Penn rested her head against the rough bark of the tree. Why in the world had she agreed to lunch? More time with Abby would give these old feelings another opportunity to rise out of her memories and break her heart all over again.

The invitation had been along the lines of the let's-do-lunch variety with no mention of a specific day. She doubted she'd see Abby again. Their paths had stopped crossing long before high school. No reason to think they'd cross again now. She blew out a long, slow relieved breath.

Peri shook his head and nipped at her collar. "You're right, Peri. I don't need to think so much about all these things, especially about that time."

She nuzzled her face against his nose and breathed in his pungent, leathery smell. "I'm borrowing trouble here, worrying about something that will never see the light of day. John's done nothing but be a kind friend.

He wants to learn his new community, and we're the ones he's recruited to help him. End of story."

A twig crackled as she rose to hug Peri. "Thanks for helping me sort all this out, buddy. You're very wise, you know that?"

Peri snorted and stepped forward.

She laughed. "Wise and modest, too." She wrapped the reins around her fist. "All righty, let's go home. I think I need some cookies."

~*~

Penn led Peri into his stall and freshened the water bucket. She offered him a sugar cube on her flattened palm. "Here you go, sweetie. A nice snack after a great ride." She stroked his snout and kissed him at the tip of his nose. "It was a great ride, wasn't it? We'll go again soon. I promise."

Choosing a brush from a nearby shelf, she raked it through the black mane. "You were spectacular today."

"How do I warrant a compliment like that?"

Flinching, she dropped the brush. Flutters in her chest chased away the peacefulness she'd garnered from her time with Peri. She bent to retrieve her brush, but John arrived first, grabbed it and appropriated the grooming duty. Concentrating on the small star on Peri's forehead, she clutched the bridle.

"Not scaring people to death might be on the list." She scooted to the other side, putting Peri between them.

"The list?" He focused on his task, leaving Penn to snatch a glimpse of John's ivy-colored polo stretched over his chest.

Her heartbeat quickening, she nuzzled her nose under Peri's ear. "Of how to earn a compliment."

John winced. "Sorry about that. Jancie saw you come home and suggested I come down and see you."

Penn flattened her hand against the horse's flanks, drawing strength from the heat emanating from him. "Wait. Start from the beginning. You were with Aunt Jancie?"

"And Winnie. I'd called earlier. Found out you weren't home. They invited me over to wait for you."

"So you visited with the aunts?" She clenched a hank of Peri's mane. How long had he been with them? What did they talk about? More details about her childhood?

"Yeah and ate a ton of cookies in the process." He patted his stomach. "Too many, I'm afraid. They won't let you eat just one."

"Welcome to my world."

"Glad to be here." John, his attention fixed on the horse, transferred the brush to his left hand and worked on Peri's front leg.

Not able to think of a response to his words, she ignored them. "You've done this before."

"My grandparents always had horses. My little brother's a trainer. I can bluff my way around equestrian circles."

"So...why are you here?"

"Get right to the point, huh?"

"I've noticed you do that, and it usually works better than beating around the bush, or the horse."

He rewarded her with a grin.

"Cute joke." He dragged the brush along Peri's withers down the back to the dock of the tail. "Here's the deal. I need your help."

"My help?"

He slid around Peri, repeating the brush strokes on the other side. "And your aunts, too."

She lowered her chin. "I'm sure they've already agreed."

"Nope. I haven't asked them yet. I kind of thought the same thing—they'd agree, and you'd be stuck." He glanced at Penn. "I wanted to ask you first. If you agree, then we go to the aunts."

Good of him to give her first right of refusal. "OK, what is it? You got plans for your wraparound porch? You need extra hammer-ers?"

He snorted. "Come on. That paper bag floor was your aunts' idea. And they offered your help. I didn't ask."

"True. But you're asking now."

"Not for that. Still looking for an easy set of directions by the way."

"Landscaping, then. They're both master gardeners."

"No, but good to know. My yard's a mess."

She smiled. "Well, don't mention it unless you want us showing up with shovels, rakes, and flats of flowers." She tilted her head. "What do you need?"

"Actually, it's my boss who needs the help."

She froze. "John, I'm not—"

"No, no. Nothing to do with the airport or flying." He rested his arm on Peri's back and faced her. "My boss has box seats to the Pirates game this weekend, but his niece is getting married. Since he can't use them, he gave them to me. Four tickets behind the catcher. Sweet, huh?" He grinned at her, hope shining in his eyes.

Sweet all right. The aunts would dance a jig and

hug his neck and bake a couple batches of celebration cookies. They'd been to a few home games before but never sat behind home plate.

"You don't have to fly him?" An edge crept into her voice.

"Nope. Wedding's in Oakmont."

She weighed her options. Saying *no* would produce loads of guilt from denying her aunts this opportunity. A *no* would also mean another boring night at home with accounting books piled beside her, but saying *no* now could help her withstand John's charms.

Not that he'd be charming her anyway. He clumped them together, the aunts and the scared-to-try-new-things geek.

Saying *yes* would mean raves from the aunts, a spectacular view in arguably the most beautiful stadium in the country, a break from accounting law, and...more time with John. That thought pumped adrenalin through her body, made her feel more alive than she had in...since...her whole life. And that thought petrified her, just like his vocation. She opened her mouth, but he held up his hand.

"Uh huh. Before you think up a reason to say, 'no,' let me remind you that the Pirates are in first place, as of last week anyway. And did you hear me say, 'seats behind the catcher?'"

"I don't have to think up a reason to say 'no.'" Her eyebrows knitted together. "Why'd you think I'd refuse you anyway?"

Peri stepped sideways, reminding her she hadn't fed him yet. She hoisted a bag of oats.

John took it from her. "Let me help." He poured the oats into the trough. "Because your aunts usually have to talk you into things that involve me." John's chin trembled, and he sniffed, feigning tears. "I'm getting a complex."

A laugh sputter from her lips before she could rein it in. "That's not true, but I'm sure a big, strong man like you isn't bothered by the likes of me."

He caught her gaze. "You'd be surprised then."

Laughter withered in her throat. Why did he say things like that? And look at her like that? Then ask the aunts to tag along with them? "Oh, really?"

"Yes, really. Now quit with the suspense. Yes or no? Boring night at home alone or exciting night with me at the ball park." He weighed his hands like a balance again, raising and lowering each one as he spoke.

"Well, the thing is, I really do have to study for my CPA exam." She fingered the mane between Peri's ears.

He ignored her for his oats.

"Penn, you can't study every minute of every day. You need breaks. I think I'm brushing proof of what I'm saying." He smoothed Peri's back.

She sighed an exaggerated surrender. "OK. I agree. The game will be fun. Thank you for thinking of us."

"Fantastic. You're welcome. Your enthusiasm is overwhelming me, by the way." He placed the brush on the shelf over the stall. "Let's go tell the aunts."

"Fine, but I'm warning you. At the very least, they'll hug you. They jump up and down and clap, too." She cocked an eyebrow. "They'll probably kiss you."

"I should be so lucky. As long as they don't offer me another cookie, let them kiss all they want."

~*~

John caught Penn's gaze over the aunts' celebration and winked. They missed the exchange because they were busy dancing a do-si-do in the middle of the kitchen, singing a jaunty version of *Take Me Out to the Ball Game* complete with harmony.

Penn's eyes twinkled at their joy.

They punched the air as they sang, "For it's one, two, three strikes you're out at the old ball game" and slumped in the wooden chairs with breathless smiles.

"Oh, John. If I had the energy and could rise from this chair, I'd kiss you again." Winnie patted her chest. "Give me a minute to catch my breath, and I think I can go for another round."

John grinned. "Take your time, Winnie." He raised darkened eyes to Penn. "I never mind waiting for a kiss." He broke eye contact, giving Penn space to process his words.

Jancie cackled. "Penny, don't keep the man waiting, for heaven's sake. Give him a thank you kiss."

A flush colored Penn's cheeks, making him wish she'd obey her aunt. Her knuckles turned white around the counter top edge behind her.

His heart panged for her discomfort.

"She already thanked me out with Peri."

The relief that sagged her shoulders pierced his ego. What could he do to win her over? How could he help her trust him?

"Pish posh. This gift deserves tons of thanks."

"Jancie." Winnie howled from her chair, her hand clutching the bodice of her blouse.

"What is it, Aunt Winnie?" Penn sprinted to kneel

beside her aunt. She covered Winnie's hand with both of hers. "What's the matter?"

Winnie's eyes zeroed in on John. "What time's the game?"

"Aunt Winnie?" Penn felt the old woman's forehead.

Winnie waved Penn's hand away. "I'm fine, honey. The game, John. What time does it start?"

"Four o'clock, I think" He frowned. "Why?"

She eyed her sister. "Our Women's Missionary Board meets downtown Saturday."

"You're right, but I don't think it's all day, is it?" Jancie sifted through a pile of papers on the counter and pulled out Sunday's bulletin. "Now let's see." She scanned the announcements section. "Here it is. Supposed to be over at three o'clock." She raised the bulletin in triumph. "Perfect."

"We'll already be downtown, so we'll just visit until game time. We'll meet you two at the stadium." Winnie glanced back at John. "What time were you planning to pick up Penn?"

"How about I get here around three? That'll give us plenty of time with traffic and parking."

"Fine, but I'll—"

John crossed his arms in front of his chest and smiled. "I'll drive. You drove to Hartwood, remember? It's my turn."

The aunts belted out another chorus of *Take Me Out to the Ball Game,* and the subject closed.

~*~

"I'm not getting on that thing." Stubbornness oozed from Penn's stiff jaw, her crossed arms pressed against her pretty pink blouse. Her tennis shoes were rooted to the sidewalk.

He had to treat her gently. John knew that. He had to reason with her. He had time. "Penn, I'm sorry, but we don't have a choice. David's visiting his family. Your aunts have your car while theirs is being serviced. We have to ride my bike."

"No, we don't."

"The aunts don't have tickets. If we don't go meet them, they don't get to eat a hotdog behind home plate." He raised his eyebrows. "You don't want to deprive them of that experience, do you?"

"Don't try to guilt me into riding your motorcycle."

"I'm not. I know you don't want to disappoint them."

She backed up another step. "You go ahead. I can watch the game on TV."

"Penn. Don't be stubborn. You know you want to go." He inched toward her, and she retreated. "Listen to me. You've got the wrong idea about me. I've told you before. I'm not a daredevil. I promise I'll be careful, and you'll be safe. I won't go over the speed limit. I have a helmet for you." He extended it toward her.

Her eyes narrowed. "I'm not stubborn."

John chuckled.

Her chin jutted forward.

"I'm not." She squeezed her arms tighter around her mid-section. "I'm just careful."

"I'm careful, too. Let me prove it to you." He glanced up the street. "What if we take a short ride around your neighborhood? Let you get the feel of the bike."

She chewed the inside of her cheek.

Maybe he had a chance. "I'll go slow. You can tap my back if you get scared, and I'll stop."

Her gaze flickered away. The color rose around her cheek bones.

Ah, maybe the bike wasn't the only thing that made her jumpy. Maybe the thought of holding on to me made her chew her lip. Maybe she wasn't as disinterested as she'd acted.

"What about it? A little spin first, then we see how you're doing?" He held out his hand. "Can we try it?"

She hiked her purse strap higher on her shoulder but stayed put.

"I can stow your purse in my saddlebag, OK?" He slid his helmet on and snapped the chin strap.

Still no movement from Penn. At least she hadn't run back into the house.

"Come on, Penn. It'll be great." He offered her the helmet. "Let me help with this."

She allowed him to tug the helmet over her head and tighten the strap. His fingers lingered against the soft skin under her chin.

Her eyes searched his face, but he focused on fiddling with the helmet. Her breathing sounded shallow, and the pulse in the side of her throat pumped at a crazy speed.

John whispered, "Trust me." He led her down the sidewalk to the bike. "Let me get on first. I'll hold it up for you." Sliding close to the gas tank, he gave her a wide berth on the seat and offered his hand. Hers was cold as the glass of milk he'd had for breakfast this morning. After she settled herself, he waited for her to hug his waist.

He craned his neck behind his back and saw her

left hand fisting a handful of floral shorts material. "Like this." He pulled her arms around him, resting her hands against his stomach. *There we go. That's what I'm talking about.* "Hang on to me. If you want to slow down or stop, just tug my shirt. Got it?" Interpreting the non-response as an affirmative, he eased the bike back down the driveway. Perfect.

A beautiful day in Pittsburgh. The Pirates were on a nine-game winning streak, and Penn's arms holding on to him felt exactly right.

16

Penn wobbled off the bike and let John unhook the helmet. Although she stood on firm asphalt, her entire body vibrated with the memory of the engine's rumblings.

He ruffled her curls crushed from the helmet. "You OK?" He studied her face. "What'd I tell you? Fantastic, right?"

She hugged herself against the sensory overload and moved her head. Not exactly a nod or a shake.

"You were great, Penn. You leaned to the left with me when I needed to turn left." He shifted left. "You leaned right when we needed to go that way." He tilted that way.

Not wanting to end on the pavement, she'd clutched him, leaning whichever way he did. She'd closed her eyes the entire ride, trying to forget she rode the back of a two-wheeled monster. Trying to forget she was smack up against John. *Impossible.*

His woodsy cologne permeated her senses. Underneath her fingertips, his strong abs demanded her attention as they rippled and rolled with each turn.

"You're a natural bike rider, lady. Way to go." He held his palm high, waiting for her to hit it.

She lifted hers about as high as her shoulder, so he lowered his hand to hers, tapped it but didn't let go. "I'm so proud of you, Penn." He bent to kiss her cheek. "Seriously. I know you were scared, but you rode anyway. The aunts will love it."

He'd kissed her.

She dragged her shaking hand from his and clutched her throat. Shaking from the ride or from his kiss? The telltale prickles of heat dotted her neck and rose to her face. Her cheek tingled where his lips touched.

"Let's go find your aunts." He retrieved her purse for her.

How could he expect her to move when she was still recovering from the ride? From his kiss?

His kiss.

He could expect it because the kiss was a celebratory act. An upgrade from a pat on the back. He demonstrated his pride with a peck on her cheek. No big deal.

For him.

"Penn?" He bent toward her again. Questions flickered in his eyes. "You OK?"

No. She tugged the bottom of her blouse, fluffed the curls still clinging to her scalp. Throwing her shoulders back, she adjusted her purse. "Sure. Let's go."

~*~

Penn spotted the aunts first. Easy as finding a spot on a ladybug. "There they are." She pointed toward the Roberto Clemente statue to the two fans decked out from head to toe in Pirates' paraphernalia, complete with baseball caps and black and gold shoestrings in their sneakers.

They'd assured her wearing sports gear to a women's church conference wouldn't be a problem.

"Dress is casual nowadays. Besides, when they ask us about our getup, we can share the news about our seats—behind home plate."

John scanned the crowd, following the line of her finger.

"See the ladies reading the programs?"

"You mean the ones with the Pirates caps, t-shirts, shorts, and waist packs?"

"Exactly." She stepped toward them.

"They both got programs?"

"It's better that way. Believe me."

At that moment, Winnie turned a page, glanced up, and spied them. "Yoo-hoo, Penny. Here we are."

Jancie closed her book and waved as they approached.

"Yay. You found us." Winnie gathered Penn into a hug.

A grin played around John's mouth. "It was easy. You're right where you said you'd be." He reached into his pocket for the tickets, spreading them like a fan before them.

Winnie tucked the program under her arm and accepted a ticket from him. "Thank goodness you remembered the tickets." She kissed hers and wiggled her eyebrows.

Jancie accepted the ticket with a curtsy. "John, you'll have to give us your boss's address so that we can write a thank you note, OK?"

"Sure thing, but I already told him how excited you were and thanked him, too."

Winnie zipped her waist pack. "All well and good, but we want to send a card."

Penn stuck her ticket in the side of her purse. "Where'd you park?"

"In the Sixth Street parking garage. Easy-peasy to walk right over Roberto's bridge to the park."

"Roberto as in Clemente, I assume?"

Penn nodded. "The official name now is the Roberto Clemente Bridge."

"We love our legends." Jancie nodded up at the statue. "A great player. An even greater human being." She strained toward a gate. "Let's go get settled. I'm ready for a hotdog. Anybody else?"

Penn laughed. "It's not time for dinner yet, Aunt Jancie."

"It's always time for a hotdog in a ball park."

~*~

John crumpled the foil hotdog wrapper and dropped it into the cardboard food tray. He contemplated the shade creeping toward first base and wished it would creep a little faster over home plate. At least a slight breeze stirred through the park making the summer afternoon pleasant. His companions, one in particular, contributed to the delightful day.

He opened the wrapper to his second hotdog.

Penn licked pizza sauce from the corner of her mouth.

"This is a beautiful park. I think it may be my favorite, and I've watched games in several stadiums, including Fenway."

"I won't disagree with you on that point, John." Jancie dabbed mustard from her chin. "You won't find a prettier view of the city either. Just look at that gorgeous downtown."

Winnie tugged a tissue from her waist pack and

cleaned her glasses with it. "Don't forget Mt. Washington."

"My sister loves to take out-of-town guests riding on one of the inclines to the top of Mt. Washington."

John squinted toward the inclines across the river. "Yeah. That view might be nice, but here, you get a ballgame with the deal."

"You'll have to come to another game when there're fireworks. It's a spectacular show." Penn lowered the promotional batting practice cap they'd received when they entered the gate. Cute look. *Not.* But at least the cap concealed her helmet-head hair-do.

Winnie and Jancie had scrunched their original caps into their waist packs, donning the free ones instead.

The organist signaled the starting lineup, and they joined in with the applause. The cheers rose exponentially when Neil Walker was announced for second base.

"Did I miss something?" John's eyes narrowed as he followed the baseballs flying from mitt to mitt.

Jancie peered through miniature binoculars. "Neil's a hometown boy, grew up right down the road in Gibsonia. Did he graduate with you, Penn?"

"He graduated from Pine-Richland, two years before me. It was a big deal when the Pirates drafted him right out of high school."

Winnie accepted the binoculars from Jancie. "What a good boy. His mother is friends with one of the ladies in our group. Always has such nice things to say about him. About his whole family. You know, this great, big baseball star lived at home with his parents until, well, not too long ago."

John caught the sidelong look between Winnie and

Penn and Penn's arched brow. That exchange piqued his interest. He'd love to know what that look meant.

~*~

Penn ignored the zero to zero game for a minute and watched her aunts instead.

After finishing their hotdogs, they bought soft pretzels with mustard during the second inning. Now, at the bottom of the fourth, they munched on peanuts. Both balanced bags of peanuts between their knees, pointing to the field and sharing their considerable baseball knowledge with John.

Accommodating, he commented on the game when they swallowed or took a breath. "You ladies certainly know your baseball. I'm impressed." He accepted some peanuts from Winnie.

"Fascinating game. Thinking man's game, you know." Jancie, never taking her eyes from the field, cracked a peanut shell and popped the nuts into her mouth.

"You're absolutely right." John winked at Penn, and she dropped her peanut.

Winnie cupped her hands around her mouth. "Here we go, boys. Let's start something."

Neil Walker walked up to the plate and tapped his bat. The crowd cheered. He waited on a foul ball.

"Way to keep your eyes on it, Neil."

"That's right. Be patient. It'll come. It'll come."

Rocking on his feet, Neil raised the bat above his shoulder and whacked the next ball over the plate, a lead-off double down the left field line.

The crowd jumped to its feet, and both aunts lost their bags as they cheered for the hometown hero.

"That's the way to do it. Yes, sir."

The next player grounded out to groans from the on-lookers, but Andrew McCutchen dropped a single into left field. Then Garrett Jones walked.

The energy from the crowd coursed through the park.

"Hoo, baby. Neil is ready to score, and I'm ready to see it. Bring it home, guys. Bring it home."

Penn chuckled, happy that the aunts were completely lost in the game. She leaned over to John and caught a whiff of his aftershave. Her arms tingled at the memory of the ride. "Can you tell they're bored silly? Why did I think they'd have fun?"

John grinned. "I'm enjoying watching them as much as the game."

Chris Snyder stretched the bat above his head, and then approached the plate. He crouched and waited for the pitch. He snubbed a foul ball to the left and watched a strike fly by him.

"That's OK, Chris. You take your time. Don't swing if it don't sing."

John's laughter boomed across the rows in front of them.

"Here we go. Here we go."

The pitcher elevated a change up, and Snyder capitalized on it. He swung, and the bat kissed the ball, sending it flying through centerfield.

The crowd roared.

Jancie snatched off her cap and swung it over her head. "That one's in the Allegheny."

From her vantage point, the ball looked as if it did sink into the Pittsburgh river.

"My goodness. Did you see that?" Winnie seized her niece's shoulder. "A grand slam. We saw a grand slam in person, Penn."

Winnie lunged toward John, teetering Penn in her wake. Winnie grabbed his midsection, jumping with him in the middle of the row.

Jancie wiped her eyes. "How sweet, John. A grand slam." She slumped back into her seat, fanning herself with her cap. "Oh, my. What a fabulous time we're having. Four to zero. Four. To. Zero." She clapped her hands like a middle school girl who'd just received tickets to see the latest pop star. "We're on our way to a ten-game winning streak."

"Don't count your chickens before they hatch. We've got five innings to go." Penn patted Jancie's knee.

"Oh, ye of little faith. We just witnessed a grand slam. The boys have too much energy now to lose this game."

The four to zero score held until the top of the seventh when the Cubs chipped into the lead with two runs after a home run batted a double in. Another hit put a man on first. Snyder cut off the next right field hit and powered it to second base to close out the inning.

Although the Pirates had a few hits in the following at bats, they couldn't score from them.

The top of the ninth breathed possibility into the Cub's dugout when the first two at bats resulted in players on first and third. Two quick outs tempered the hope. Starling Marte extinguished any lingering hope with a sliding catch on a pop up to end the game.

Jancie whooped as she stood. "How sweet. We swept 'em three games. That keeps us at the front of the pack. Right, sister?"

"Yes, indeed-y. October, here we come." Winnie adjusted her waist pack. "John, we always watch the

World Series. Every year. This year we'll have a party if...no, when, the Pirates get into the dance. You're invited."

"I told you about counting those chickens." Penn rubbed Winnie's back.

"It's called believing. Having faith. These boys have got it. You'll see."

"All right. Well, now we have to think about getting home in this traffic. I guess I can ride with you and save John a trip to our house." Penn ignored John's quick glance in her direction.

"Wait a minute, Penny." Winnie sputtered and sought her sister's eyes.

Jancie shook her head. "Sorry, sweetie. The backseat is full of church materials. We don't have room for you. John won't mind bringing you back to the house, will you, John?"

"Absolutely not. I expected to." John arched a brow in her direction.

"It's just that...the motorcycle..."

"You rode his motorcycle?" Both aunts dropped their jaws. "That's tremendous. How'd you get her on it, John?" Winnie slapped him on his back. "Good for you."

"She wanted to. She loved it." He winked at the aunts. "She can't wait to hop on and hold me tight again."

Penn gasped and twisted her ring.

The aunts hooted, sending her a hopeful glance.

"Just like Aunt Cassie."

Penn rolled her eyes at the reference to her legendary great-great aunt. A sepia photograph of her leaning against an early motorcycle graced the mantel of their living room fireplace at the house.

Family legend insisted she'd ridden the bike all the way to Kill Devil Hills on the Outer Banks, including a short stint on a ferry boat, to meet up with a co-ed she'd met at a fraternity party at the University of North Carolina at Chapel Hill. No proof beyond the picture had ever surfaced, and the picture showed only her lounging against it, but the aunts proudly maintained the truth of the story.

"Come on, sister. We need to make tracks. It's been a long day." Jancie covered a yawn with her palm. "It'll take thirty minutes at least to get out of downtown, and we've still got to cross Roberto's bridge."

"You're right, but it's a beautiful night to be in a beautiful city." Winnie winked back at John. "I said, 'it's a beautiful night, John.'" She cut her eyes toward Penn.

Penn cringed, and John squeezed her shoulder. "You're a good sport." He whispered into her ear, raising goose bumps on her arm. He pivoted to the aunts. "A beautiful night indeed."

17

John slowed the bike as he swerved on to Oakland Street.

Penn's chest ached at the inevitable end of the night. She snuggled against his back and breathed in more of his faint cologne. She tightened her arms around his waist. His abs stiffened against her wrists.

Earlier today, she'd clung to him for fear of her life. She'd focused on every car that passed them, every bump in the Pittsburgh streets, every time he'd added gas to bring the bike to the speed limit.

Tonight—blame it on the sun that baked her brain out there behind home plate, or the exhilaration of the win, or the knowledge that she'd ridden on the back of a motorcycle all the way to Pittsburgh, or blame it on whatever—but tonight was different. On the ride back, she ignored everything except him.

His black hair curled out from under his helmet and rippled with the breeze. His cologne smelled woodsy, calming her like time spent with Peri.

Riding on the back of his bike won her over to new experiences. She'd ride with him to the moon and back. At least to Pittsburgh if he asked her.

John signaled a left and coasted to a stop in her driveway.

The house waited, dark and silent.

He pushed the kickstand down and caught her eyes in the mirror, peeking over his shoulder. He smiled, unclicking his helmet strap. Dismounting, he reached under her chin. "Home safe and sound. What'd I tell you?"

Home, yes. Safe and sound? Her *thump thump thumping* heart didn't think so. She removed the helmet, handed it to him, and raked her hand through her curls.

He offered his hand to help her off the bike and rested against it, half sitting, half standing. He shook his head. "Ferris wheels and roller coasters. Now riding motorcycles. What's next? Bungee jumping?"

"Ab-so-lute-ly not!" Penn shivered at the thought. Or maybe it was because he still held her hand.

"Don't knock it until you've tried it."

She sucked in a sharp breath. "You are a daredevil."

"Nope. Just enjoy having fun."

"Yeah, me, too. Like Scrabble, Monopoly, Pictionary…"

"I had fun today. Those aunts of yours are a trip." His thumb, arcing over the back of her hand, distracted her, robbing her of a proper comeback. "Speaking of your aunts, what was that exchange today about living at home? If you don't mind my asking, that is."

She steeled herself against the prickles zinging up her arm from. What was the answer to his question? "Oh, they don't want me to move out. They love reminding me that Neil Walker, Major League Baseball Star, lived at home until not too long ago."

"You want to move out?" His warm gaze, trained only on her, wreaked almost as much havoc on her insides as his touch did.

She blinked and peered over his shoulder to break eye contact. "It's not that I hate living here. I don't. If I can pass the CPA exam and get a job in Pittsburgh, they can move back to North Carolina. They've sacrificed for me enough."

"But do they want to move back?" He cocked his head, searching her face.

"Most people their age think moving South is the Holy Grail. They have a hometown and old friends down there."

His voice was warm and without accusation, he persisted. "Have they told you they want to move?"

"No, but—"

"Uh huh. Why can't you work in Pittsburgh now?"

"You need to be a CPA to work in the big firms downtown."

"You teach now, right?" He shrugged. "So transfer to one of the city schools."

"Yes, but..." She grimaced. "I couldn't do that. I love my students at Mars High. I couldn't jump ship to teach at another school." She pinched her lips together.

"But you could take a job in another field."

Why couldn't he understand? "Yes, because I wouldn't be choosing other students over them. I'd be choosing the job my degree is in." She tried to free her hand from his grip, but he held on. Captured her other one, too.

"Hey. I'm just asking questions, not judging you." He drew her toward him. "Don't be upset with me, OK?" He jiggled her fingers. "I'm a writer. I ask questions."

She stared at his hands surrounding hers, her heartbeat pounding in her ears.

He released a hand, nudged her chin up. "Penn. Look at me."

She raised her eyes and swayed toward the intensity in his.

"Penn, I..."

He brushed her lips, a brief, tentative contact that surprised and thrilled and disappointed her all at the same time. She didn't want a quick, apology kiss. She wanted a real one. Clinging to him, she waited, reluctant to move and ruin this fairytale scene.

His eyes swept over her face and settled on her mouth.

An emotion she couldn't discern flitted across his features, and he bent toward her again. He tipped her head, threading his fingers through her curls, cupping the nape of her neck. This time his lips were sure and strong.

Against her better judgment, she'd dreamed of this moment, had played and replayed a simulated version between the pages of her accounting books, on rides with Peri. She sighed against him and let herself sink into his embrace, answered the questions his lips asked of hers.

She forgot promising herself not to fall for him, forgot everything but how strong his arms felt around her, how fast his heart thumped underneath her palm. She trailed her fingertips up to his cheek, his day's growth of stubble scruffy under her fingertips.

His arms circled around her, but he broke the kiss, dragging his mouth over to another tender place. "Yeah. I think you might be a little daredevil." Husky and fervent in her ear, his whispered words revved her pulse another notch.

What had she done? She'd let him kiss her, kissed him back. Liked it. And wanted him to do it again. She squeezed her eyes shut.

"As much as I'd like to stay and test the daredevil theory, I know when to call it a night." He slid his hands to her shoulders, shuffling her backwards but holding her near. "Plus, I need to get ready for tomorrow."

"Tomorrow?" What day would that be? Hot and cold flashes dashed through her limbs stealing any cohesive thoughts. Sunday maybe?

"I have to fly out tomorrow afternoon."

Penn froze. The hot and cold flashes pinged to a halt as if she'd been doused with a bucket of ice water. Right. Flying. Planes. A pilot. The reason she'd planned to protect her heart. *Think of something to say.* "A long trip?"

"Supposed to be back Thursday." His thumb caressed her shoulder blade. "What if I call you then?"

He wants to call. A good thing right? She plucked at the scooped neck of her shirt.

But Thursday. Almost a whole week. A weight settled in her chest. "OK."

He laughed. "Don't sound so thrilled." He secured her helmet on the back of the bike.

She swallowed to dislodge the lump in her throat and pressed her ring into her palm.

"I'll call you when I get back." He swung his leg over the bike and kicked the starter lever. The engine obeyed the command and purred.

"Fine." Her manners resurfaced. "Thank you again. For the tickets. And the game."

"My pleasure." His dimple flickered with his grin. "You're welcome for the ride, too."

~*~

John rolled the bike down the driveway to the street. He chanced one more glance her way and waved.

Still twisting her ring. But…during that kiss, she'd let go of it long enough to hold onto him, to touch his face. Responding to him as if she enjoyed it. Nice. His cheek still tingled. So did his lips.

He twisted the handle grip, and the biked surged forward. His waist felt empty without her arms around him. On the way down to Pittsburgh, her fists had clenched against him the entire thirty-minute ride. On the way home, however, she'd twined her fingers and hugged his midsection, her sweet fragrance wafting around him.

During the initial ride, her rigid body perched on the seat, straight as the brace he'd worn on his leg as a child. After the game, she'd snuggled right up to him so fast and so close, he'd almost asked her name.

But he didn't want to spoil the moment by teasing her, a surefire way to get her rubbing that ring again, so he'd simply enjoyed the feel of her body up next to his.

He understood her hesitation. Motorcycles exuded a dangerous reputation for a lot of people. His mother tried all of his teenage years to talk him out of buying one, but he'd changed her mind with a few rides and a few more daisy bouquets.

John rounded the corner to Clay Avenue, he powered down as he approached his house.

He'd won over his mother. He wanted to win over, Penn, too.

Unlocking his back door, he entered and flipped on the light switch. As much as he wanted to let his thoughts center on Penn, work called. Throwing his keys onto the counter, he flopped in front of his laptop to check the weather and write his flight plan.

Thoughts of Penn, as sweet as they were, would have to wait.

~*~

Penn reclined in her bed with the ceiling fan stirring the warm air of her room. She listened to the aunts bustling around the kitchen and smelled the coffee waiting for her in the glass carafe.

She rolled to her stomach and let her thoughts run toward John. Again. She'd managed to study through the week, but today was Thursday. He said he'd call on Thursday.

Her heart raced at the thought. She stuffed her pillow under her chest, rested on her elbows and let her mind wander to last Saturday night in her driveway. When he'd kissed her. And cupped her cheek. And kissed her. And hugged her to him. And kissed her.

The aunts had played their hand very well. They'd suspected something but hadn't pushed the conversation that night or at breakfast Sunday morning. She waited for a question all afternoon, but none came until she stepped on the first stair on her way to bed Sunday night.

Jancie called from her floral wingback chair in the den. "Penny, you never told us. Is John a good kisser or what?"

Lucky for Penn, her hand gripping the railing steadied her when she tripped on the second step. "What?"

Winnie abandoned her book. "You heard her. I

know you did. You almost fell up the stairs, girl. Come in here and tell us all about it."

Stalling for time, she wracked her brain for a way to avoid what she knew was coming. "All about what?"

A coy smile danced around Jancie's mouth. "About his kiss. That's what."

Penn hesitated at the threshold. "Are you two out of your minds? What makes you think—"

"Give it up, girl. We know he kissed you." Jancie laid *Jane Eyre* under the reading lamp.

"I was going to say, 'what makes you think I'd let him kiss me?'"

"Well, if he tried and you wouldn't, you're goofier than you look when you wake up in the mornings." Winnie slid a bookmark between the pages of *Pride and Prejudice* and clasped her hands on top of the cover.

"Thanks very much." Penn huffed at the indignity of that statement. How to move the conversation to a safer subject?

Jancie waved her to join them. "Come sit down. You know it's true, and we're one-hundred-percent sure he kissed you. We've waited all day, and you've been stubborn."

Expecting to rue the conversation, she entered the den and parked on the navy couch.

"Spill, Penn." Jancie crossed her ankles on top of the ottoman in front of her chair. "Tell us how it felt to be in his arms."

"Aunt Jancie, stop." She couldn't face her aunts. She snatched up a magazine on the coffee table, hiding behind it.

"She's blushing, Winnie."

Winnie reached toward her and held her hand.

"Penny, dear. Don't be embarrassed. John's a wonderful boy. He's the real deal."

Penn licked her lips. "Um." How to proceed? She smoothed curls around both ears, fluffed them, and smoothed them again.

"So he kissed you?" Jancie persevered like one determined to discover the secret ingredient of a coveted recipe.

Honesty. Maybe honesty would end this nightmare interrogation. "Yes, he kissed me good night when he dropped me off."

Jancie slapped the arm of the chair. "I knew it!"

"A grand slam and a kiss all in one day!" Winnie hugged her book to her chest.

"And a motorcycle ride." Jancie wiggled her index finger at her sister. "Don't forget that."

"Exciting, dear." Winnie slumped into her chair. "Thank you for sharing with your old aunts. Now get along to bed before it gets too late."

"That's it? I thought you wanted details." Penn's mouth gaped at the jackknife in their interest.

Winnie giggled. "Sweetie, we were just teasing you. That's your private business. We don't want to pry."

Cocking an eyebrow, Jancie stopped mid-reach for *Jane Eyre.* "Unless, of course, you want to share more."

And the interrogation ended as quickly as it had begun.

Penn flipped over and scooted against the head board. It was too early in the game to talk about John and how she felt about him. She wanted to hoard the feelings to herself and ponder them in secret. Like now. She hugged a dotted-swiss pillow sham, remembered his cologne, and tingled all over again.

~*~

Penn grinned her way downstairs and into the kitchen to greet her aunts. The small TV on the counter played in the background delivering the morning news. She poured a glass of orange juice and reached for a mug of coffee. "What smells so divine?"

Winnie closed the oven door and set a baking stone on a trivet. "We made cheese scrolls out of crescent dough." She offered one to Penn. "Try it. See if they're any good. We're taking a batch over to the ladies' group this morning. What do you think?"

Penn bit into one and moaned. The pinwheel stuffed with cheddar cheese and Italian herbs melted in her mouth and tingled awake all of her taste buds. "These are fantastic. Why haven't you ever made them before?"

Jancie lifted one from the stone. "We just found the recipe in one of those cookbooks we bought from the used book booth. Good, huh?"

Winnie fanned her hand, shushing them. "Let's hear the weather for today."

Conversation stopped just as during their childhood when their father, a farmer, listened to the forecast.

Jancie swallowed the last bite. "Ooh, looks like we're in for storms today."

Penn's heart seized at the mention of storms. "Storms? When?" She crouched at the TV, inches away from the small screen.

"Not till this afternoon it looks like. We'll be fine this morning, sister."

"Penny, what is it? You look as if you've seen a

ghost." Jancie rubbed the top of her shoulder.

Winnie patted her hand. "You're fingers are cold as ice. What's wrong? You're not afraid of storms. You always loved a good thunder boomer."

Penn chewed on her lip. Her lapis ring rested on her dresser top. "John's supposed to fly home today."

The sisters exchanged glances.

Winnie squeezed Penn's hand. "What do weather people know? It probably won't rain a drop. John's a careful pilot. He'll be fine. Don't worry."

Penn slammed her hand onto the table. "Don't say that. You don't know what'll happen." She dipped her chin. Yelling at her aunts? Excellent way to behave.

Jancie didn't flinch. "You're right. We don't, but we do know the One who can take care of us. Let's pray for peace and comfort for us and safety for John as he travels. We can trust in God, the Creator of this world and airplanes, too."

Penn closed her eyes to keep from rolling them. Who took care of her parents twenty years ago?

"Don't you go down that negative path, Miss Penny." Jancie called Penn by the name she used when she meant business. "I can tell by the smirk on your face where your mind is going." She moved beside Penn and brushed curls away from her face. "We can't read God's mind. We don't know why our tragedy happened, but I do know how grateful I am that He allowed me to be a part of your life. So we're not thinking negative things right now. We're going to pray."

And they did, with the scrolls forgotten on the table and the news streaming in the background, the aunts hugged Penn and prayed.

18

Penn scooped a ball of rocky road ice cream into a pink, cut glass ice cream dish and scanned the sky outside the kitchen window. Although it was three o'clock, time for her afternoon snack, the time seemed later.

The sky held an overcast tint all day, a common occurrence for Butler County, Pennsylvania, but the morning's forecast painted the clouds more ominous than annoying.

She resisted the compulsion to check the weather on her laptop and dragged her spoon across the top of the ice cream. She spread a dollop over her tongue but didn't taste the chocolate-y treat. Her mind skipped to thoughts of John.

He'd repeatedly told her that he was careful, not a daredevil. He wouldn't fly in unsafe weather, but what if...? What if his boss needed to get home and urged him to fly in questionable circumstances? What if he dangled a bonus in his pay if John would fly against his better judgment?

Would John work for someone like that? Would the idea of extra money, right in the middle of refurbishing his house...? Would a bonus be enough to entice him? What if—?

The aunts burst through the back door. "Thank goodness. We made it, but the rain's on our heels."

As the kitchen darkened, Penn glanced out the

window again.

The sky, no longer overcast, framed roiling, black clouds overhead. The tree limbs swished back and forth. A few knocked against the house.

She rose to get a better look as a strike of lightening lit up the backyard and illuminated the room. A booming clap of thunder immediately followed the flash, vibrating the house.

Winnie shivered. "That was right on top of us. I couldn't even start counting seconds." She always counted the seconds between a lightning strike and the sound of thunder, multiplied the number by seven, and shared how many miles away the lightning struck.

Jancie switched into big sister mode. "Everybody to the basement. Now."

Penn grabbed her laptop with one arm.

Jancie seized the other, leading her toward the basement door.

They huddled on a worn, paisley couch, moved down when the new one upstairs took its place several years ago.

Penn opened the computer with trembling fingers, ignoring the tears wetting her cheeks. She reached for the ON button, but Jancie covered her hand.

"We don't need that thing yet. We need to pray first." Jancie wiped her face with a crumpled paper towel stuck in her pocket for the trip downstairs.

The house vibrated above them with each thunder crash. As the crabapple trees slammed against the back of the house, Winnie opened the prayer with praises and thanksgiving for God's omnipotence, for His provision and sovereignty.

Jancie chimed in, praying for peace and comfort. She prayed for safety for people in the storm's wake.

She cloaked Penn's shoulder with her arm and prayed for John's safe deliverance.

Penn's aunts' soft but firm voices blanketed her. She could have been six years old again. The words swirled around her, their resonance and meaning wooing her to peace. The panic racing her heart, stealing her breath retreated. She envisioned John smiling, his eyes crinkling at the corners, a dimple appearing in his cheek.

Jancie's *amen* brought her back to the present and reignited the storm smoldering in her chest. Penn fingered the ON button, and Jancie kneaded her shoulders.

Waiting for the computer to wake, she groped for her ring. Empty finger. Why did she decide not to wear it today?

The local TV station website flashed on the screen. The Doppler radar glowed with reds, greens, and oranges filling the screen. The headline screamed *Wild Weather* in red type. Thunderstorms. Wind. People had already posted tornado sightings, but none had been confirmed.

Reading over Penn's shoulders, Winnie gasped. "Pittsburgh had tornadoes before. Remember, Jancie? In 19-what, 1998, I think."

"John's out there in that." Penn wanted her voice to sound strong and firm, but she lacked the energy. Her heart jammed in her throat. Waiting tears stung in the tip of her nose.

"We don't know that for sure. Don't borrow trouble, honey." Winnie kept her voice soothing, but her white knuckles were strangling a lumpy throw pillow relegated to the basement with the couch.

"He said he'd call when he got back. Why hasn't

he called yet?" She tunneled her fingers through her hair, grabbing hanks and tugging against her scalp.

Jancie halted Penn's hand, removing it from the tangles. "I believe you just answered your own question. If he said he'd call when he got back, he isn't back yet."

"Or maybe he can't. Maybe he's out there in this...this—"

"Stop." Jancie closed the laptop. "I mean it. We don't need any more of that. We know we've got a raging storm." She rose with her hands on her hips. "I tell you what we're going to do. We're going to think positive thoughts. What's that verse, Winnie? About thinking good things? Tell us. We need to hear it now."

Winnie recited the verse from Philippians without stumbling. "Whatever is true, whatever is noble, whatever is right, whatever is pure, whatever is lovely, whatever is admirable-if anything is excellent or praiseworthy—think about such things."

"Exactly right." Jancie smiled at her sister. "Thank you, dear."

The tremors in Penn's fingers expanded into her arms and down her legs, and a faint whisper of nausea flitted in her stomach. She lurched into the basement's half bath just before her ice cream made a repeat performance. After rinsing her mouth and face, she returned to the couch, ignoring the aunts' words of comfort. Her mind fast forwarded ahead of this situation.

No plane crashes had been listed on the news website, but her mind traveled down this road years before today.

Once when she was about eight and the aunts were folding laundry in the basement, she'd spent some time nosing through things that didn't belong to her — the aunts' purses, envelopes on the kitchen desk. She'd found yellowed newspaper clippings of her parents' crash in the family Bible, tucked within the flimsy pages and stored on the bottom shelf of the hall bookcase.

She'd never seen the articles before and surmised, because they were hidden in the back of the big Bible opened only on Christmas Eve, the aunts didn't want her to see them. She'd kept her find a secret. The pictures haunted her for months afterward until she'd confessed to Dr. Suzie.

Thank goodness for Dr. Suzie — always listening without judging, offering gentle advice with scripture verses and a lollipop, too. The appointments with her had been a haven especially in the first few years after the tragedy. Maybe she should call Dr. Suzie again. Would a children's therapist agree to chat with a twenty-six-year-old?

Common sense told her she was over reacting. She and John weren't dating. They were getting to know each other. They'd enjoyed time together and one kiss.

But she'd let her heart open up to John in a way she hadn't before. Refusing to listen to common sense, she'd let her heart look forward to being with him, let herself enjoy his arms around her.

If her body reacted this way — shaking, heart pounding, not-being-able-to-breathe to a scenario that hadn't been proven yet, and to a person just beginning to mean something to her, how would she handle his flying if they began dating? She covered her face with her hands.

The aunts closed in around her. Hands warmed her back and her forearms.

"Come on, honey." Jancie kissed the top of her head. "Those old thoughts aren't good for us."

"I can't help it." Penn leapt from the couch with so much force Winnie toppled against the padded arm. "Do you think I want to think about plane crashes and...and..." She stopped pacing in front of the glass block window, but nothing showed through the opaque cubes. She pressed her sides.

"Of course, you don't. None of us do."

"I don't want to." She threw back her shoulders. "And I'm not going to." She'd been happy before John Townsend ever zoomed into her life on his stupid motorcycle. She'd be happy without him again.

No more roller coasters. No more crazy rides on the back of his bike—or hugging him during those trips. Or losing herself in dark-eyed smiles with a dimple. Or melting into his kisses.

No more John.

~*~

Her elbow on the accounting textbook, Penn gazed out her bedroom window. She surveyed the storm's havoc in their backyard. No real damage, thankfully. Mostly debris, branches, and green leaves scattered over the grass.

A few trees at the back of their property lay broken on top of each other near the shed, unscathed by the trees' crash landing.

Peri, also unaffected by the earlier storm, munched on wet grass in the adjacent corral.

They'd have to have help to clear those trees. Plenty of men at church owned chain saws and were always willing to help widows and orphans and anyone else who needed a hand. She drew a slow breath. Maybe the youth group could help clean up the yard, a good summer service project for a Saturday afternoon complete with frozen yogurt afterward.

She'd successfully reassured the aunts that she felt calm after the storm, but they'd still tut-tutted when she declined to sit with them, choosing to retreat to her bedroom instead.

Alone in her room, she'd considered all the details of her dilemma, placing the pros and cons on an imaginary scale. That exercise brought a pang in her heart as she remembered John doing the same thing in their conversations about lemons and lemonade and again when he asked her to the baseball game. The baseball game. The first time he'd kissed her.

The last time, too.

~*~

John stretched his hands over his head, enjoying the pull on his lats. Returning home at midnight wasn't his idea of the perfect trip. Returning in one piece after the monster storm they'd encountered was. He poured himself a glass of milk and glanced through the week's worth of mail on the counter David had gathered for him.

The storm, one of those freaky summer ones that popped up with all the advance notice of a cat burglar, had sidelined him and his boss the last hour or so of the home stretch. They'd waited at an airport in West Virginia scrutinizing every update on the weather channel and all local news reports. His eyes burned with computer screen fatigue.

Most of his body burned with some kind of

fatigue. A stressful week emotionally and now physically. Two rejection e-mails greeted him Tuesday morning. Not a good feeling despite reciting an old professor's adage that rejections weren't personal. If the query rejections weren't personal, why did they sting so much?

He rubbed his temples and remembered the e-mail accepting a longer article for a start-up travel magazine and another requesting a sample of his writing for an on-line magazine. Not bad. One article sold and possibly another.

He drained his milk and licked off the liquid mustache. His whiskers tickled his tongue. A while since he'd shaved. Long day. Glad to be home.

Home.

He'd told Penn he'd call her when he got home.

Too late now.

He'd call first thing tomorrow morning. He smiled. It felt good to have someone to share good news. He couldn't wait to see her again. He wished he could ride over to her house right now, throw some stones up to her window, if he knew which one it was, that is, and wake her up.

She'd come down to the front porch, and they could spend some time on the swing again.

Nice.

He grinned, remembering last Saturday night and their goodnight kiss. Would she have a hello kiss for him?

Another grin.

He'd call tomorrow.

No...later today.

Maybe they could get together tonight or Saturday.

He bounced his leg as he considered possible restaurants.

Yeah. It was good to be home.

19

Grace and Trudy hopped out of the church van and sprinted toward Penn. "We're here to help, Miss Penn." They waved matching purple gardening gloves before wiggling their fingers into them. "Just let us know what to do."

"Is Peri here today?" Trudy folded her hands together like a prayer. "Can we go see him? Can we pet him?"

Quivering on tippy toes, Grace added her two cents. "Was he scared in the storm? Can we feed him, please?"

Penn breathed in the pungent scent of fresh wood as she sent up a thank-you prayer. These girls would be fine distractions today. Their giggly selves and manual labor just might keep her mind from wallowing about John and the cellphone she'd turned off yesterday.

"Yes, Peri's here. He's fine. Storms usually don't bother him. He's brave. I already put some oats in his trough, but we can visit him for a minute before we get started."

Jack and another boy she didn't recognize hopped off the van.

Andy called a final admonition to work hard and flicked his fingers in a salute from the driver's side window. "Hi, Penn. I'm taking the rest of this group out to Mrs. Jeffries' place."

He shifted into reverse. "Just give me a call when the job's done, and I'll come back to pick 'em up." He edged the van down the driveway.

"Will do. It'll be after lunch. My aunts are preparing a feast. Thanks, Andy." Penn swiveled back to the girls, but something caught the corner of her eye. Glancing in the street, she found only Andy, idling the van in front of the mailbox. Andy threw his head back, gave the thumbs up sign, and eased the van forward revealing a black motorcycle on the other side of the street.

Her heart seized.

John lounged on top of the motorcycle.

He was alive. *Thank you, God.* She gripped the edge of the porch for support.

Alive and handsome as ever. She wanted to run to him, jump into his arms, and hug him till he begged for mercy, but that couldn't happen.

Not now. Not ever. She stuck her feet to the ground.

The girls. Get the girls out of earshot. "Grace, you and Trudy can pile up the twigs and small branches in the backyard."

The boys sauntered up the driveway. "Jack, you and your friend can load the cut wood into Mr. Blanton's trailer. He's already back there sawing the trees into firewood for his heater."

As if on cue, a chain saw sputtered to life behind the house.

"I'll be back to help in a minute." Penn pointed Grace toward the backyard.

"OK. Hey, John. Are you helping, too?" Grace called over her shoulder.

"We'll see. Now go. The morning's racing by."

Penn crossed her arms and pressed them into her stomach before she faced John.

"I guess I see now why you were busy yesterday." He surveyed the scarred trees in Elbert and Maud's yard next door. "Too busy to turn on your cell. Or answer your land line." He swung back to her. "Mars got a pretty wicked storm on Thursday, too, huh?"

She caught her breath. So he had been in the storm. She sent another thank-you prayer. Two in the space of minutes.

"A pretty intense one." She studied the grass instead of making eye contact. "You made it back safe and sound, I see."

He reached for her chin. "Penn, look at me."

She stiffened when his fingers touched her skin.

~*~

John dropped his hand. A frown lined his forehead. What was going on here? He scrubbed his chin. She looked more pained than happy to see him. What happened to the warm, happy Penn he'd kissed right here on this very driveway only a week ago?

"Hey, Penn. It's me, John. What's up? I mean, besides your yard."

She grimaced, licked her lips.

He could almost visualize the wheels turning in her head, searching for an answer. What was the deal? Was she shy because of the kiss? She didn't even have a smile for him.

Two steps forward, one step back.

"It's just...we've got a lot going on here this morning."

"Yeah. Andy told me the youth group was

spreading out all over town to help with the clean up today. I'm here to help, too." He stretched on beat up leather work gloves.

She retrieved floral canvas gloves from her back pocket, her attention on them instead of him. "Umm, that's very kind, but...but I think we've got it covered."

"John!" Winnie burst through the front door. "You made it back." She grabbed the hand railing and descended the steps as fast as she could. "We were so worried about you flying in that storm." She flew to him with open arms.

John jerked his head toward Penn. They were worried about him flying in the storm? Was that the reason behind the cold shoulder today? He watched emotions play across her ashen face.

Of course, she'd been worried. She'd lost her parents...

"We tried not to worry. We prayed and prayed, and, of course, God is faithful." She squeezed so hard he lost his breath for a second. "Thanks be to God. You're here."

He delighted in Winnie's enthusiasm. Now that was a greeting.

Why couldn't Penn have welcomed him like that?

Maybe add a little kiss, too.

How could he reassure her that he'd been safe on Thursday? That he never took chances when flying was involved. That he cared about getting to know her.

John spread his arms wide. "I heard you needed help, so here I am."

Winnie still held onto his waist. "Fabulous. What a sweet friend you are. Right, Penny?" She urged him toward the backyard. "Penn. Right?"

Penn remained rooted in the middle of the

driveway. "Yeah, sure. Thank you."

Not exactly enthusiasm, but she didn't chase him off her property either.

Winnie quirked an eyebrow at her niece. "We do need help. Our yard's a sight, but many hands make light work." She grunted as she picked up a broken twig. "After, we'll have lunch. You can stay for lunch. Right, John?"

Having no plans for today beyond showing Penn he wanted to be with her, he surveyed the debris in the yard. "I'm here for as long as you need me." He'd prove to her he wouldn't jeopardize their relationship or friendship in any way.

Penn climbed the steps onto the porch with her mouth set in a straight line.

He had his work cut out for him. The backyard cleanup would be a breeze compared with warming the frigid expression on Penn's face.

No problem. He'd had to work hard all his life.

He could handle the challenge.

~*~

Penn slid the last salad into the refrigerator. Somehow, she'd made it through the morning without much interaction with John.

He'd claimed the chain saw from George Blanton, so the seventy-year-old supervised the guys in loading his trailer.

She and the girls, with the aunts, cleared the branches and large twigs, piling all of it by the street for the garbage collectors who'd come by on Tuesday.

With Mr. Blanton's extra rakes, everyone helped rake the yard.

Winnie and Penn took over kitchen detail. By 11:30, the yard was groomed again, and lunch beckoned with chicken salad, pasta salad, potato salad, spinach salad, a fruit salad, and an assortment of deli sandwiches.

As they'd laid out the serving utensils, Penn chided her aunt. "I told you yesterday when you were making all these salads that we weren't serving the whole youth group, just a handful of teenagers."

Winnie harrumphed. "Good thing we made all we did. George and John have worked like mad all morning. They'll be starving, but we'll have plenty." She bit a rolled turkey slice.

They did have plenty despite Jack and his friend piling two sandwiches on their plates before they ate one bite. Everyone scarfed down the food if it were the first meal after a long fast.

Jancie and Winnie glowed as the teenagers shoveled in the food.

Now the teens waited for Andy to collect them for one more afternoon clean up job. The boys lounged on the couch complaining of stomachaches while the girls flitted about the family room examining knick-knacks.

Screams pierced the kitchen.

Penn dropped the plastic wrap into the rack on the back of the cabinet door and called to the girls from the kitchen. "What is it?"

Trudy pointed to the mantle. "Look at this old picture. It's a woman on a motorcycle—in a dress!"

"They found Aunt Cassie on the motorcycle." Winnie pushed a chair under the table and followed Penn and Jancie to the girls in front of the fire place.

Penn fingered the frame. "She's my great-great Aunt Cassie."

"It must run in the family." John entered the family room, his eyes on the picture.

Penn startled at his voice and forced her gaze back to the photograph. How did he move from the yard to inside so quickly? Last time she checked, and she was checking on Mr. Blanton, not on John, he stood by the trailer, securing the chains.

Winnie lowered the silver frame from the mantle and dusted the glass with the corner of her apron. "This is one of my favorite pictures. She was a pistol, or so I'm told. She rode that contraption all the way from Oxford, North Carolina, to Kill Devil Hills to see a beau. In 1929, if you can believe that. A few months before the Depression started."

Grace craned toward the picture. "Wow. She was pretty, too."

"That runs in the family, too."

Penn snapped her gaze to John, but he oozed charm all over Jancie who giggled like she was Grace's age.

Jancie swatted his forearm. "John, I do like you coming around here."

A honk sounded out front.

Jack wobbled off the couch. "Hey, you guys. Andy's here. We need to roll."

"Wait, wait." Jancie sprinted to the kitchen and returned with four baggies of celebration cookies for the teenagers. "Thanks again for all your help."

The teens closed the front door, and Mr. Blanton cracked the back one. "Just wanted to say, 'I'm gone.'"

This time Winnie dashed to the refrigerator. She retrieved a plastic container. "Here. Take some of the chicken salad. Don't worry about returning the tub."

A smile lit the wrinkles in Mr. Blanton's face.

"When I said it rivaled my late wife's salad, I wasn't fishing for—"

Winnie fiddled with the collar of her chartreuse blouse. "I never thought such a thing. Please take it and enjoy. Thank you so much for your help today."

"You're very welcome, Winnie. I was glad to." He adjusted his cap. "I suppose I'll see you at church tomorrow."

Winnie smoothed back her hair and waved to Mr. Blanton. "I'll be there."

Penn didn't have time to contemplate the sparks flying around the back door. The hairs on the back of her neck prickled.

John approached her from behind.

Jancie, halfway up the stairs, called to Winnie to come look at something in her room.

Penn closed her eyes. She wasn't ready to face John alone.

20

John rolled his neck and waited for Penn to face him. Would he have to talk to her back?

Her back straight, she pivoted, her arms folded in front of her. "Thank you for your help today."

"You're welcome." He hooked his thumbs in his belt loops.

"We appreciate it so much." She stepped toward the front door.

He shuffled backwards to let her pass. "Glad to help."

"We could never have cleaned the whole yard by ourselves." She closed her hand around the glass door latch.

John tilted his head toward her. "Looks like you're ready for me to go."

She snatched her hand from the latch and stuffed it into her pocket. "Oh, no. It's just—"

"Let's sit on the swing a little while, OK?" He advanced toward the door.

She chewed the inside of her cheek. "Well..."

"Just for a bit. We didn't get to talk today."

She slumped her shoulders. "OK."

Not an encouraging sign.

Penn led the way to the swing, crushed herself against the wooden arm.

Giving her plenty of room, John nixed the idea of swinging. He fingered a scratch near his watch where a thorn had left its mark earlier in the morning. He blew out a long stream of air. *I need some wisdom here, Lord.*

"Penn, we can take this slow and talk about Trudy and Grace, talk about the fantastic lunch, or whatever. Or we can get right to it and talk about what's wrong today—I mean besides losing trees in the storm." He rubbed his chin. "What'd you think? Which way do we go?"

"What do you mean, 'what's wrong'?"

"Good. That's what I wanted to talk about, too." He stretched his legs in front of him and brushed off a wet maple leaf sticking to the laces on his work boots. He leaned back, folding his hands in his lap. "What's up, Penn?" He kept his voice light. "When I left last Saturday night, I thought things were great. We had fun at the game, right?"

She nodded.

"Yeah. A lot of fun." Go slow. Don't be aggressive. "And…after the game…" He held his breath.

She shifted her body to face the front yard.

Retreat. He'd pushed a little too hard.

No problem. He'd leave the kiss alone.

For now.

"When your phone went directly to voicemail and no one answered at the house either, I had some questions because I told you I'd call you when I got back. Then I got here this morning and…" He shrugged. "Let's just say, not exactly a welcoming greeting."

She dipped her chin and worked on the cuticle of one nail.

He didn't want to make her uncomfortable. He simply wanted answers. Humor. That's the ticket. "Except for Winnie. Now she knows how to make a guy feel welcome." He chuckled. "I wonder if that's how she'll greet Mr. Blanton at church tomorrow?"

Her mouth twitched. "You noticed that exchange, huh?" She picked at the hem of her faded blue shorts.

"Yeah. I notice a lot of things, Penn. Like how you seemed upset all morning, going out of your way to avoid me." He furrowed his brow. "What's wrong? Did I do something or say something to hurt you?"

She wiped her hands along her thighs.

"You're hands are shaking." He clasped hers. As much as he wanted to wrap his arms around her and comfort her, he didn't want to risk her bolting for the front door if he did. He inched his leg closer to her. "Penn, let me help you."

"You didn't hurt me, but..."

"But what?"

"John, when that storm came up Thursday afternoon, I knew you were up there. Flying your plane." She covered her face. "It was awful."

"Winnie said the storm was bad here, but you guys prayed and—"

"Yes, that's true. They prayed, and they were calm. I was physically ill. I threw up, John."

"I've told you I'm careful. I don't—"

"You don't what? You don't think my dad was careful?"

"Of course not. I wasn't going to say that." He flexed his fingers, an image of David's punching bag hanging in his basement floated before him. John counted to ten. Her words were unfair, but she wasn't thinking clearly. He could feel the fear emanating from her even now. He tempered his voice. "I don't take foolish chances, Penn, not with flying. I'm careful, cautious. I follow every rule."

"I know. You've told me. You were careful with me on the bike ride. But, John, my dad wasn't reckless either. And look what happened...I lost my mom, my dad, and my..." She pressed the back of her hand to her mouth.

"Penn, I'm sorry. I can't imagine that loss. Don't want to, but—"

She shook her head. "I don't want to relive it. Again and again." She raised glassy eyes to his. "That's what I did, John, all afternoon Thursday and into the night. I was in therapy for years to get a handle on this tragedy, and one afternoon brought everything back. The one saving grace was that the news didn't carry a plane crash, but I didn't know where you were. Maybe you'd crashed at the front end of your trip."

"But I didn't, Penn." He spoke quietly and carefully, determined to convince her. "We were flying when this rogue storm blew up. We landed at an airport near Charleston well south of here and waited it out. I would've called—"

"That's the point. I didn't know you were safe. I couldn't stop the images..." She covered her eyes.

"That's where faith comes in, doesn't it? Faith that God will take care of you, take care of me. Faith that I'll use the intelligence God gave me and heed the weather. That I'll be careful."

"It's so easy for you to sit here and talk to me about faith when you still have both your parents. When you haven't been through what I've been through."

He flinched at the pain shrouding her words. "You're right, Penn. I don't know what you've been through, but I do know that God is faithful. From my own experience."

John raked his hands through his hair. "Listen. This is an easy fix. I'll call before I leave, and when I land. You'll know what's happening with me so you won't worry."

"Don't you understand?" Her dark eyes pleaded with him. "There isn't a fix. Easy, quick, or otherwise." Penn flattened her lips. "I can't do this. I knew it from the time I found out you fly."

She was scared. She had a right to be, but how could he convince her to take a chance on what he felt between them?

"Penn, let's figure this out. We enjoy being together." He brushed her wrist with his fingertips. "Let's at least try—"

She leapt from the swing, clanking the chains. "No. I can't. I'm sorry..."

John reached for her, but she shrugged away from him.

He rammed his hands in his pockets.

"So...what do we do about us?"

"John." Her plaintive whisper cut at his heart. "I'm sorry. Please understand me. I wish I could push those pictures out of my mind, but I can't. And I don't want—can't—have another night like I had Thursday." She squeezed her arms across her chest.

If only she'd let him comfort her. His arms ached to hold her. Maybe holding her would assuage the tight feeling in his chest, too.

"I get that." He stared at the ceiling fan over the entryway, circulating the humid air. He wiped his hand across his mouth. "Does this mean you'll avoid me from now on, ignore me if we see each other some place?"

"No. Of course not." Her eyebrows bunched

together under her curls. "We're still working on the Apple committee together."

"Right." Lots of awkward fun times ahead.

"And don't forget church."

"We can't forget church." Why did he feel like she was breaking up with him? They hadn't even gotten started. She hadn't let them.

"I wish you'd—"

"I can't, John." She jutted her chin forward.

He'd see that look before.

"Right. Sorry." He cleared his throat. "I better get moving then. It's been a...it's been a day." He gripped the handrail and glanced back at her.

She hadn't moved, still hugging her arms around her waist. "Thank you again for your help."

"No problem." He descended the steps. "Glad to do it." *I wish you'd let me do more.*

~*~

Penn plodded to the door. Her feet dragged, as heavy as her heart. She entered the foyer and caught the aunts halfway to the kitchen. The creaking of the door alerted them to her, guilt flushing their cheeks.

"I guess you heard everything, so I'm going upstairs." She stepped toward the stairs.

"Oh, no. We couldn't hear everything."

Jancie swatted at her sister. "Hush, Winnie. Penn, honey, we didn't mean to eavesdrop. We saw the last bag of cookies and didn't want him to forget them. We were bringing them out when we realized...we realized..."

"You were having a serious talk." Winnie clutched the plastic bag of cookies to her waist.

Fatigue pressed against Penn's shoulders. "Serious, yes." The physical labor this morning had worn her but not as much as the emotional toll of being near John and not allowing herself to enjoy his presence. The final conversation had zapped any last thread of energy. "I'm wiped out."

Winnie gestured toward the kitchen. "How about a cup of tea, dear?"

Penn clutched. "I'm not hungry."

"You don't need to be hungry to have a cup of tea."

The back of her throat burned with tears demanding release. Her nose stung, signaling that the release was near. She needed to escape to her room. Quickly.

"Aunt Jancie, I—" Too late. Her stoic countenance collapsed.

"Come here, sweetie." Jancie swept her into her arms, and Winnie stroked her back. She breathed in the faint scent of moth balls and perfume, a constant with both aunts. She burrowed her head and succumbed to the tears.

The aunts murmured and fretted, caressed and patted, but the comfort she found in their arms was a poor substitute to the arms she longed to feel around her.

~*~

A knock on his front door roused John from the golf game blinking on his flat screen TV. When David left to buy some groceries, he hadn't mentioned expecting anyone. He snagged a t-shirt from the back of the couch and tugged it over his head.

Winnie and Jancie, sheepish smiles plastered across their faces, waited on his stoop holding a bag of cookies.

"Hello, dear. You forgot these yesterday, and we missed you at church this morning, so we thought we'd bring them by." Winnie wiggled the bag in front of him.

Jancie lowered her chin. "We don't have your number or we'd have called first."

"No problem. Thank you." He accepted the bag and chose a cookie. "I didn't hang around after church." He peered over their gray heads but saw only their empty sedan parked in front of his house.

Jancie entered the foyer. "She's not out there."

"She's riding Peri." Winnie brushed his arm as she passed by.

The lie that he wasn't looking for Penn died on his lips. "Right. Come on in, ladies." He stuffed the whole cookie in his mouth.

Winnie surveyed the seating options. "We'll come in just for a minute. We wanted to say 'hello' and thank you for yesterday and bring you the cookies."

Jancie placed her hand on her hips. "We wanted to see how you're doing."

He smiled at her. "No beating around the bush for you, huh, Jancie? I like that." He slid several sections of the Sunday paper off the couch and corner chair, stacking them on the coffee table. "Have a seat, ladies."

They perched on the edge of the couch. "So. How are you doing?"

John chose the Amish twig rocking chair David had bought last week. He shrugged. "I'm fine. Disappointed." He leaned his forearms against his thighs, clasped his hands. "How's Penn?"

"Miserable."

"Winnie." Jancie laid a hand on her sister's knee. "I'd say 'subdued'."

"She's also miserable, if you ask me." Winnie patted her hand and pushed it away.

He grimaced. "Sorry to hear that." He stared down at his hands.

What had these two women cooked up? "I suppose you know about our conversation yesterday?"

"Yes, we heard it."

Jancie elbowed Winnie. Jancie elbowed her back. "We were bringing the cookies to you when we accidentally heard you two on the porch. We didn't mean to listen."

"Of course not." John rubbed his upper lip to prevent a grin. "I guess it wasn't really confidential. No harm done."

Jancie shifted on the couch. "That's where we think you're wrong. Sorry, dear. No offense."

"None taken."

"Penn is..." Jancie glanced at her sister. "She's been through a lot. We've told you about her history, but she's got a lot on her mind this summer with the accounting exam she's studying for and the Apple festival."

"She's not thinking clearly. She's exhausted most of the time lately."

"We just hope you'll—"

John gripped the arms. "Ladies, Penn was pretty clear about not—"

"We know what she said. We just wondered if maybe...over time..."

He rocked backwards. "I appreciate how much you love her. I know you want her to be happy, but I don't think I can do that job for you." He rubbed the back of his neck. "I'm a pilot. Yes, I hope my writing takes off and becomes my main source of income. But, ladies, the fact is—I love flying. I can't change that."

"We don't want you to give up on Penny."

Something glimmered behind Winnie's glasses.

Please, please, please don't cry.

"I think she's terrific. Give it time and maybe we can work out a friendship—if she wants to." That's what he kept telling himself about the knot in his chest lodged there since yesterday afternoon. *Give it time. It'll go away.*

"You're such a good young man, John Townsend. We're going to miss your visits." They rose.

Don't say that. You don't know me as well as you think you do. If you did… He gripped the spindly arms of the rocker. *Stop. Don't go there today. Not now.*

He unfolded himself from the sloped seat and led them to the door. "I'm sure I'll see you around. I can't go too long without a celebration cookie or a cinnamon roll, you know."

"Don't you worry about that. We'll keep you supplied—even if we have to do it on the down low!"

He laughed and hugged both of them. "I appreciate that you came by."

"You take care."

He watched them walk down the steps and waved to them as the car crawled along the street. He'd miss seeing them as well, another kink in the knot tangling up his chest.

21

Penn ransacked her closet for something appropriate to wear. *What do I wear to lunch with someone I've avoided for the past twenty years, give or take?* She spread out the gathers of a yellow sundress.

No. Too perky.

How about a lilac blouse to go with a pair of grape capris pants?

No. Too purple-y.

She settled on a skirt swirled with fuchsia, aqua, green, and blue and topped it with a hot pink cotton sweater. Bold colors. Good. Strong colors would make her feel strong. Wouldn't they?

Why did she agree to this lunch with Abby? She'd been caught off guard as she thumped the watermelons at the farmer's market last weekend.

Abby stood with a basket of peaches on her arm, looking sweet and interested and...like someone she used to love.

When Abby asked her, Penn's heart pinged, and for a split second she'd wanted a best friend again. "Sure. When?" popped out of her mouth before she realized the commitment she'd made. *Lunch. Only lunch, not a relationship.*

She slung a straw purse over her shoulder, kissed the aunts who grinned like Christmas morning, and headed out the door.

Parked in front of the Mars Sandwich Shop, she

cracked the window and braced herself for the heat. A squeal from down the street arrested her attention.

Abby, dressed in scarlet shorts, black top, and black sandals, jogged toward her. "Penny, you've still got Gretchen?"

Penn blinked away tears pricking behind her eyes. *Not now, tears. Not now.*

"I've always loved this car." Abby trailed fingers along the hood. "I was so jealous of you."

"Jealous?" Penn blinked. "Of me?"

"Uh huh. Remember what I drove? I bought my granddad's green sedan for two hundred bucks." She wrinkled her nose. "What a dad car. Or, I guess, granddad car."

"It wasn't that bad." A faint picture flickered in her mind of a green car with a silvery, goopy top. Not a very handsome ride.

"Do you remember the top and that silver gunk globbed on the roof? Dad insisted it waterproofed the ceiling." She shuddered now, ten years later. "It was horrible. You got to bebop around town in this cutie." Abby swept another long glance at the blue Volkswagen. "I'm so glad you've still got her."

Penn's mouth gaped. "Bebop? You thought I bebopped?"

Abby dropped her keys into her purse. "You know what I mean."

She really didn't.

"Are you hungry? Because I'm starving." Abby headed toward the cafe. "I hope they have a vegetarian choice."

Opening the door, Penn tinkled the warning bell. "They've got pretty much whatever you want."

Aromas of kosher pickles and pastrami mixed

with pumpernickel and sour dough greeted them as they lined up by the counter.

Several minutes later, they munched on their selections, a tomato, fresh mozzarella, and pesto on sour dough and a portabella mushroom with balsamic vinegar on whole wheat, in silence.

Abby twirled the fancy toothpick, relieved of its duty of holding the sandwich together. "I'm glad you agreed to come today, Penny."

Penn sipped her frozen green tea.

How could she answer? Truth.

"You took me by surprise. I didn't know what else to say."

Abby grabbed her napkin and hooted behind it. "Honesty. I love it. I could always count on you to be honest."

Penn scrunched her face. "What do you mean by that?" She bit the end of her pickle spear, the brine fighting a bit with the sweet balsamic.

"You don't remember?" Abby swirled her straw through the crushed ice and root beer.

"Remember what?" Penn laid down the pickle and wiped her fingers.

"Our last conversation. Pretty much anyway."

Penn furrowed her brow, splayed her fingers against the tingling in her chest. Their last conversation? At the Parkers' house? After the tragedy?

"Do you mean...right after...?"

"Good grief. Not then. We were about eight maybe. Walking to Brownies after school. I waited for you because I knew you'd be by yourself."

Alone.

Yes, she remembered that part.

"I told you I missed you. You said you missed me, too. I said, 'Good. Come to my house after school on Friday. We'll play dolls.'" She dipped her chin but held Penn's gaze. "Do you remember what you said?"

Penn shook her head.

"You said it was too hard. Being with me made you sad." Tears pooled in Abby's eyes. She widened them to keep the tears from falling.

"I have no recollection of that conversation."

Was Abby serious? Why couldn't she remember?

"It's burned into my brain, for sure. I skipped Brownies, ran home, and cried all afternoon."

A wave of sadness rolled over Penn and settled around her heart. She hurt for the two little girls, struggling to find their way in the wake of her family's tragedy. She folded the end of the wax paper draped over the plastic basket. The remainder of her sandwich no longer appealed to her. "I'm sorry."

"No need to apologize. You were honest. I appreciate that about you."

Penn pushed away the basket. "I thought you avoided me."

"Why on earth would I do that?" She slid her hand close to Penn's, stopping before touching it. "We were best friends, for heaven's sake."

"Because I was the orphan." Penn winced at the weak argument in her words.

Abby's mouth dropped. "What? Penny, you had your sweet aunts who bought you Periwinkle, the coolest horse in the world by the way, who took you on summer trips, who made those delicious cookies for every bake sale we ever had. What did I do to make you think that way?"

Nothing. Not really. She'd just always felt that

way, the outsider. She couldn't speak around the lump in her throat. She'd pushed people away, not the other way around.

Abby nudged Penn's knuckles with hers. "Penny. Oops. I'm sorry. Missy said you go by Penn now. I'll have to get used to the new name." She smiled. "It fits you."

"Don't worry." Penn waved away the apology. "The aunts call me Penny half the time. No. Most of the time."

"I'm glad we had a chance to talk." She glanced at her chunky white watch. "I need to get to the 'burg.'" She raised shining eyes to Penn. "Do you think we could try it again sometime?"

Penn checked her own watch. Should she rush into another lunch with Abby? This one wasn't so bad. She'd learned something about her past, something that shifted a couple of the broken pieces of her heart into place.

"I think that'll work." She smiled. Tentative, yes. But a real one. "Yeah. Let's try it again."

~*~

John slammed his gloved fists against the speed bag hanging from the basement ceiling. Left, right. Left, right. Left, right. If the pounding rhythm of the bag and the gloves didn't chase away the heaviness in his chest, maybe it'd exhaust him instead.

The ache underneath his ribcage strengthened daily. Would it be a permanent companion?

One pummeling strike walloped the bag into the ceiling tiles.

The sound alerted him to the pressure he asserted

on the anchoring screws. He caught the teardrop shaped ball with both gloves. How long could David's handyman skills withstand this beating?

Save the bag. Cool it.

A glance at the clock radio resting on a bare, particle board side table reminded him David would be home from work within the hour.

He swiped his wrist across his damp brow. A good workout always helped him unwind after several hours in a cockpit, loosened the kinks in his muscles, cleared his mind. He fooled himself for a while that he burned off steam after this morning's flight. Now, however, he conceded other demons fueled his efforts.

Jancie's words floated through his mind, mocked him. "You're such a good young man, John Townsend."

Yeah, right. If she only knew.

Unhooking the straps with his teeth, he stuck his glove under the opposite arm, slid his hand free, and chucked the gloves into a corner.

A good guy wouldn't have hurt someone like Penn. She barely made eye contact with him today at the Apple meeting. A hello nod comprised their interaction. The sadness circling her eyes looked familiar, probably matched his own.

John grabbed his water bottle and sank onto the bean bag chair. He remembered the names people had tagged on him as he chugged his water—committee member, youth group chaperone, criminal nabber. Uh huh. A nice cover. He knew the real John.

Long, auburn hair teased his memory. He crushed the bottle, crackling the plastic and cascading the remaining liquid over his arm. Bolting upright, he flicked off the droplets.

John bounced from the bean bag and gripped a pair of twenty pound dumbbells. He didn't want this memory. He felt bad enough with Penn's reaction. He didn't want to walk down memory lane.

He rammed the dumbbells toward the ceiling but couldn't push the memories into the corners of his mind. They were sixteen years old...

Grunting against the weights and the memories, he pushed the dumbbells up again and again until his muscles trembled with the effort.

Lowering them to the linoleum, he dropped into a straight back chair, his head in his hands. What a sweet summer they had. His first girlfriend. Really—his only one. He'd had girls who were friends since then but kept himself purposefully at arm's length.

He rocked on the back legs of the chair and heard his mom say, "Four on the floor, John," but he ignored the faint admonition ringing in his brain.

The call came a few days into their junior year. Her dad died before leaving for work as a state patrol officer. Massive heart attack.

John squeezed his eyes shut, and the big, burly man filled his mind again. Scary to a sixteen-year-old boy but always nice, personable.

He crashed the front legs to the floor. What happened to the vow they'd made at youth group? The vow to...not to...

Grabbing a jump rope tangled near the weight bench, he clamped the handle in his fist. He coiled the rope around his elbow, up over his palm, under his elbow again until he knotted the end, securing the rope. He shrugged his arm free off the coils, pressed the loops together.

Although the memory of that time shined as clear

as the chrome on his motorcycle—he could still see her pink sundress, smell her favorite bubblegum—he refused to relive the details. He tossed the jump rope aside. It slapped the floor beside the discarded gloves.

The warnings of his parents, his youth pastor chimed in his ears. "You're spending too much time together. Give her some space."

She didn't want space and neither did he. He wanted to help her, to take away the pain that dogged her every day. He wanted her to be the happy girl who watched movies with him, flirted with him at the pool.

But she'd never be that girl again. Her dad died, and they'd crossed the line, broke the promise they'd made less than two months earlier.

Thank God—again—she hadn't become pregnant.

Absolutely. Thank God. But that news hadn't removed the awkwardness between them. Hadn't helped them talk or make eye contact.

Then before Thanksgiving, she was gone. Moved back to her mother's family in Iowa.

He scrubbed his chin. The whiskers scratched at his palm. He sank onto his knees.

God, I'm so sorry. I know You've already forgiven me, but I'm sorry I let these memories come back. I don't want these memories.

He twisted the sweaty t-shirt away from his clammy chest.

Therefore, there is now no condemnation for those who are in Christ Jesus because through Christ Jesus the law of the Sprit of life set me free from the laws of sin and death.

He loosened his grip on the shirt.

A sweet promise from the Bible. A sweet release of the guilt.

Upstairs, a door slammed. David, home from

work.

He drew in a long breath and shifted on his knees. *Thank You for forgiving me.*
Now help me forgive myself.

~*~

Sitting at a red light, Penn drummed her fingers on the steering wheel, impatient to arrive at the coffee shop to meet Abby, the second time in a week and a half. "Can you believe it, Gretchen? I'm actually looking forward to seeing Abby again." Where was the old dread? The sad feelings? Maybe she was finally growing up.

Or not...talking to her Volkswagen as if Gretchen were a real person, something she'd done since she started driving by herself.

The aunts had played very cool with the news of the rekindled relationship with Abby. They smiled, hugged her, but left her without the twenty questions game they so loved to play. Maybe they were growing up, too.

Abby embraced her when they met outside the shop. "Thanks for switching from lunch to coffee. My hours changed at the clinic, but I didn't want to cancel on you."

They were waiting for their skinny cappuccinos to cool when Abby dropped a bomb. "So I'm dying to know about the dreamy man you were with on the Fourth. Missy says he just moved here."

Penn prayed a quick thank-you prayer. Her hands rested in her lap safe from the coffee mug that would have crashed into a hot, drippy mess at the surprising words.

Of all the possible topics of conversation, Penn never dreamed John would be the first one Abby chose.

She breathed in the soothing aroma of coffee. "You mean John?"

"That sounds right. Tell me about the dreamy John." Abby raised the over-sized mug and sipped her drink.

What to say? Except for one Apple meeting, she hadn't seen him since the storm clean up. Three weeks.

Kind and personable, he nodded hello when they made eye contact but didn't walk her out or chase her into the parking lot for a chat beside Gretchen. Instead, he hung in the meeting room, sharing a joke with Jacob.

He'd been present in her mind, however. How many times a day did she have to banish thoughts of him? Her brain assured her she'd done the right thing, nipping in the bud whatever had started between them. Her heart, however, argued the point, pushed tears from her eyes several times the first week.

The aunts had been oddly silent about John. She'd caught furtive glances and an occasional raised eyebrow between them, but they hadn't probed her with questions. She couldn't believe they gave up their idea of John as a suitor so quickly.

"What do you want to know?" *And why does she want to know?*

"Look at you blush. What's the deal with you two?" Abby leaned her elbows on the table, rested her chin on top of her hands. "He looked pretty interested at the parade."

She grimaced. "I'm not blushing. It's the steam." She fanned her hand over the mug. "We're on the

Apple committee together. That's all."

Abby cocked an eyebrow. "Yeah, right."

"No, I'm serious. Nothing's going on. If you're interested—"

"Penn. I'm seeing someone. You'll have to meet him."

A lightness swelled in her chest.

"Then Missy..."

"Not Missy. She's too...too Missy for a guy like John."

"A guy like John?"

"Missy, and you know I love her, is flighty, looking for the next good time. John is a solid, stand-up guy. He's a relationship guy. He doesn't do the speed dating thing."

That observation warmed her. Would John agree with Abby? "You got all that from the maybe five minutes you met him?"

"What can I say?" She grinned. "I'm that good."

Penn rolled her eyes. "Uh huh. Did you know he bungee jumps?"

"Cool." She rubbed her hands together. "I've always wanted to do that."

The bell signaled another customer.

Abby glanced at the door and sucked in a quick breath. "Don't turn around, but guess who's coming for coffee?"

Penn didn't have to turn around.

Abby's grin and the hairs on the back of her neck radioed that John had entered the shop.

When he stepped into her peripheral vision, she cut her gaze toward him. He hadn't seen them. His attention centered on the menu board.

"Aren't you going to say, 'hello?'" Abby swiveled

toward John and opened her mouth, but Penn grabbed her hand.

"Wait."

"What?"

"Just...he'll probably see us in a minute." Penn's thumb found her ring.

Abby lowered her eyebrows but acquiesced and studied her mug.

John ordered and moved to the end of the counter and into Penn's peripheral vision. He surveyed the room and jolted when his gaze found their table. He worked his jaw.

Hoping for nonchalance, she glanced in his direction and waved.

He approached their table, handsome in his faded cobalt golf shirt.

"Good morning."

"Hello, John. You remember Abby?"

"Sure. Nice to see you again." He nodded to Abby then swung his gaze back to Penn. "How ya' doin'?"

"Fine. Thanks. You?" She gripped the coffee mug with both hands.

"Good. Good" He rubbed the back of his neck.

Abby's eyes swung from Penn to John.

"Well, I—"

The barista called out an order for a regular coffee.

"My order's up. I better get it. Good to see you both." And he was gone.

Abby arched an eyebrow at Penn, but she waited until John exited the cafe before speaking.

"What in the world was all that about? Can you spell awkward?"

Penn sipped her lukewarm drink. "What?"

"That wasn't the same Penn and John I witnessed

at the parade a few weeks ago. What's up?"

"A lot can happen in a few weeks." With her fingertip, she wiped away the smudge of watermelon-colored lipstick from the mug, transferred it to her napkin.

"What do you mean? He still likes you, Penn. I can see it all over his face." Abby slid her forearms across the table.

Penn traced the rim of her mug.

"You like him, too. I know it. Did you have a misunderstanding?"

Penn snorted. "No. No misunderstanding. Everything's perfectly clear."

"Speak clearly to me then. What are you saying?"

"He's a pilot, Abby. A pi-lot." She said the word slowly to emphasize her point. To convey the implications behind the word.

Abby sat back.

"That happened a long time ago."

Penn straightened her spine. "Are you saying I should be over my parents' death? That I can just go willy-nilly along with my life like—"

"Of course not. That's not what I'm saying at all." Abby pressed her lips together. "Penn, you had a terrible tragedy. I know...I was there when you got the call." She grabbed Penn's hands, wouldn't let go when Penn strained against her. "This tragedy doesn't have to define your entire life. That's all I'm saying."

Penn narrowed her eyes. "Don't analyze me. I'm not a case in one of your textbooks." She yanked her hands at the same time Abby let go. A spoon flew off the table.

Heads whipped toward them from every direction. A tow-headed little boy who looked to be about four-years-old skipped to their table, picked up the spoon for them, and sprinted back to his mom.

Abby mouthed, "thank you," to the mom since the little boy's face disappeared between the folds of his mother's skirt.

Penn trembled at the edge of her chair clutching the strap of her purse. "I've got to—"

"Don't leave yet, Penny. Please. I didn't mean to make you mad. Let's talk about something else."

Penn trained her eyes on the table. "I'm fine. I just have to get back to studying."

"I promise. No more talk about John or anything. You choose the topic. Just stay a little bit longer."

She pressed the familiar scrollwork on the side of her ring. "I'm not sure—"

"We've got the awkward first meeting and the first lunch out of the way. We've set up the parameters of what we can and can't talk about—"

"You're talking like a counselor again."

"That's what I am."

She pushed back her chair. "I don't need a counselor. I have one. Thank you."

Abby caught her wrist. "I don't want to be your counselor. I want to be your friend."

Penn's heart constricted. "Why?"

"Why? Because I love you. I always have. I've missed you for almost twenty years. I was hoping that now as adults—"

"That I'd be over my past and ready for sleep-overs again?"

"No. Good grief. You're a tough one, Penny." She sighed. "I was hoping that as adults we could forge an adult relationship. That we could go shopping together, commiserate about jobs together, dish about boyfriends, you know. Regular friend stuff."

Regular friend stuff.

What exactly was regular friend stuff? Whatever it was, it sounded good. Her heart twisted at the idea of a real friend. She'd had a few friends in high school and college but none like Abby had been to her the first few years of her life.

Tears tickled the back of her eyes.

"I'm not that great a shopper."

Abby barked a laugh. "Sweet. Then I can teach you." She bit her lip. "That is, if you want me to."

Penn twisted the purse strap.

A new door, an important one waited for her to open. Was she ready? She wanted to be. She prayed to be. Another broken heart piece shifted, touching a longing she'd buried a long time ago. "Sounds good."

22

"Wait. Wait. Wait." Jancie's voice halted Penn on the first stair step.

"Aunt Jancie." Penn pushed the whine out of her own voice, dialed up a warning instead.

Winnie joined the conversation. "Now, Penny. We've been good. We haven't asked you anything about Abby, but you've seen her twice. How's it going?"

"Come in here, and let's chat."

Penn squeezed the railing. "I really have to—"

"Study—we know. Five minutes won't make or break you." Jancie rapped the table. "Come here."

Jancie's command contained an added dimension. Something beyond normal curiosity. Her interest piqued, she entered the kitchen and found both aunts at the table, the portable phone between them.

"Sit down and chat with us for a few minutes. Are you hungry?"

"No." She glanced at the clock above the refrigerator. Ten thirty. Something was up. They never ate between breakfast and lunch.

"So tell us about Abby. How's she doing?"

"She's fine. We talked."

"That's good. I hope she'll come by here soon."

Penn divided her gaze back and forth between her aunts. "What's up with you two?"

Raised eyebrows. Shrugging shoulders. "What do

you mean?"'

Feigned innocence.

Penn crossed her arms. "You're sitting at the table in the middle of the morning, asking me if I'm hungry—in the middle of the morning. What's going on?"

The aunts exchanged glances. Jancie took the lead. "We were planning to tell you. We wanted to hear about your morning first."

Winnie folded her hands. "We got a phone call from home. Your granddad has been experiencing some...health issues."

Jancie shared the facts. "He's had chest pains and shortness of breath for a while. He's going in for some testing."

Winnie supplied the emotion. "Heart disease is a problem for our family, you know. Both our parents died from heart attacks."

The family stories resurfaced in her brain. Her great-grandfather dropped to the ground while walking in his backyard after breakfast one June morning. Her great-grandmother died in her sleep after struggling for years with heart issues.

Winnie pleated the edge of a place mat. "Penn, we want to go down and check on Graham. Spend some time with him."

She calculated how many days she had left to study. "When do you want us to leave?"

"Not 'us,' honey. Winnie and I can go. You need to study, and the festival is coming up. We're waiting to hear back from him about the date of the tests and what happens next."

Jancie stroked the bottom of her neck. "The doctor could treat with medicine, with a stent, or with open heart surgery, I suppose. We haven't decided when we'll go yet."

"But—"

"No, buts. We'll go down for a few days. You won't miss studying or the last minute work on Apple Fest."

Winnie cleared her throat. "We're just a little worried about one thing, however."

"What's that?" Besides their brother's health.

"You've never stayed here by yourself before. We thought maybe if you and Abby are becoming friends again, she could come over and stay with you."

"Aunt Winnie. I'm twenty-six-years old for Pete's sake. I can stay by myself. Don't worry about that." *Probably she could.* "But I should go with you. That's a long way to drive."

"Eight hours divided by two isn't too bad. We'll leave early and take our time." Jancie cupped Penn's hand. "Maybe all of us can go back down over your fall break. He should be well in to recovery by then."

Penn examined the hands covering her own, the prominent veins circling around the brown age spots dotted on top. She loved these hands, hands that petted her when she was upset, made cookies and cinnamon rolls, held her when she was scared.

A homesick feeling fluttered in her chest. She didn't want them to go without her. She missed them already, didn't want to be separated from them. What was wrong with her? Wasn't that the plan she worked toward every day?

Study for the CPA exam. Take the CPA exam. Pass the CPA exam.

Get a fancy job in Pittsburgh. Move to a cool apartment on the North Side. Why did that plan seem unattractive today?

"Sweetie pie, don't look so sad. We're not leaving today. We just wanted you to know what was up so you wouldn't feel blindsided when we start packing."

"Maybe—depending on the schedule for his tests—I can go. I mean, the preliminary stuff for Apple Fest is already finished. I don't absolutely have to be there—"

Jancie frowned. "Of course you have to help, Penny. You can't leave your committee people in the lurch."

"Yes, indeed-y. With Linda still hobbling around on that bum leg of hers, Clara will be relying on your help that day. Many hands make—"

"Light work." Penn propped her cheek on her fist. "I know."

~*~

Penn lay on her bed with her feet propped on top of her pillows and her head at the foot, a favorite position of hers ever since she read about Pippi Longstocking sleeping this way. Pippi, a favorite fictional character during her childhood, possessed a joy de vivre that Penn admired and envied when she was ten, and, if she were honest, envied now.

She worried a hangnail on her pinky finger. How could she consider letting the aunts drive all the way to North Carolina without her? Shouldn't she be with her grandfather also?

Not that she'd ever felt close to him. She'd enjoyed visiting him, but he worked through most of the vacations she spent down South.

She didn't absolutely have to be downtown during

Apple Fest. By that point, every detail would be in place. Plenty of volunteers would oversee every aspect of the day. Still, she hated to let down Clara. The other side to the argument was avoiding John. She wouldn't have to see him.

Like today.

A surprise.

An awkward surprise.

This morning he'd looked so handsome. Her breath caught thinking about him. His dimple still flashed when he smiled, but he'd seemed uncomfortable and sad and aloof.

She didn't relish the idea of going through another uncomfortable scene. On Apple Festival day they'd have plenty of time to run into each other. Penn didn't want to have to avoid him. She didn't want awkwardness to sit between them like a third wheel every time they met each other. She wanted…what?

John. She wanted John, but she couldn't have him. Not as long as he made a living as a pilot.

She remembered the conversation over coffee this morning. Abby acted as if she should be over the tragedy.

How did she put it? "Not be defined by it."

Easy to tell someone that. Harder to live it.

Was she holding on to the tragedy? No. She was a hardworking, contributing-to-society adult. So what if she didn't like roller coasters and bungee jumping. Plenty of people avoided those activities.

But what if the tragedy were holding on to her?

That sounded like a counselor thing to say.

But seriously. What if she was allowing that period in her life to define her identity? Label her. The orphan. The little girl who lived with her crazy aunts.

And still does.

She'd been the one to don those labels so long ago.

Could she choose new ones now? Could she be the woman who tried new things, loved grape leaves...dated a pilot?

A shudder tripped up her spine. She exhaled a long breath to slow her accelerated heartbeat. She flipped over and raised onto her elbows. She had to think of something else. She grabbed her planner.

A week until her CPA exam. Two weeks until Apple day.

She'd be so happy when the exam was over. It'd been hanging over her for months now. Eighteen to be exact. She'd passed the first two parts to the exam a year and a half ago. Six months ago, she passed the third part but failed the fourth. Three months ago, she'd failed it again. If she didn't pass the last part this time, she'd lose credit for the first two parts and have to retake those.

She massaged her temples in a vain effort to release the pressure working to suffocate her.

Don't think about Apple Fest. Get through the exam.

After the exam, she'd have plenty of time to explain to Clara about missing the festival. She'd done her part beforehand. Someone else could man the entertainment fort during the actual event.

She had a good reason for not attending. Her grandfather's health. She couldn't help it if that reason also lent itself to steering clear of a handsome pilot who, no matter how many times she warned herself against him, still tugged at her heartstrings.

~*~

Jancie slapped her hands on her hips and stomped her lime-green tennis shoe. "You are not going to miss that exam. You've studied all summer long."

Winnie waved her index finger from the couch. "You've paid for it, too. You won't get those hard-earned dollars back, either."

"We're leaving in the morning after we see you off for the test. His surgery is first thing Monday morning. We'll have plenty of time to get there and visit with him beforehand."

"Fine. I'll leave after the exam and meet you there." Perfect idea.

"Do you remember how exhausted you are after those tests? No, ma'am, you have no business driving like that."

Penn ground her molars. "Then I'll drive down on Sunday." She flopped beside Winnie and propped a foot on the coffee table.

"No, Miss Hardhead." Jancie swiped her foot off the table. "You most likely wouldn't get there in time to see him Sunday night. You need to stay here, recover from the test, and we'll call you with updates."

"And don't forget. You've got responsibilities here. Like your students. Like last minute Apple Fest details. The doctors can handle their jobs without your presence, hon."

Penn pouted. "You're going." Being thwarted by her aunts chaffed her.

"He's our only brother. Of course we're going to see him before he has open heart surgery."

Winnie rubbed her forearm. "I can't believe he has four blockages."

"Five if you count the little one on the back side of his heart." Jancie raised her palms. "What does that man do? Mainline fried chicken and gravy?"

"You know he walks three days a week. Like the doctor told you last summer. If you've got bad pipes, you've got pipes."

Jancie harrumphed. "Great bedside manner, that man."

Penn scooted to the edge of the couch. "Since you two have it all worked out, I guess I'll go—"

"Study. We know."

~*~

Penn sank into a puddle of fried brains in her foyer Saturday afternoon. Thank goodness, Gretchen knew the way home from the testing center. Besides the all-encompassing fatigue eating away at her, however, she felt positive about her exam results.

She hated admitting it, but she was relieved she had nothing left to do today except crawl onto the couch. She could sleep there if the stairs seemed too daunting tonight. She hoisted herself onto the worn cushions and lay spread eagle waiting for sleep. Maybe when she woke up she could manage the remote and watch an infomercial, anything that didn't require processing thoughts.

A trilling ring shot through her dream and jerked her upright on the couch. She seized the portable phone from the tray on the side table and mumbled a hello through a mouth dry as silica gel.

"Penny. We made it." Winnie's voice crackled in her ear.

"Where?"

Winnie chuckled. "In Oxford. At your grandfather's house. Where did you think we'd be?"

"You drove the whole way?" Penn rubbed the sleep from her eyes.

"Sure. It was a beautiful day for driving. We took turns. Two hours on. Break. Two hours off. Teamwork. Right, sister?"

"Let me talk now." Penn heard Jancie in the background. "Penn, how was it? How do you feel?"

"I'm fine. Wiped out. I think I did pretty well. I can't believe you drove the whole way." Not exactly true. She'd had a feeling they might. Had hoped they wouldn't.

"We had fun. We stopped at the cute little ice cream shop in Berkley Springs for a smoothie brunch. Then ate a late lunch in Fredericksburg. We stopped another time after we passed Richmond and then pushed through. Easy-peasy."

Easy-peasy. Her aunts. Her heart flipped over with love for them. She missed them already.

They put her grandfather on the phone for a quick chat. Never one for small talk or big talk either, her grandfather seemed more reserved than usual tonight.

Understandable.

The aunts hopped back on the phone for a quick good night, and they were gone. The silence when they hung up accentuated the loneliness of her house.

She roused from her lounging position on the couch and slogged into the kitchen. Not hungry at all but needing comfort, she spied her reward in the back of the freezer—a carton of cappuccino chocolate chip ice cream.

Ice cream left over from a study session break last week. About a third of the carton remained. Perfect. She grabbed a soup spoon from the drawer and padded back to the den, ready for some mindless television.

Living alone had definite advantages. Number one—no one groused about eating ice cream for dinner. Number two—no one minded if it came straight out of the carton.

She licked the spoon and pressed the button on the remote.

23

Penn checked her phone after every class Monday afternoon, expecting to hear news of the surgery. The call came early in the evening. Startled by the ring, she dropped the crust of her chicken salad sandwich.

"We've just been in to see Graham."

She tumbled out the questions that had been crowding her mind all day. "How is he? It took forever. How are you? I thought you'd have called hours ago."

"Take it easy. We're exhausted. He's still in ICU and still groggy from anesthesia." Jancie sighed. "He had a hard time, Penny."

Penn clutched the phone with both hands. Although she didn't know her grandfather very well, she loved him. "What do you mean?"

"The surgeon was closing about, I don't know, one o'clock or so, when he found bleeding he couldn't stop. They had to go back in and find the cause. Five hours later, the doctor stabilized him, and they let us in to see him." Jancie exhaled a deep breath. "It's been a long day, honey. He'll be in ICU for a few days and then move to a regular room. We'll stay down here a little longer than planned."

Penn made a noise, but Jancie cut her off. "Do not even think about coming down here. There's nothing you can do. You've got students to worry about. Graham's in good hands." Fatigued dripped from

Jancie's words.

"But—"

"But nothing. Clara needs you, too. You are not a person who shrugs off responsibilities. Help her this week."

"But—"

"While he's in ICU, he can receive two visitors for about ten minutes every other hour. I'm not sure how much he'll remember of this time anyway. You need to be where you are."

Penn's stubborn streak flared. "You know I don't need your permission to go down there."

Jancie's big-sister voice kicked in gear, large and in charge. "I do know that, but it sounds as if you need me to give you good advice. I'm doing that. Stay there and do your work. We'll keep you in the loop. If anything changes, we'll call immediately. OK?"

Penn didn't like surrendering, but she recognized the truth in Jancie's words. "OK."

"That's all I've got tonight, honey. Poke us with a fork 'cause we're done. We're going back to the house and come up here to Wake Med tomorrow morning. Love you, sweetie."

Again, the homesick feeling swelled inside her as she pressed the off button. Why? She gathered her dinner dishes from her table, in her house.

Her home. The only home she'd ever known.

It just didn't feel like home without the aunts in it with her.

~*~

They called twice a day with updates. On Thursday, her grandfather moved into a regular room.

240

Penn capped her marking pen and pushed the quizzes aside. "So, I guess that means you can start home tomorrow?"

The shine from living by herself had tarnished days ago. She was ready to see her aunts, ready for something besides the chicken salad they'd left her in the refrigerator, ready for conversation around the table while she ate something she hadn't warmed up from a can.

"Honey, no. We're staying her a few more days."

"A few more days?" Penn clenched her teeth. "You'll miss the festival."

"Penny, we figured we'd miss it this year when we found out about your grandfather's surgery. We hate to, but we've been to the other ones."

Jancie added her two cents from the background. "All the other ones."

"The doctor won't talk about going home any time soon. With what amounts to a double surgery on Monday and all that time in ICU...well, we'll just have to wait and see. He's supposed to walk down the hall and back maybe tomorrow. Can you believe it? He had open heart surgery Monday, and they want him walking already." Winnie tsked into the phone. "Anyway, we'll get him settled back at the house and then maybe drive up sometime next week. We'll just see how everything goes."

A slight growl escaped Penn's throat. Turmoil churned her insides. She wanted her recuperating grandfather to be cared for, but she wanted someone else to do it. She missed her aunts.

A click indicated Jancie had joined the conversation on an extension. "You have fun on Saturday. Don't worry about us."

"Ask her if she's seen John." Winnie whispered but not low enough for Penn.

Penn pressed her hand against her galloping heart. "I heard that."

"Well, have you?"

"No. He missed the meeting on Tuesday." A disappointing, boring meeting without John. "If he's working," also known as flying, but she avoided saying the word out loud, "he might not be back for Saturday."

"Pish posh, Penny. John's not the kind to renege on a promise."

"And neither are you."

"He'll be there."

"And so will you. With bells on. Make it the best festival yet. Take lots of pictures so you can show us when you tell us all the stories."

"Uh huh." Tears blurred the quizzes waiting for her.

"Sweetie, you sound kind of blue. Are you OK?"

Penn uncapped the pen, recapped it. "Sure."

Silence over the phone lines. Were they eyeing each other? Deciding which course of action to take with her? *Be positive. Be kind. Be an adult.* "So. Grandfather's going to be fine?"

"Yes, honey," Jancie's voice soothed her. "And so are you."

True. And they'd be home soon.

And things would get back to normal.

~*~

From the beginning, Clara insisted the committee meet downtown in the park the Friday night before the festival to attend to any last minute details or problems.

Penn arrived late after a long student conference. As she joined the group, a movement caught her eye.

John approached the group with Missy.

So...he wasn't out of town on a flight. Looked as if he'd make the Apple Fest after all.

Clara gestured to the volunteers. "Hello, everybody. Thanks so much for coming tonight. The Sub Shop has generously donated sandwiches and chips for our dinner, so dig in. I've got your assignments right here."

She waved a stack of pages. "Your name and job are highlighted, so pick up a sandwich and a sheet. Oh, and don't forget to grab a volunteer t-shirt to wear tomorrow. We'll be visible to anyone with a question. By the way, thank you to Design & Print for the shirts. Any questions?" Clara scanned the huddled group with a quick sweep of her eyes. "Good. Let's finish up, and I'll see you here bright and early in the morning. Thanks, people."

While Penn waited for the rush on the sandwiches to subside, she snagged her assignment sheet. Highlighted, her name coupled with Jacob Doran's. Partners. Their assignment—chalk off booth locations for vendor placement. Buckets of sidewalk chalk lined the curb.

She found Jacob in the memorial section of the park beside a ship's bell. The bell was donated to the town when the USS Mars, part of the US Pacific Fleet, had been decommissioned in 1998. He gestured to the bell as he conversed with Al Martin. A Korean veteran chatting with an Afghanistan veteran. The small-town vision warmed her heart.

Missy skipped up to her, and John trailed behind. "Hi, Penn. Ready for tomorrow?"

"Think so. We better be, I guess." She glanced at John.

He acknowledged her with a half-hearted smile. "How's your grandfather doing? Are your aunts home yet?"

"Better. He may leave the hospital tomorrow. They said they'd come back maybe early next week."

"Good." He folded his assignment sheet and stuffed it in his back pocket.

Missy swished her blonde ponytail behind her back. "Abby said she enjoyed her lunch with you. She's hoping you two can get together again soon."

Penn shuffled her foot. "Me, too."

Missy tugged on John's sleeve. "Well, come on, John. Grab a bucket. Let's start dividing up Grand Avenue. See you, Penn."

John waved and followed Missy. A breeze stirred and ruffled Missy's ponytail. Several strands of blonde hair fluttered against John's arm as they strolled together toward Grand Avenue.

Penn winced, and hugged the chalk bucket against her chest.

Missy and John. Penn and Jacob. The luck of the draw? A sign? A statement?

You had your chance, Penny girl.

Be happy, John.

"Hey, Jacob. You ready to chalk off the other end of Pittsburgh Street?"

~*~

Her clock peeled at five thirty Saturday morning,

interrupting a dream featuring a motorcycle. What an annoying buzz. She slammed down the alarm button and buried her face deep into her pillow.

John's bike?

Probably.

Who else had stalked her mind over the last few weeks?

No matter how much she tried, he seemed to push to front and center of her thoughts.

She shoved back the sheet and threw her legs over the side of the bed. Five thirty?

Clara had extracted promises from the whole committee to report downtown at no later than six fifteen. What more could they possibly do in the final two hours before the opening festivities?

Her grandfather improved every day. The aunts would be home soon. She expected the exam results soon. *Just survive today, and no more volunteering with John again.*

And maybe he and his motorcycle would stop visiting her dreams.

From the edge of the bed, she rolled her shoulders. Waking up was never the easiest part of her day, and lately without the aunts, beginning the day was worse than usual. No muted giggling tripped up the stairs. No robust coffee aroma wafted under her door to tease her awake. No good morning song. Just her and silence. Not exactly satisfying.

Forty-five minutes later, she sipped on a cup of coffee at the information table.

The committee circled around Clara, armed with a whistle, clipboard, and two-way radio.

Clara raised the clipboard. "Here we are, people. Our Apple Fest. Aren't you excited?" She waited for several seconds until a few people realized the question wasn't rhetorical. A smattering of yeahs and a few hand claps skittered through the group.

Penn adjusted the lid of her cardboard cup.

John chatted with Missy at the edge of the circle.

Her heart tightened.

You pushed John away, remember? To Missy?

She swallowed some coffee, but the sweet liquid didn't fill the emptiness swelling inside her.

Be happy, John.

She wanted to be happy, too. She thought moving to her own place after she passed the CPA exam and working at a fabulous new job would make her happy, but after this week, questions pricked and challenged those thoughts. Maybe she could work downtown and still live with the aunts. Plenty of Butler County people commuted.

Her students' faces floated in front of her. Just this week, three students had already caught her after school for individual tutoring that turned into more of a counseling session. So many problems and the school year barely started. The thought of leaving them, of not being able to help struggling students made the coffee taste bitter in her mouth.

Penn forced the daydreams aside and listened to Clara's instructions.

"So we'll keep rotating from my schedule. If you don't remember where you start, I have the master list here." Clara waved the clipboard over her head.

John glanced up and caught her staring. He offered a quick smile, waved, and resumed his conversation with Missy. Somehow, he succeeded in looking cute in the stupid yellow volunteer t-shirts mandatory for everyone on the committee.

Missy rocked it, too, of course, with white denim shorts.

A burning sensation spiraled from her stomach through her chest. Pretending to take another sip of coffee, she offered her back to that scene and contemplated the long day stretching out in front of her.

Three hours later, the festival was well under way. Puffy white clouds floated in a lazy cornflower blue sky. Perfect weather. The temperature huddled around seventy-five degrees. A beautiful day to be outside.

Penn hoped the aunts were having a good day.

At noon, Clara invited the volunteers over her two-way radio to eat the pizza located in the information tent.

Hunger knocked in Penn's stomach at the mention of pizza, and she ambled toward the tent, checking on booth vendors as she passed. She arrived at the tent as John appeared from the opposite side of the street. Without Missy. She grabbed a slice with mushrooms and bit the tip. He phone jingled in her pocket. Aunt Winnie's name flashed across the screen. Grandfather update at lunch. Perfect timing.

"Hi, Aunt Winnie. How's everything this morning? We've got a great day here." Penn took another bite and chewed as she waited for the response.

"Oh, Penny..." Winnie dissolved into tears.

Fear gripped Penn and roiled the pizza in her stomach. "Winnie, what is it? What happened with Grandfather?"

John's head snapped toward her. She lowered her voice and stepped farther away from the tent.

"Aunt Winnie, calm down. Tell me what

happened."

"P-P-Penny. Not-not Graham."

"Not Grandfather? Put Jancie on. Let me talk to her." Penn clutched the phone in a death grip.

Winnie wailed into the phone.

"Please, Aunt Winnie. Tell me what's wrong. I can't help if you don't tell me." Blood pounded in her ears. Trembling racked her legs.

Breathe in. Breathe out. Breathe in. Breathe out.

Footsteps signaled John. With his hands in his pockets, he waited at her elbow, concern marking his face. He didn't touch her, but his presence calmed her, helped her slow her breathing.

She dropped her voice and forced the panic from it. "Aunt Winnie. What's happened?"

Winnie drew in a shaky breath. "Jancie."

Penn waited and listened to few more sniffles. *Jancie?* Icy chills tiptoed up the back of her neck.

"She had a heart attack." Fresh sobs poured out of Winnie.

The pizza fell from her hand. "Aunt Jancie had a heart attack?"

But her aunt Jancie was healthy. She complained about little aches and pains when it suited her, but she hardly ever needed a doctor.

Penn brushed her temple. She felt lightheaded with the scrambled thoughts in her brain. She pressed her free hand against her other ear, concentrating on every word. "Aunt Winnie, how is she?"

John stepped closer and laid his hand on her back. The warmth seeped through all the way to her heart. She raised rounded eyes to his. His mouth flattened to a determined line.

Penn gripped the phone with aching fingers. Panic

drummed a frightening beat in her chest. "Where is she? Tell me something."

"In Wake Med. The doctor's operating right now. Everything happened so fast..." Sobs strangled the remaining words.

"I'm coming. I'll be there as soon as I can. Call you later. I'll see you soon. I love you, Aunt Winnie." Penn covered her face with her hands, the cellphone hot on her cheek.

John gathered her into his arms and stroked her hair. "I'm so sorry, Penn. What do you want to do?"

"I'm going to them." A whimper escaped, smothered against his chest. He hugged her tighter.

"Penn, listen to me." John spoke against her ear, his breath warm and comforting. "I can get you there fast. Let me take you."

She stilled. "On your motorcycle?"

"No, Penn. I can fly you. Let me do that."

She shoved his chest. The pizza worked in her stomach threatening to rise again.

He held his arms around her but loosened his hold so that he could meet her gaze. "Hear me out. It's what? Eight, nine hours by car? I can get you to your aunts in under three."

"Have you lost your mind?" She strained against him to no avail. "Have you forgotten—?"

His muscular arms felt powerful around her, exactly the opposite of her wobbling insides.

"I haven't forgotten anything. Listen to me. I know what a monumental thing it'd be for you to fly—"

"Let me go. I've got to get started."

He lifted her chin with gentle fingers, concern and determination ruling his gaze. "Penn, think about it. By the time you pack, get gas, and get on the road, it'll be ten o'clock tonight before you get there, and you'll be exhausted. Three hours, Penn. I can get you there this afternoon."

She dropped her head onto his chest, strong, solid. How could she consider flying in a plane? How could she not consider this gift? She remembered Winnie's sobs. "I want to get there fast. I just don't think—"

"Let me help you. I can help you, Penn."

She nodded against his chest.

That signal set John in motion. He called to Clara, hovering by the pizza boxes and scanning her clipboard. "Clara, Penn's had an emergency. We've got to go. Sorry about leaving, but her aunt's in the hospital in North Carolina."

Penn didn't hear Clara's response.

John hadn't waited for one.

She held onto him like a piece of lint on a black suit. She focused on the sweet feeling of letting him take charge and ignored the chorus chanting in her brain. *Flying? No way. Flying? No way.*

John led her away from the pizza and the crowd and her responsibilities, but he couldn't lead her away from the memory of her aunt's sobs.

Could he lead her all the way to a seat on his plane? She shuddered, and John's arm tightened as they walked toward home.

24

John skidded the blue Volkswagen to a stop in front of his house. When he'd left her in her family room, Penn had intended to pack for the trip. His throat ached at the memory of her ashen face, her stooped back as she ascended the stairs.

He had to help her.

Praying for help and wisdom, he grabbed a couple of shorts and shirts, his shaving kit and Bible, stuffing all of it into a duffel bag. He tossed the duffel into the back and crammed himself into the driver's seat. Gripping the steering wheel, he bowed his head before cranking the engine. *God, thank You for this opportunity to help Penn. Please help her to trust me. Please help her to trust You.* He raked his hands through his hair and pointed Gretchen toward Penn's.

The porch creaked under his feet. He rang the doorbell. No answer. Peeking through the glass in the front door, he found her, head in hands, in the middle of the couch. He banged on the door and tried the knob. Unlocked.

"Penn."

She jerked and raised glassy, red-rimmed eyes toward him.

An overnight case waited beside her feet.

"Let me take your bag. If you've forgotten anything, we'll buy it down there."

She remained seated, motionless except for her

thumb working on her ring.

"Penn, I've got everything squared away. Let's get going. The faster we leave, the faster we'll be there." He stooped for her case.

"I can't." She licked her lips. Panic pinched her face. Tears flooded those big brown eyes. "I thought I could, but I can't."

"No problem. I'll drive you." Eight hours, give or take. "Come on. Let's get going." He held his hand for her.

Color flooded her cheeks. "You'll come with me?"

"You're in no condition to drive." He settled beside her. "I love them, too, Penn."

Fresh tears swelled. Her phone buzzed from her purse. She wrangled it open and dug for the device. Winnie again. The words mangled together, and the sobs wrenched his heart.

She hung up and dropped her face on her folded arms. "I have to get down there. Now."

"Penn." He spread his hand across her back.

"I have to fly." She sucked in a breath. "But I don't know if I can do it."

"Let me help you, Penn. We'll do it together." He pulled her off the couch and into his arms. He held her in a tight hug, wishing he could transfer peace to her trembling body. "Let's go."

John glanced at her as he parked the Volkswagen at the airport. Her hands wrapped around her seatbelt in a white knuckled grip. Her breaths reduced to short puffs, she stared straight ahead.

He shifted the stick into park and turned off the ignition. Taking her freezing hands into his, he caressed her fingers. "You can do this, Penn."

Penn's eyes darted to him, a dazed look fighting

with their beauty.

He cupped the side of her neck. "Penn, listen to me. I'm a careful pilot. It's clear weather all the way down. Nothing stirring in any direction for miles. You'll be with your aunts before you know it."

She blinked.

"Let's pray. I usually do before I take off, but I think we need to now."

She closed her eyes.

"God, we need to get to Oxford. Please lead us safely. We need clear weather the whole way. Penn needs peace and comfort now. Help her to relax and trust You."

~*~

Penn thanked God for John and his prayer, a simple one—straight forward and to the point—just like John himself.

Thank You. Thank You for John.

"I have to file our flight plan. Let's go inside, OK?"

Would her legs carry her inside? Doubtful. Something in her face must have conveyed her apprehension to John.

"Hang tight. I'll grab our bags and open the door for you."

He helped her out, and wrapped a strong arm around her waist. Both their bags bounced against his other side as they entered the receiving area. The smell of cleaning supplies attacked her olfactory glands as soon as they stepped inside.

Penn pressed her nose into John's chest to replace the chemical scent with his. He didn't wear cologne today nor by the looks of his scruffy whiskers did he use aftershave. He smelled of soap, clean and spicy, and something else. Today he smelled like strength.

She drank in that smell. She needed as much strength she could get.

A petite, blonde woman manned the front desk.

"Hi, Reesa. I need to file my flight plan."

"Hey, John. You got a great day to fly."

He plopped the bags in front of the reception counter but kept his arm around Penn. "That's just what I was telling, Penn. Reesa, this is Penn Davenport. Penn, meet Reesa—manager, pilot, instructor—she keeps us all straight."

Reesa smiled at her, and Penn's mouth quivered.

"You got that right." Reesa wiggled a pink tipped finger at John. "And don't forget it, pretty boy."

"Do you have the weather on the radar screen? I wanted to show Penn our route."

Reesa turned the screen toward them. "Sure thing."

"See, Penn." John pointed to the map of the eastern side of the country. "All clear from Vermont to Florida. Not even any small green blips. And look to the west. All the way out to Illinois, Missouri, Arkansas. Nothing." He squeezed her shoulder.

"Fall's usually a great time to fly, honey."

Says you, a pilot, instructor, the keeper of the airport. Penn pushed her arms against her stomach, her eyes darting from Reesa, to the door, and back to the radar screen.

Reesa leaned against the counter. "I mean every now and then you do need to keep your eye out for hurricanes down there in the southeast."

John pulled her closer and kneaded her forearm. "But—" The tone of his voice held a warning.

"Nothing's brewing out there on the Atlantic today." Reesa raised her palms. "No tropical storms. No hurricanes."

"Right you are—" A voice boomed from behind them. "John, glad I caught you." Striding toward them, a burly man, ruddy faced and barrel chested, stretched out his hand. He grabbed John's shoulder and pumped his free hand. "So you have to be Penn. I've heard so much about you." He engulfed her hand and winked at John.

John gestured to the older man. "This is James Dunbar, my boss."

His eyes kind and sure, James Dunbar emanated enthusiasm and energy. In normal circumstances, she'd have enjoyed meeting him. Today was nowhere near normal.

"You got a great day to fly."

Again with the "great day to fly" mumbo-jumbo. Was this refrain for her benefit or regular pilot banter?

"Take the Cirrus, John." He nodded his head toward the hangar. "It's fueled up and ready to go. After you called me, I ordered it for you."

"But I—it's more…"

"No, buts." He flicked away John's protest. "Don't worry about the fee. I'm taking care of it, the whole thing."

"But—"

"Quit with the 'buts' already. Let other people help, too, son."

"Thanks, boss. This is great." He angled his head toward Penn's. "We just got an upgrade."

"Now? At the last minute?" Penn breathed through her nose to slow her breathing. She fought lightheadedness.

He chuckled and squeezed her shoulder. "It's a good last minute thing, Penn. Trust me." John filed the flight plan and chatted with James.

Penn rolled "trust me" and "great day to fly" around in her mind.

"All right. We're set." John patted the counter and glanced down at Penn. "I have to do the pre-flight check. Do you want to wait inside or come watch?"

Neither. She wanted to be back at home with her head stuck into Peri's neck smelling leather and sweat and cold wind in his mane, her aunts baking celebration cookies in the kitchen. But she wasn't at home. She was in this airport trying to breathe while John—kind, capable, special John—stroked her hair and waited for her answer. If only she could speak.

Reesa rescued her. "You go get started, John. Let Penn visit the ladies room, and I'll bring her outside in a few minutes. OK?"

John lifted her chin to meet his gaze. "OK?" He rubbed his thumb across her cheek.

She nodded.

"All right. See you out there in a few."

He hoisted the bags and for the first time in fifteen minutes, her legs supported her without help. Loneliness stole all the strength his presence had afforded her. Her knees wobbled, and she clutched the counter to steady herself as he disappeared through the glass door.

Reesa rounded the end of the counter and hooked her arm through Penn's. "This way." She led her to the bathroom.

As Penn emerged from the bathroom, Reesa caught her hand. "Penn, I just met you, but I feel like I know you a little. John's mentioned you."

Penn arched a brow.

Reesa raised her hand. "Now, wait. Don't get your hackles up. He's a gentleman. He thinks a lot of you."

Penn's traitorous heart warmed at the words.

Reesa fingered a pendant on a silver chain. "I know this trip will be difficult for you."

Difficult? Try vomit-inducing. Breath-stealing. Life altering. Penn clamped on the inside of her cheek to keep from screaming. Her fingers clawed her arm.

Reesa reached for her hand. "John's one of our best pilots. He doesn't play around. I'd fly with him any time. And as a pilot myself, I don't say that about everybody." She hooked a lock of her blonde bob behind her ear. "Let me tell you something. I pray every time one of our planes go out. I'll do the same today, and I'll be praying for you the whole way." She laid her hand on Penn's shoulder. "You can do this, honey."

~*~

Penn's icy fingers refused to buckle the seatbelt correctly.

John pushed her hands to the side of her lap. "Let me do that for you." He buckled the seatbelt and adjusted for a snug fit. "Good."

"Do we get parachutes?"

He cocked his head. "Would you jump if you had one?"

She bit her lip.

"Exactly."

She pointed to a dial. "What's that?"

"The vertical speed indicator. Shows the rate that the plane is climbing or descending."

She tapped the next dial. "That one?"

"Airspeed indicator. Shows the speed of the plane in relation to air around it."

"That one?"

"Attitude indicator. Shows the relationship between the wing, the nose position, and the natural horizon."

None of this information made any sense to her, not when she struggled to breathe and forced herself not to claw her way out of the plane. She didn't understand John's explanations, but questions replaced the ones he answered. She glanced at the ceiling. "What about that red-handle thingy?"

John hesitated. "It's a parachute for the plane."

"Oh, ha ha. Very funny, John. I get your message. No more questions." She faced the window.

John tugged her chin back to him. "I don't think you're stupid, and I don't mind your questions." He hesitated again and narrowed his eyes. His thumb trailed from her chin to behind her ear. "Ask all you want."

She shook her head, and he threaded his fingers into the curls brushing her neck. "No. Maybe it's better not knowing." She leaned into his hand and concentrated on the soothing pattern of his fingers through her hair, a difficult feat with her stomach knocking on the bottom of her lungs.

"You can do this. I know you can. You're stronger than you think."

She pressed her lips to fight the bile bubbling in her stomach.

"Think about this summer, Penn." He counted with his left hand. "The Ferris wheel, the roller coaster, my bike..." He shrugged.

"It's a great big leap from a motorcycle to a plane if that's where you were going with that line of thinking." Penn rounded her lips and pushed air out of her mouth like expectant TV moms in Lamaze classes.

He chuckled. "I guess you're right." He sobered. "You ready?"

She pushed her back against the seat and straightened. "Is it time?"

"You tell me. I'm ready when you are."

"Do you have a barf bag?" *Please, please, please. Do not throw up in front of this man.*

He reached behind her and handed her a white paper bag. "Whatever you need."

"I just don't know if—"

"Let's pray again." And he did.

For peace. For comfort. For safety. Quick. Short. A text to God instead of a letter.

"Don't go for long, winding prayers, huh?" She'd love a chatty, rambling letter right now.

"I told you I like to get to the point." He leaned over and brushed her cheek with his lips. "You can do this, Penn. Close your eyes and try to nap if you want."

"Are you kidding me?" Her esophagus had closed to the point of making swallowing a chore. Her lungs worked as if a one-hundred-pound weight lay on her chest. Red arcs cut into her palm from the constant pressure of her fisted fingers. Napping while her body went wacky? *No way.* "Closing my eyes might make it worse."

John replied, but she didn't quite understand him. She glanced toward him. He spoke into his microphone, not to her. He radioed Reesa to request clearance for takeoff. While she took inventory of her body shutting down, he'd set things in motion for her nightmare.

The plane slowly began to roll forward. She opened the barf bag and folded down the top. *Just in casey.* Her heart beat as if she'd just tagged home plate after dashing around the bases. She sucked air into her lungs with the same fierceness she needed after a homer.

She gripped the arm rests, and words she thought she'd forgotten drummed in her mind. *Yea, though I walk through the valley of the shadow of death, I will fear no evil...* Words of the twenty-third Psalm. The aunts had recited the King James Version to her every night of her childhood after reading a bedtime story.

When was the last time she'd said it? She couldn't remember, but she repeated them as she kept her eyes pinned to the bag resting in her lap.

Lead me beside the still waters. She needed calm and quiet.

For Thou art with me. She needed God with her right now.

Thy rod and Thy staff they comfort me. Absolutely need comfort. Divine comfort.

The words tumbled over and over in her mind. By the time she'd recited the Psalm four times—or was it five?—something changed about the plane. What did that mean? She chanced a quick peek away from the bag, and saw John's hands adjusting knobs, turning dials, finally resting, one on his thigh and one on something that looked like a joystick.

What did he call it? A yoke.

She loved looking at those hands. Long, tan fingers. Capable when driving the motorcycle or buckling her into her seat. Firm and comforting when he led her away from the questioning eyes at Apple

Fest. Soft and tender when he cradled her cheek. She longed for them to touch her now.

"OK, Penn." He shouted above the engine noise. "We're at cruising altitude." He reached over and grabbed her hand, still cemented to the armrest. He wiggled his fingers under her palm, loosening the grip and engulfed her hand in his. "That's better, don't you think?" He focused back on the windshield, not expecting an answer.

Good. Her brain still wasn't up to signaling words to her mouth. Her eyes peeped away from her lap and trailed over the dials, emphasizing her location.

In the sky.

In a plane.

Her eyes skittered away from the dials and landed on the glass beside her.

Bad mistake.

Penn gulped in air and worked for the armrest again.

John refused to let go, holding steady. "You're doing fine."

Says you. She swallowed and forced herself to concentrate on his thumb and the pendulum path he traced on the back of her hand.

25

Penn's fingers throbbed from gripping the armrests for over two hours. Her breathing slowed to close to normal, but Penn couldn't relax her aching fingers. Waiting at the ready on her lap, the barf bag remained folded and pristine, empty.

Thank you, God, for keeping me from using that bag.

At least some of her dignity remained intact. No throwing up in front of John.

Thank you, God, for the Bible verses, too.

For the first hour, the Twenty-third Psalm marched through her thoughts, like a platoon on maneuvers. The phrases, as familiar as the scrollwork on her ring, echoed in her brain without effort.

Psalm twenty-three repeated until metamorphosing into another verse, one she'd learned as a child in Vacation Bible School. *I will be with you always.*

Always meant anytime, even in a plane. Right?

More verses reverberated in her mind.

Be strong and courageous. A command, perhaps? Was she strong with her fingers squeezing the life out of the armrests? Did she exhibit courage by entering the cockpit, sticking her behind in the seat, allowing John to take off without clawing herself out the door?

So...a command, and she was being obedient. Obedient to the point of being in a plane.

In. A. Plane.

What in the world was she, Penn Davenport, doing in a plane, for Pete's sake?

Going to her aunts. Her sweet aunts who loved her more than she could imagine.

Her stomach churned. She swallowed.

I'm coming. I'm coming. Please hang on. Please be all right.

John shifted and spoke into the microphone. He glanced over to her and smiled. "Just got clearance for landing. We'll be there in a few minutes. You're doing great." He raised his thumb high between them.

Her heart jumped to her throat and chased every single Bible verse out of her mind.

The landing.

"You'll hear some sounds in a minute and maybe feel some light jolts. That's just the landing gear moving into place. Everything's good."

The plane bucked, and John adjusted the yoke. She swung a desperate gaze to him.

He shook his head. "That was a thermal. We just flew through a cloud."

Weren't clouds supposed to be soft and fluffy? Soft and fluffy shouldn't rock a plane like that.

A mechanical groan sounded from underneath the plane before a slight jolt startled her. Her gaze flew to John again.

"Yep. Landing gear's in place." He pointed in front of the plane's nose. "When we bank to the left in a minute, you can see the airport if you want to look."

Shaking her head, she clamped her eyes shut. Pinks and blues appeared inside her lids. What were those verses? Disjointed images swirled through her mind.

God, please help me. It's almost over. Help me, God.

Land this plane safely.

The verses drifted gently and quietly into her consciousness.

I am with you always.

She relaxed, opened her eyes. John's hands worked the controls. He reached over and patted her knee. Warmth soothed its way through her magenta capris.

He held out his hand, an invitation.

Her hand remained planted on the armrest. She shook her head again, keeping her eyes centered on the controls, not the window.

John smiled and caressed her knee before adjusting a knob. He grabbed the yoke and banked left.

Another verse floated into her mind. Her body listed to the left. A wave of nausea rolled over her. She pinned the bag waiting in her lap and swallowed again.

Landing. The only thing standing between herself and the sweet, solid earth. Landing. Fear popped in her chest and spread like an ink spot on a white shirt, speeding her pulse, robbing the air from her lungs. Whispering, she drew strength from the words. "When I am afraid, I will trust in You." The first verse she'd ever learned in Bible School.

She'd secretly practiced it all week, and on the final day with the families in the sanctuary, she walked up to the platform where the director stood and recited the whole verse. The surprise and joy on her aunts' faces as she said every word without hesitation thrilled her more than the small silver cup she'd won for memorizing the verse.

Jancie and Winnie. They loved her so much. What was happening with them right now? Tears prickled, and she dragged her thoughts from them.

She remembered instead the director placing the cup in her hand. The cup had turned out to be tin in actual fact, but Penn loved it. It resided on a shelf in her bedroom today. When she got home—if she got home—no. No negative thinking. When she got home, she'd move the cup to her dresser, a daily reminder of…of this ordeal? Of the Bible verse? Of God's faithfulness?

Another slight jolt jostled the bag in her lap. She watched it move and lifted another thank You prayer she hadn't used it.

Yet.

The engine noise changed. New, unfamiliar noises filled the cockpit.

John's voice sounded louder, easier to hear.

A movement in the corner of her eye moved her attention to the window. Before she thought about what she was doing, she looked out the window. Green things whipped by. She focused and realized the green things were trees. Trees?

She swung her gaze back to John, grinning and working the controls. "On the ground. Safe and sound. Thank You, Lord."

"We landed?"

"Yeah. Where were you?"

"I…I mean…I felt a little bump. Was that it?" Her arms and legs trembled like the congealed salad languishing in her refrigerator back home.

"It was a pretty sweet landing if I do say so myself. But…as we say in the business, any landing you walk away from is a good landing."

Penn slumped against the seat and watched the parked planes come into view. She'd just flown in her first plane ride. And survived. *Praise God from Whom all blessings flow. Praise be to God.*

And John.

Penn glanced at him. His gaze focused ahead, concentrating on his task as he taxied the plane to a parking place, but his face stretched wide in a victory grin. He leaned back in his seat, and pressed the pedals with his feet. "Penn, babe, we're here. You did it. I knew you could."

She didn't do anything but hang on for dear life. Hang on and trust John to fly the plane as he said he could.

And God, of course.

She'd trusted God to carry her through. Those verses hadn't surfaced in years, but they'd come to her exactly when she'd needed them, dormant until a time such as today.

Just like God. He'd always been with her whether she acknowledged Him or not, loving her, helping her, carrying her through every rough patch.

Praise be to God.

Indeed.

~*~

John cut the engine and unbuckled his seatbelt. "Hang on. I'll come round and help you." He leaned toward her and kissed her forehead. "You did fantastic! Great job, Penn."

Thank you, God.

He hopped out the door, sprinted around the front of the plane, and climbed up on the wing to get to her.

Thank you, God.

Her head lolled against the seat. Her face was as

white as the clouds they'd flown through. He opened the door and grabbed the buckle.

"I'm so proud of you. Can you believe it?" He removed the harness from her shoulders, tossed the barf bag to the floor, and tugged at her legs to get her to exit the plane.

She met his gaze. "I don't know if I can stand."

"I'm right here to help you. You made it this far. I'm not going to let anything happen to you now." He set her feet outside the door and reached for her arms. "We'll just take it slow and easy."

She slid forward and edged to the wing.

He hopped to the tarmac, gripping her calf. "I'm right here, Penn. I've got you. Come on down."

"Seriously, John. I don't think I can move."

"You don't have to." He stretched up and grabbed her waist, lifting her to stand beside him. "I got you, Penn. Stand right here until you get your land legs." He gathered her to him, so proud of her and thankful for the great flight that his heart pumped like he'd just bungee jumped off the Perrine Bridge in Idaho.

He kissed the crown of her head, breathing in the scent of flowers. He kissed her temple and trailed his lips to the frantic pulse in front of her ear. "Can you believe it, Penn? We're here. Great job, babe."

Shifting to meet her eyes, he brushed curls away from her face. Before he could think about what to say next, Penn rose on her tiptoes and reached behind his neck. She tugged his face down, clamping her mouth to his. She pressed into him, twining her fingers into his hair, with a kiss that meant business.

Adrenaline from the landing pumped in his veins and ramped up with the shock of her kiss.

He cradled the back of her head and answered her

as he'd wanted to since the first time he'd sat with her on the front porch swing. A shiver that had nothing to do with the landing tingled the back of his neck.

Their trip was only partially over. They had to get to the hospital and find out the state of things with Jancie, and they'd do that. But right now for a couple more seconds, he wanted to revel in Penn's being in his arms and kissing him.

She felt so good crushed up against him. His hand traveled her spine to the small of her back, and he let himself fall into the deepening kiss.

Her sigh brought him back to his responsibility. Get her to her aunts. He dragged his mouth to her cheek and rested his chin on the top of her head. She laid her forehead against his chest. Her crazy breathing keeping pace with his own.

"Penn, as much as I want to pursue this new development between us, we need to get going."

She burrowed her face into his shirt. She didn't want to let go yet. He tightened his arms around her. Good. Neither did he.

He stroked her hair and let her have a few minutes. After that kiss, he needed calming, too. As he stood, he felt a warm wetness seep into the front of his shirt. Concerned, he lifted her chin. Smudged tears matted her eyelashes and highlighted her cheeks.

"Hey. What's wrong?" He dried the tears with his thumbs, cupping her face in his hands. "Penn, talk to me. You've barely said a word since we took off. What's wrong? You were a trooper on the plane, and that part's over." He smiled at her.

Silence.

"You didn't bump your head on the way out, did you?" He inspected her curls, appreciating their softness again. "What's wrong?"

She whispered into his damp shirt, "I don't know."

~*~

That was a bold face lie.

Her entire body had been suffused with trembling when the plane had taxied to a stop. The tremors had stolen her muscles and left al dente noodles in their places. Without John's help, she was certain she'd never have been able to exit the plane.

The plane.

She'd flown in a plane. The enormity of what she'd just accomplished hovered just outside her comprehension.

Before she'd had a chance to process the flight, get her land legs as he'd suggested, John began exploring her profile with his kisses. The tremors that had slightly subsided returned like swarming bees looking for a new hive.

And then.

And then she'd kissed him like…like she'd just passed her CPA exam, or won a million dollars, or flown in a plane and survived.

The adrenalin had to go somewhere, and she'd poured it into kissing the daylights out of him. When he broke it off, her body and mind overloaded with sensory feelings, culminating in a liberating catharsis all over the front of John's shirt.

He massaged her shoulder. "You've had a tremendous day. Unfortunately, it's not done. Some of your family is supposed to be here to pick us up."

"What?"

"Reesa called some numbers I gave her and radioed me that somebody, Benjamin, I think, is taking us to the hospital."

"Benji and Alice." Sweet Benji and Alice. Always together. Always helping, bringing casseroles, visiting shut-ins, chauffeuring sick ones to doctors' appointments.

"Right. Family?"

"They're my aunts' first cousins on my grandmother's side."

"You ready to go find them, or do you need more time out here?"

She wanted to stay right here in John's arms. Not think about what was facing her with her aunts. Not think about anything but him.

Penn covered the wet splotches on his ivy colored cotton shirt and felt the heat from his chest on her palm. She arched her neck, regarded his dark chocolate eyes, and lowered her gaze to his mouth that lifted into a smile.

More zings skittered down her spine.

He slid his hand over her arm and spread his fingers over her hand. "Come on. I'll walk you in and come back for our bags." He tucked her under his arm, close to his side, safeguarding, supporting.

Benji and Alice appeared at the glass double doors, waving and smiling. "Penny, dear, so good to see you. Wish it could be in better circumstances." Both of them surrounded her with a bear hug as she and John crossed the threshold. "She's doing all right. She's out of surgery. The doctor placed two stents in to repair two blockages on the left side of her heart."

"Thank God." So much to thank Him for—especially in the past couple of hours.

26

Penn's nose twitched at the antiseptic smells wafting in the hospital corridor. Alice pushed the elevator button. "We can go right up to the heart patient waiting area. That's where we left Winnie. The preacher stayed with her."

Penn relaxed against John as the lights blinked the floor numbers. Exhaustion swelled to every pore of her body. She snuggled into his shirt, searching for the familiar clean, spicy scent.

Thank you, God, for this man beside me.

The doors pinged open and spewed a crowd of men and women in scrubs.

John shuffled her out of the way.

Alice led them onto the elevator. "We told her she ought to get something to eat. She won't be able to see Jancie till she wakes up. But you know Winnie. Stubborn. Said she'd wait a while."

John nudged her. "You need to eat, too. You had a couple of bites of pizza before you got the call."

Although her stomach felt empty, it rejected the idea of food. A picture of the barf bag that had journeyed with her to North Carolina appeared before her eyes. Triumph curled her lips. The bag, clean and empty, waited for someone else, not her. She'd conquered that bag.

Conquered.

What a special, powerful word.

But John had to be starving. "We'll get something in a little bit, OK?"

Alice led them to a group of chairs behind the reception desk. Winnie sat crocheting in a chili-colored hospital room chair, chatting with a man Penn assumed to be the pastor.

Penn raced out of John's hold and draped herself across Winnie's lap with a fierce embrace, the hook bouncing on the carpeted floor.

"Oh, Penny, girl. I'm so glad you're here." Winnie extracted a wadded tissue from her shirt pocket and dabbed her eyes with the damp shreds. "And so fast. How in the world? No traffic, huh?"

Penn stroked her cheek. "I made it, Aunt Winnie. I'm here."

"I'm sorry I was in such a tizzy when I called you, honey. I just...I just didn't know what to do." Winnie buried her head into Penn's neck and sobbed.

John handed her fresh tissues snagged from the side table and greeted the pastor.

When the sobs subsided, Penn wiped her aunt's face with the new tissues. "I'm here. We're going to handle this together." She guided Winnie to the olive love seat. "Let's sit and tell me everything."

Benji took Winnie's vacated chair, leaving John and Alice to the paisley couch perpendicular to the loveseat.

Winnie removed her glasses and wiped the lenses on her shirt hem. Replacing them on the bridge of her nose, she gasped. "John. Oh, Johnny boy, you're here, too?" She blew her nose. "I thought I was done with the crying, but I just might have to start all over. I can't believe you're here." She wiped her eyes.

"Couldn't let Penn come alone. I'm glad to be

here, Winnie."

Alice assumed hostess duties, introducing the pastor before he left for more hospital visits.

Winnie grabbed Penn's hand and nestled her head on her shoulder. "It's been a long day, Penny."

Alice took charge again. "Why don't ya'll go down and get something to eat? The cafeteria has pretty good food. Benji and I can stay right here and wait in your place. We'll call if the doctor calls. Probably be a while still before she wakes up."

Benji slid back in the chair. "We'll call the minute we hear something." He wiggled his flip phone and dropped it into his chest pocket.

Several minutes of cajoling later, the three of them negotiated the maze of halls to the hospital cafeteria.

At the checkout line, John unfolded his wallet.

Managing her tray with one hand, she stilled his movements with her free one. "Let me pay for you. Let this be the start of what I owe you."

He frowned. "For what?"

"For the...for today..." The idea of her...flying...in a plane...

"First off, letting a woman pay for my meal," he shook his head. "Not the way I was raised up, as they say. Second, today's on me—and my boss. So don't worry about that."

Winnie, holding her tray with a tuna salad sandwich, joined them.

Penn tabled the argument.

Over a few nibbles of a quinoa salad—her feet may have been back on the ground but her stomach hadn't completely landed yet—Penn listened to Jancie's story.

Winnie managed to relate it without fresh tears,

but her chin trembled, and her voice broke a couple of times.

Jancie had complained of heartburn but blamed it on the Mexican food they'd eaten. She'd been up several times during the night and about eight o'clock started wondering about going to the emergency room. About nine, Winnie convinced her to call the rescue squad. She'd had the heart attack on the way to the hospital.

"I followed in our car behind the EMTs. I found out after when I came in from the parking lot." She sniffed and wiped her nose with her napkin.

"Aunt Winnie, I'm so sorry you had to go through all this by yourself. I'm here now. We can face it together. Right?"

Winnie pushed away her half-eaten sandwich. "I'm ready to go back up when ya'll are."

John, with two cheese burgers fortifying him, gathered the plates and glasses and stacked them on a brown plastic tray. "Let's go."

Five minutes after arriving back at the waiting area, the doctor called for Winnie, but she asked Penn to take the call.

Prickles stung Penn's chest as she and John proceeded toward the phone.

Penn came back and offered a tentative smile to the waiting group. "She's awake but groggy and can have two visitors for ten minutes."

Alice rose, adjusting the skirt of her dress. "Thank God. You two go right on ahead. We'll stay here and get to know John."

Penn searched John's face. He opened his arms for her. His breath warmed her ear. "You'll be fine. I'll be here when you get back."

She snuggled close to his chest, listening to his heartbeat. She released her hold and missed his solid strength immediately.

"Aunt Winnie, you ready?" Penn enfolded her aunt in a side hug and walked with her to the locked door that led into the ICU.

When she saw Jancie lying in the bed, Penn's heart sank. She stopped inside the door.

Jancie looked pale and tiny. Frail and old. Vulnerable without her glasses.

Winnie strode right to the bed and grabbed her sister's arm.

Jancie's eyes opened, squinted and tried to focus. She shifted her head to see both of them. "Hey..." her voice croaked. "Penny, you're here?"

"It's me, all right." Penn pushed her legs forward, kept her voice light. "Didn't want to miss anything."

"Be glad you missed this."

Winnie perched on the edge of the bed. "How do you feel, sister?"

Jancie lowered her eyelids. "Like a freight train sat on my chest."

Penn smiled at the mixed metaphor. "The doctor says everything went fine. You'll be good as new in no time."

Jancie snorted, weak, but reminiscent of her old self. "That sounds like 'one size fits all' to me."

"We'll let you get some rest. We're not supposed to visit over ten minutes."

Her chin trembled. "I wish you could stay."

"We'll be back bright and early tomorrow. With bells on. Don't worry." Winnie straightened the sheet and smoothed the pillowcase.

Penn hugged Jancie goodbye, and her aunt

whispered, "I'm glad you're here. She needed you."

~*~

Standing on her grandfather's front porch, Penn savored John's arms around her. His heart beat slow and strong under her palm. *Thank you, God, for John.* How would she have managed today without him? She'd probably still be driving somewhere on I-85.

Instead, she'd trusted this man who promised to deliver her to her aunts safely and quickly, who even now kept her from sliding to the porch in an exhausted heap.

His warm breath tickled the curls springing around her ear. "You need to get some sleep. Winnie wants to get back up there bright and early tomorrow."

She did need sleep. Waking up in her bedroom on Oakland Street this morning was eons ago. She needed to think about John, too. What did today's events mean for them? Did it change the way she felt about him? No. Did it change the way she felt about flying? *No. Maybe.*

It was too much to think about right now. She needed to call for a substitute teacher for Monday, for sure. Probably for the whole week. She needed to— Peri. She gasped and jerked upright.

John tightened his hold. "What is it?"

"Peri. I completely forgot—"

He settled his head back in place on top of hers. "Already taken care of."

"What?" How could she forget Peri?

"I called Andy before we left. He knows horses. He's got it covered."

She rocked back on her heels. "I can't

believe…thank you, John." She cupped his cheek. "Thank you for everything today. I don't know…I can't…but I will pay you, John. It's too much."

He pressed his thumb gently against her mouth. "You don't have to thank me. And, no, you won't pay me. Let people help you." John leveled his gaze with hers. "You were tremendous today. You are the bravest person I know, Penn Davenport." He splayed his fingers against her back.

She closed her eyes. "I'm not brave. I was scared to death the whole time. I can't believe I didn't throw up."

"Whenever I had to do something hard, my mom always quoted her favorite author, Mark Twain. 'Courage is resistance to fear, not absence of fear.' Babe, you resisted your fear and won."

"I really don't remember much of anything except the Bible verses rolling around my mind. The whole time. I haven't thought of those verses in years, but today they came back with a stubbornness that sank in and stayed for the whole flight."

"That's God, Penn." He brushed back the hair from her face. "Listen. I've got to roll. Alice and Benji are waiting for me."

Her stomach clenched. Her chest tightened with a new heaviness. She didn't want him to leave. The ten hours they'd shared seemed like a lifetime. "Do you know how to get to their house?" She plucked at his shirt sleeve, enjoying the hard band of muscle underneath.

He grinned. "Alice insisted on writing down directions even after I told her I had my phone." He kissed her forehead with a light brush of his lips. "Get some sleep. I'll see you in the morning." He moved to the front steps.

She wrapped her empty arms around herself. "What time?" A question to keep him talking and on the porch.

"Eight or eight thirty? Call me when Winnie decides."

Ten hours before she could see him again. She pressed her lips together. "You've got her keys, right?"

He dangled them from his left hand. "Yes, ma'am. Get inside and go to bed. Now."

"OK. Yes, sir." She saluted him. "Will do." She rubbed her ring as taillights blinked in the darkness.

27

After dressing and downing a glass of orange juice, Penn checked the front window every five minutes until John arrived at eight o'clock.

Dropping them at the hospital, he insisted they go up without him while he checked out the town. He promised to come back for lunch and visit with Jancie after they'd seen her first.

Sleep had agreed with Jancie. Color painted her cheeks again. She reclined on her pillows more like a queen than a heart patient. Her glasses gave her the familiar take charge attitude people expected from her.

Penn released a breath she'd held since exiting the elevator. Jancie was back. The two sisters, her sweet aunts, teased each other, smiling and holding hands.

She left them to visit her grandfather roomed on the floor beneath Jancie's. She hadn't had the energy yesterday evening to venture a trip to his room.

He greeted her with a booming 'hello' and a weak hug less robust than ones from her childhood.

A couple of minutes into their chat, his cellphone rang. He glanced at the screen, wrinkled his nose, and apologized for taking the call. That was the grandfather she remembered.

When she returned to Jancie's room, she heard a rich laugh that scattered tingles like dropped gum balls up and down her back. Her heart flipped over, and she curbed her grin into a more sedate, welcoming smile.

"Look who's here." Jancie's cheeks glowed pinker. "And he brought me flowers." She pointed to an arrangement of daisies, chrysanthemums, and three yellow roses with pink tips. "Lovely. He's made my day. I love flowers from a man."

John winked at Penn.

Her aunt wrinkled her forehead. "I'm confused about something, though. Winnie says both of you came yesterday. Together. But you're using our car. Not that we mind one bit, but what's the matter with Gretchen?" Jancie raised her eyebrows.

Penn played with the curls at the back of her neck. She opened her mouth and closed it. The subject of her flying had to be addressed sooner or later. Why couldn't it be later? How would the aunts take the news?

Jancie seemed to be bouncing back at record time, and Winnie hadn't cried since yesterday afternoon.

She sent a wide-eyed plea for help from John.

"Penn and I came down together. We had a good trip. A good day to travel."

Both aunts tilted their heads.

"On the motorcycle? You rode the whole way on the back of a motorcycle?"

John raked his hand through his hair. "Well, no, not exactly..."

Penn inhaled and let the words tumble out in a rush. "John flew me down in a plane."

Two mouths dropped wide open. Surprise crackled through the room.

"What?"

She shrugged. "You heard me. I flew on a plane. John flew it. He got me here faster than we could've driven. I got on a plane and didn't throw up. We landed, and we're here." She picked an imaginary piece of lint from her blouse. *No big deal. Yeah, right.*

This news, shocking and unbelievable, shouldn't be unveiled now, especially when they'd already experienced an emotional roller coaster first with their brother and now with Jancie's health scare.

As the aunts continued to stare, the familiar panic awakened somewhere around her heart and spread to impede her lungs. Her gaze latched onto John.

He moved from his place beside the bouquet of flowers and pressed his hand in the small of her back. The heat of his palm permeated her body, a shield against the panic, an anecdote to the trembling. "She was fantastic. She had a goal—" He gestured toward them. "Get to her aunts as fast as possible. She set her mind to it and accomplished it." He rubbed his hand up her back, settled on her shoulders. "She didn't even need medicine."

"I could have had medicine?" Why hadn't medicine occurred to her yesterday? She could have been knocked out in the back instead of gripping the armrests for all she was worth.

He jostled her. "You didn't need medicine. You had your Bible verses, remember?"

"True, but..."

He chuckled. "You didn't even need the Cirrus."

She cocked an eyebrow. "Ah, wasn't that the plane we flew on?"

"Yes, but it's a special plane, Penn."

"Special?" Indeed. It had ferried her to her aunts.

"Remember that red handle in the roof?"

A frown cut across her brow. She didn't want to relive that experience, was working on forgetting it.

He lowered his head. "You asked about all the

dials and knobs, the red handle in the ceiling."

Not a significant clue. "Don't know what you mean."

"I told you it was a parachute for the plane, and you thought I was making fun of you."

She remembered that part. Again, pain tightened her throat at his teasing her, tittering on the edge of hysteria.

"Penn, a Cirrus plane is equipped with a parachute for the whole plane in the event of problems, a safety net, so to speak. James knew that. And knew about you and flying. He upgraded us from the Cessna to the Cirrus, to give you that safety net. But you didn't need it. You did it by yourself. With those Bible verses and the love for your aunts." He slid his hand to her neck and kissed the top of her head. He whispered, "You need some time with your aunts." John brushed away tears from her cheeks. "I'll leave you ladies to chat. I'll be down in the cafeteria." He kissed her temple and left.

Penn dropped onto the bed with her aunts and cried until she was spent.

With all three sobbing, they emptied the box of tissues and resorted to paper towels from the bathroom.

When the storm subsided, and she lay scrunched between them like too many celebration cookies crammed into a cookie tin, she sighed, spent but renewed. The aunts held her hands, and peace and happiness washed over her like a warm wave.

"Penny, I don't know what to say." Winnie wiped underneath her chin with a damp washcloth. "I hate that you went through what you did to get here. You did it because I was in such a state—" She twisted the cloth in her hands.

"I got on that plane because I wanted to be with you as fast as I could. John offered to drive Gretchen, but I chose the plane. Nobody made me." She said the words as much for Winnie as for herself. She had chosen to fly. John hadn't forced her. He'd offered. Suggested. She'd made the decision.

"That John." Jancie reclined onto the pillow and closed her eyes.

Penn clutched at the hem of the sheet. "Aunt Jancie. We've worn you out."

"No, but I am going to rest a minute." She slid up the sheet. "Why don't you go find John?"

"I think I'll rest, too." Winnie stretched her legs beside her sister and tucked her head on the pillow.

A good idea. Let them muse and chat on yesterday's miracle.

~*~

Penn found John typing notes on his iPad in a back corner of the cafeteria. Wisps of his dark hair fell in front of his eyes as he concentrated on the screen.

As she approached, he raised his gaze and smiled. "Everything good?" He offered a chair.

"I think it's going to be."

His eyebrows met. "You've been crying."

Her hands flew to her face. How could she not think to put on lipstick at least? "Sorry. I'm sure I look a mess."

"You always look good to me, Penn."

She smoothed her cheek. How did she respond to that statement? She'd come back to it when her emotions stabilized. When the sharpness of the flight had mellowed. "It's been an emotional two days."

He closed the tablet. "We need to talk."

Not yet. She couldn't think straight yet. Yes, she'd flown in a plane, but she didn't know what that meant for her future.

For their future.

"Has the doctor been by?"

New topic. That was quick…

"He made his rounds first thing this morning. Before we got here, Jancie said."

John rubbed his chin. "Do you have an idea about your schedule this week? When she might be released? What the word is about your grandfather?"

He wanted to talk about this week, not about what the flight had meant to her, to the two of them.

Thank you, God, for saving me from embarrassing myself.

That made sense. He hadn't kissed her, really kissed her since they'd landed. He'd kissed the top of her head, her temple. Reminiscent of a brother's touch.

In fact, the kiss after the landing had been her doing. She'd dragged him to her, initiated it. Not John. She planted that kiss on him before he could refuse. True, he'd responded, but—

"Penn. Are you OK?"

"Yes." She shook her head to wipe that kiss out of her mind. "Umm, she might be able to leave tomorrow."

He fiddled with his phone lying next to the iPad. "And then what?"

"I figure she'll need a few days to recuperate before going home. My grandfather's doing fine. He's being released sometime this week, too."

She stiffened. "John, I get what you're asking.

When I texted her, my department head gave me the whole week off. I'm hoping we can drive back maybe Friday, but you don't have to stay that long. I'm sure your boss needs you."

"He called while ago to check on you. He says to tell you good job for flying yesterday. Reesa's thrilled, too."

"They're nice people." She rested her chin on her palm. "When do you have to leave?"

"I don't have to leave. I can stay as long as you need me."

And there it was. Good, kind John, still helping her.

"Thank you. You've been such a help. I couldn't have—"

He held up a hand. "Penn."

"I know. I'll stop. But you can go back. You don't have to worry about me."

"Worry about you? The bravest girl I know? Are you kidding? I thought if I hung around long enough somebody might start baking something. I'm looking to snag a celebration cookie, or a cinnamon roll, or—"

She smiled. Maybe the smile would offset the ache in her chest. "I'm sure some baked goods will be coming your way. You can count on that."

28

Joy bubbled in Penn's chest the following Saturday afternoon as she glided her aunts' green sedan into their driveway.

Home again, home again. Jiggety jig.

Finally.

After leaving her grandfather with frozen casseroles and a day nurse, they'd been on the road since Friday morning, turning the eight-hour drive into a two-day marathon journey. Stopping about every two hours for thirty or forty minutes, they'd stayed overnight about halfway in Winchester, Virginia.

She excited the car and stretched to release the knots of the marathon journey. A few more hours and she could climb into her own bed again.

Thank you, God.

Penn reached for Jancie in the back seat. "Let's get you inside. I'll come back for our bags."

Jancie batted her hand away, climbing out by herself. "Penny, I've told you and told you. Please don't treat me like an invalid. I'm not back to one-hundred-percent, but I'm getting there. I'm still sore, but besides that, I'm feeling pretty good."

Penn crossed her arms in front of her chest. "Fine. Just trying to help. Here. Take my bag, won't you? And don't forget the sack of Winesap apples Grandfather sent either. I'm going to see Peri."

"Don't get fresh with me, girly."

Penn grinned. Home again, home again. "Just teasing you."

"When is your young man coming by?" Winnie rolled her suitcase up the walkway.

"Hold on. I'll get that, and I've told you and told you. He's not my young man."

"John called every other day and texted, too." Winnie continued up the stairs to unlock the front door.

"He wanted to find out how you were doing." Penn held the door for Jancie.

"It's more than that." Jancie entered the family room and inhaled through her nose. "Thank you, Lord, for bringing us home." Placing her hand on her chest, she faced Penn. "I wasn't too sick to miss signals between you two."

Penn caught her breath. The connection between them wasn't her imagination? "Signals?"

"Sparks, electricity. Whatever you want to call it, the two of you have it."

Penn's heart rate kicked into high gear. "I'll take the bags up later. I want to see Peri first."

"Fine. Ignore me." Jancie sank onto the couch. "It's still true, honey."

~*~

Peri stomped in the paddock, his head and neck straining over the fence as Penn jogged toward him. He trotted to the gate and nibbled at her hair while she freed the latch.

"You missed me, huh?" She buried her head in his neck and let his warm scent soothe away all the kinks of travel as well as the strain of last week. "Well, I missed you, too, buddy. A lot. I'm so glad you're here and not visiting down the street."

She hopped onto his back and lay against his neck, squeezing him in a tight, whole body embrace.

"You look great. Andy took good care of you, huh?" Peri nodded his head. Peri—he understood her no matter what. "And were you good for him? You didn't break out and give him a scare, did you?"

No response except for the swishing of his black tail.

Penn chuckled. "Hmm. I think I know what that means."

Stretching his muzzle to the ground, Peri nipped at blades of grass.

"I've got so much to tell you, buddy. I can't even believe most of it myself." She stared toward the back of the paddock. "I should have some sort of trumpet fanfare. Words don't capture the magnitude of what happened." She stroked his mane. "All right. Here it is." She caught a hunk of his hair in her fist and drew in a deep breath. "I flew in a plane."

Peri lifted his head and neighed.

"Exactly. Thank you." She hugged him again. "It seems like a dream now, but it's true. Here's another thing. John...kissed me." She giggled and swung her legs back and forth. "It's true."

Peri clomped to another patch of grass, ignoring her chatter.

"He kissed me right after we landed. He was so excited about the good flight and proud of me for conquering my fear, for going through with the flight." A shudder raised the hair on the back of her neck. "I was pretty much still shell shocked. Anyway, he kissed me on the forehead, and then I," she buried her face in his mane. "I grabbed him and kissed him on the mouth. But he kissed me back."

Peri raised his head, cocking it toward the house.

"Oh, that got your attention, hey?" She petted his neck. "What do you think, Peri? I don't know what to think." She separated three hanks of his coarse hair and worked them into a braid. "Why do I have to like someone who flies for a living? Why couldn't I be interested in someone like Edward? All his lit students love him. We'd have the same work schedule. It'd be so easy." Edward, the lone man in the English department.

Peri neighed again.

"You're right, buddy. It'd be boring, not easy. Half the time I don't know what Edward is talking about with his Shakespeare quotations sprinkled in every conversation." She sighed. "John is different. He's fun and kind and a little bit scary with his motorcycle."

No, that assessment wasn't true.

He may seem edgy with his bike and penchant for extreme sports, but he'd always been tender and careful with her. Even with his kisses, he'd been gentle, not pushy.

Pushy described her when she'd reached up and yanked his mouth to hers. She closed her eyes. The memory of being with him warmed her.

After John left Oxford on Monday, loneliness had been her constant companion. Chatting with her aunts had been a temporary fix. When she went to bed at night, a lonesome cloak wrapped around her heart, the memory of his arms a poor proxy for the real comfort—and tingles—they created.

She released the braid and finger combed the dark mane, wishing her fingers streamed through a different mop of black hair. She flung the hanks out of her hands. *Enough of those thoughts.*

John had flown out a couple of days ago and wouldn't be back in Mars until Monday.

Monday...

She snuggled against Peri, her hand drifting over the muscles in his neck.

On Monday, she'd be back in school, catching up on a week's worth of work, trying to restore order to the possible chaos if the substitute didn't hold the students in check.

Penn looked forward to being back with her students. Her hand stilled. Looked forward to seeing her students? Interesting.

She missed those crazy kids.

How did they do all week without her? Did they understand the new principles? How far ahead did they advance in the chapter? Would she need to review before moving forward?

Penn rose to a sitting position. She *wanted* to teach.

Peri tore at another mound of grass and chomped on his prize.

She glanced back at the house and love somersaulted in her heart. Being home was the best feeling.

Questions about John and her exam score and what these new developments might mean for her future swirled about her mind in a kaleidoscope of unknowns, but she thanked God for her aunts and the life they had together.

~*~

John taxied the Cessna to its parking place and

powered down the engine. *Thank you, God, for another uneventful flight.*

James hoisted his satchel. "Good trip, man. Thanks. I'm a little stiff after that two-hour flight." He stretched his arms toward the windshield. "I need to be in town for the rest of the week. Might need you next Tuesday, but I'll let you know for sure. Go ahead and pick up some other flights if you want to."

"Thanks."

James was always good about sharing his schedule so that John could accumulate more flying hours. John grabbed his backpack. "I'm finishing up some articles, and I've got other stuff to do here. I'm grounded this week."

"Would that other stuff happen to include Miss Penn?" James grinned over his shoulder as he stuck his feet out of the cockpit.

John's insides quickened as he jumped from the wing to the tarmac.

"Well?" James met him at the nose and fell in step with him.

John hiked his backpack on his shoulder. "Maybe."

James slapped him on his back. "Maybe. Playing it cool, huh? Well, I hope it does. She seems like a keeper."

Definitely a keeper. Many times in the past week, a picture of her in the cockpit, determination warring with panic on her face, floated across his mind. His heart swelled every time. And many times this past week, his mind wandered to the kiss they'd shared.

He'd been worried she was in shock when they landed. He planned to hold her until she seemed steady, able to walk on her own. The excitement of the moment, the pure pleasure of knowing she'd succeeded in slaying the beast that haunted her, crippled her, jazzed him to celebrate with a kiss.

John waved to Reesa who listed coordinates into her microphone.

If he'd thought about it beforehand, he would have meant the kiss to be a way-to-go, good-job, I'm-so-proud-of-you reward at the end of a challenge. He hadn't thought, though. He'd just reacted to the exhilaration pumping through his veins, hugged her to him, and plopped that kiss on the top of her head.

Maybe that's what had happened with her. Maybe she reacted to being safe on the ground again. Maybe she was thrilled the challenge was over. Maybe it didn't mean anything to her. She might have forgotten about it already.

He certainly hadn't. How could he forget about one of the biggest surprises of his life? When she wrapped her arms around his neck and tugged him down to meet her mouth...so sweet. So soft. The intensity of that kiss rocked him, making him grateful for the plane supporting his back.

John retrieved his cellphone from his pack and pressed it on. No messages. He sagged against the counter. He hadn't expected to see a call from Penn, but a guy could always hope.

Her personality probably didn't extend to calling a man. Just like that kiss definitely didn't jive with her normal actions. At least in their history.

Maybe a new day was dawning.

He punched her number.

She answered on the third ring.

"Hey, Penn. I'm back."

"Where are you?"

"At the airport. Just landed. Everybody doing fine?"

"Jancie's following doctor's orders to take it easy. Winnie made a banana chocolate chip bread for my classes. Peri's stayed at home now for over a week without visiting. He's being good for us."

He chuckled. "Good horse. How're you? How did school go today?"

"Not bad. I used the banana bread as a threat. No good behavior. No good bread."

"Sounds like you've got them back in control."

"How was your trip?"

"Long. Glad to be back."

"Good."

Good for me to be back or good for her that I'm back?

Silence.

Nothing to encourage him to continue the conversation the way he wanted. He scuffed his boot along the tiled floor. *Back to square one? No problem.* He'd take a slow and steady course with her. He hoped after the trip to Oxford, they'd progressed in their...what?

Relationship? Friendship?

"OK. Just wanted to see how you're doing. I guess I'll see you. Clara said she wanted a follow-up meeting—what'd she call it? A plus/minus session about the festival. So...maybe then?"

"Yeah. She mentioned the same to me at church yesterday."

What else could he say to keep her on the line? Ask her for a date? Maybe not happening today. Maybe for the best. Ask her in person. That's the way to go. Observe her body language. Judge all the little nuances that made up Penn Davenport.

"Tell your aunts I said, 'hello.' Take care."

Awkward. What had happened to the closeness he'd felt with her only a few days ago?

Two steps forward. One step backward.

~*~

Penn hung up the phone.

Awkward...disappointing. Again.

With the click at the end of the call, the secret hope that he'd ask her for a date—a specific time to get together, not a vague, "see you"—withered like Jancie's hospital bouquets.

A date?

A date.

Flutters jostled her heart. Could she seriously consider dating him?

Maybe.

More than likely.

Yes, since the opposite was not being with him.

She'd missed him the whole week.

Penn hadn't expected him to ask her during the calls he'd made while Jancie recuperated in Oxford, but if she were honest, she'd been holding her breath waiting for him to say something like...what? *Wanna hang out sometime?*

No. John wouldn't ask her that way. Sounded too much like her algebra students.

Maybe he'd say, "Are you free on Sunday afternoon?"

No. Too formal.

How about, "I'm bungee jumping from the Roberto Clemente Bridge on Saturday. Care to come with?"

No. He'd never ask her to do something like that.
Would he?

But if he asked her out on a date...a real date
without the aunts tagging along as chaperones or
without a mission to accomplish for a volunteer
organization, would she really say, "yes?"

Her mouth curled, and she hugged her arms
around herself.

In a Learjet minute.

29

John entered the fellowship hall and familiar smells accosted him. Popcorn and teenage body odor mingling with cheap cologne. Wednesday night youth group. More than ten years had passed since he'd attended his own youth group, and the distinct scent remained the same. He scanned the room for Andy. When the weather report had forecasted rain for tonight, Andy had sought extra hands for crowd control. Would he see Penn tonight?

Maybe.

Doubled over the back of speakers, Andy inspected power cords.

A hooded boy with an electric guitar slouched on a stool.

A girl clad in a t-shirt scooted up to a keyboard.

A praise band, just like the one he grew up with.

Straightening from his task, Andy spotted John and made his way through the throng of teenagers to his friend. He grasped his hand. "Thanks, man. I really need some help tonight. Krista's too tired lately, and a bunch of the parents are tied up somewhere else."

"No problem. Glad I could help." John surveyed the room again. He smiled.

Penn chatted with a group of girls near the back.

Maybe he could catch a few minutes alone with her at some point. If everything worked to his favor, he'd have a date with her by the end of the night.

Penn's group shifted when two new girls arrived, and she spotted him.

John waved. He checked his watch. An hour until the end of group time. An hour until take-off, so to speak, or crash and burn.

The teens loved the ice breaker games. Praise songs echoed through the hall, a hipper sound than the warbling during his teenage Wednesday nights.

Showing real talent, the slouching guitarist adlibbed extra riffs to the original versions.

Andy's talk incorporated current events with Biblical truth. Perfect balance. A few teens benefited from the quiet time at the end to speak with adults.

John prayed with a football player troubled by friends who acted one way on Wednesday night and another after Friday night games.

Penn held her arm around a tall, blonde female.

Andy dismissed the crowd and several teens started folding chairs and picking up random pieces of paper from the floor.

The guitarist packed away his instrument, and still the girl poured her heart out to Penn.

John helped Andy roll the electrical cords for the speakers and waited for his turn.

Several minutes later, the blonde hugged Penn, grabbed her keys and phone from underneath her seat, and left.

He didn't waste time. He handed Andy the cord and sauntered over to Penn as she removed her jean jacket from the back of her chair. "Hey. I thought I might see you here."

"Krista asked if I could fill in for her. She sounded wiped out."

He stuck his hands in his pockets. "Everything

going well?"

"Uh huh. With you?"

"Great." He glanced around the room. Still too many eyes in the hall for comfort. "Are you ready? I could walk you out."

"Yes. Don't tell anyone, but I'm skipping choir practice. Need to check on my girls."

"Choir practice? What choir practice?" He helped her don her jacket and tugged her collar free. Soft brown curls spilled onto his fingers. Nice. He headed toward the door and settled his hand at the small of her back. Very nice. Darkness covered the parking lot, affording them a little privacy. "Hey, listen. I'm here the rest of the week. I was hoping maybe we could get together sometime."

"OK."

Not exactly encouraging. He glanced at his boots. At least she didn't say, "no."

"What about Friday night? You free?"

She winced. "Sorry. It's my turn to supervise the concession stand at the football game. Mars is playing Hampton."

Crash, but not exactly burning yet.

She bit her lip.

Disappointed?

Wishful thinking?

"Right." He rubbed the back of his neck. "Andy says it's supposed to be a good game."

She lifted her shoulder. "Maybe. I'm going because of the concessions. And to see the band."

"Gotcha." He stuffed his hands in his back pockets.

They reached her car. She leaned her hip on the door and held her purse low in front of her, not like a shield against him but loose, comfortable. A good sign.

John searched her eyes for a clue, and something positive, something…hopeful flickered in those beautiful brown eyes. His mouth went dry. He shot up an arrow prayer for help.

"How about Saturday, then?" He held his breath.

She smiled. "That sounds good."

He exhaled on a laugh. "Great. Know what'd you like to do, or do you want me to surprise you?

"Well, as long as you don't take me bungee jumping or parasailing or hang gliding or—"

"All right. All right." He held up his hands in surrender. "I get the picture. Those options are history, gone, off the list already, but we'll still do something fun. OK?"

"Sound good."

A lightness surged through his body.

Real good.

~*~

Penn shrugged out of her sage green cardigan and tied it around her neck. Cool and crisp, the autumn night in western Pennsylvania sparkled, perfect football weather outside the concession stand, but inside the cinder block walls, the popcorn machine, cheese pots for the tortilla chips, and the grill for the burgers and dogs heated the little room. She rolled up the sleeves of her blouse.

During home games, different school clubs rotated selling concessions and received a percentage of the proceeds at the end of the night. As one of the faculty co-sponsors of the National Honor Society, she supervised the teens with Edward.

Normally, the faculty sponsors hung near the back and delegated, but tonight was different. The rivalry between the two schools ensured a capacity crowd. A hungry, thirsty crowd. To keep up with the demand, both she and Edward served customers along with the teens. Nobody lounged in the back.

She placed the dollar bills in the register and swung back to her line of hungry people. John. Her breath caught in her throat. So focused on serving each customer as quickly as possible, she'd ignored the faces in the crowd.

"Fancy meeting you here. A high school football game?" She arched a brow.

"Andy came to support the players in the youth group. He invited me to tag along. Here I am—hungry for a cheeseburger."

She spread her hands on the counter. "Why am I not surprised?"

"Hello, Penn. John, right?" Abby had moved to first place in the next line over.

"Abby? You're here, too?" Who knew high school football was so popular with twenty-somethings?

"My cousin is a senior and plays for Hampton." She shrugged. "So here I am."

Penn handed the foil-wrapped burger and bottle of water to John.

He grabbed some napkins. "Thanks. So...we're still good for tomorrow night, right?"

"Sure."

He grinned. "See you then." He waded his way through the bulging crowd.

"Did I just hear what I think I heard?" Abby gave her order to the girl with the pierced nose standing beside Penn. The teen left her post to scoop chips and pour melted cheese on top.

Penn scorched Abby with a fierce look. "Ssh." That's all she needed—teens serenading her with 'Ms. Davenport has a date. Ms. Davenport has a date.'

"Fine." Abby lowered her voice and leaned close to the condiments. "Do you or do you not have plans tomorrow night with you know who?"

"Yes."

Abby squealed. "I knew it. Want me to come over to help you choose an outfit, do your hair?"

"I'm not going to the prom. It's just a—" She stopped as the teen returned with the plastic tray of chips and cheese.

"I'll be there. Tomorrow afternoon." Abby gathered her plastic rectangle of chips. "Plan on it."

~*~

Why didn't she stick to the original plan? Tell the aunts about the date five minutes before John's arrival. Too bad she let the news slip as they sipped coffee and worked the crossword puzzle over breakfast.

Aunt Winnie's ink pen hovered in midair. "What does that mean? 'You're seeing John tonight?'"

Jancie set her mug beside a saucer holding a half-eaten English muffin. "It sounds like a date to me. Is that right, Penny? You're going on a date with John tonight?"

Kicking herself, she grimaced. "He's picking me up about seven o'clock."

Winnie pushed back her chair. "Glory be. We've got to get started." Winnie strode to the sink, emptied her mug, and rinsed it three times before placing it in the dishwasher.

Penn frowned. "Wait a minute. You don't have to do anything. He's not coming here for dinner."

"That may be so, but we owe that young man some cookies." Jancie joined her sister in clearing the table.

"And some cinnamon rolls. Jancie, you can help until you need to rest. We'll take it slow. Don't wear yourself out."

"Stop. You don't need to bake anything. He's already asked me. No need to try to win him over with your baking wiles."

Jancie stared. "Penny, we're not trying to do anything. We promised him some cookies weeks ago, then everything fell to pieces." She glanced at the clock. "How much time do we have?"

"Seven o'clock."

Jancie rubbed her chin. "Definitely the cookies and the cinnamon rolls. He loves those. I know. We've got all those pecans Graham sent back with us. We could make a pecan pie. What do you think, sister?"

"Wonderful idea. Let's get to it."

Penn slapped her hands on her waist. Visions of baked goods piled high on the counter teased her. "Wait a minute." Couldn't they see reason? Understand logic? "He's one person. He can't eat all that." She scrunched the fabric of her pajama top with her fists.

"Of course, he can't eat all of it, but he'll have a good selection to sample." Winnie stooped into the refrigerator. "Do we have enough eggs?"

Penn grunted and retreated to her bedroom.

30

The house smelled like a bakery. Cinnamon mingled with butter. Sugar and chocolate melted together creating a blissful scent permeating through the closets upstairs.

Penn smiled in spite of herself, enjoying the comforting aromas. Her aunts were back. Really back.

The doorbell jingled around four o'clock. Abby, as promised, arrived with a small carry-on bag beside her.

Penn cocked her head toward the luggage. "Are you spending the night?"

Abby smirked. "Funny." She planted a quick kiss on Penn's cheek." These are reinforcements in case you get a bad case of I-have-nothing-to-wear. Oh, man." She peered over Penn's shoulder. "What's going on in here? It smells like—"

"A bakery?"

"I was going to say Christmas." She inhaled. "To die for."

"Abby." Winnie shrieked as she stepped into the family room, wiping her hands on a kitchen towel. "It's so good to see you, dear." She enfolded Abby in an eager hug. "And you're here to help Penn dress for her date?"

"Not that I can't dress myself."

"Penn, tonight is special. Calls for special effort." Jancie joined the party clutching a sampler tray of the day's baking frenzy. "Let's get this party started. I'm ready for a break from the kitchen."

Penn snagged Jancie's arm. "You're coming, too?"

"Wouldn't miss it." She headed up the stairs.

All four of them wedged into Penn's modest bedroom. The two aunts reclined against the headboard. Abby perched in the desk chair, and Penn was stationed at her closet door.

Abby broke a celebration cookie in half. "So what're you doing tonight? Casual or dressy?" She bit the cookie and moaned.

"I don't know."

Abby lowered the cookie. "You don't know?"

The aunts clapped and giggled. "Ooh, a surprise. We love it."

Abby tapped her chin. "Makes choosing an outfit harder, though."

"John's not exactly the dressy type. Casual. That's the way to go. Pants, for sure. He rides a motorcycle."

Abby's eyes widened. "Girl. That's so cool." She pinched a tiny bite of a cinnamon roll, popped it into her mouth, and licked her fingers. "My thighs are screaming, 'Quit with the butter and sugar,' but my mouth is loving this afternoon smorgasbord." She wadded up a napkin. "No more treats. Penn, show me what you've got."

Abby nixed four pairs of pants until Penn produced a pair of black crepe pants. "These are nice. We could work with these."

The aunts agreed, but their heads lolled on the headboard.

Penn paraded blouses and shirts and sweater sets before Abby, but none sparked any interest for her. Running out of clothes and time, she dug in the back of her closet and discovered a blouse she hadn't worn since last fall. An amethyst scoop-necked blouse. It featured long, billowy full sleeves. She'd forgotten how much she liked it.

"Not bad." Abby fingered the fabric. "I like the material. Try it on with the pants."

No second command chirped from the bed. Penn glanced at her aunts. Both napped, heads resting against each other.

When Penn donned the outfit, Abby issued more directions. "Walk back and forth a few times." Abby studied her like a specimen in one of her medical cases. "Hmm mmm. I like the way the hem flutters when you walk. How do you feel in it?"

Penn shrugged. "I don't know. Fine, I guess. I always liked this blouse."

"Good, but can't you get a little more excited? Oh, I know. Wait." Abby dropped to the floor beside her satchel, extracting blouses and scarves and boxes until she found the objective. "Ah ha. Here it is. Wrap this around your neck." She shook out a beautiful gauzy violet, pink, and cornflower scarf. "I bought it in Milan during a summer study abroad session."

Penn caressed the silky scarf. "I love it. Are you sure you want me to wear it?"

"Try it on and let's see." She squared Penn in front of the full-length mirror on the back of the closet door. "Wrap it like this." She wound the scarf loosely twice around her neck and fiddled with the ends until they hung straight in a nonchalant way.

She peeked over Penn's shoulder. "What do you think? She fluffed the folds and stepped back.

"I love it." The blouse and pants looked fine alone, but the scarf added interest.

Abby hugged her. "I do, too. It's classy and fun at

the same time. You have to wear it."

Soft snores sounded from the bed.

"See? The aunts agree. It's unanimous." Abby peered at them. "They're out cold. Did they bake all day?"

Penn's heart pinged for them. "Don't blame me. I tried to get them to stop before the pecan pie. Then they saw the spotty bananas, and we had chocolate chips, so of course we needed a banana bread to round off the other three deserts." She pivoted in front of the mirror. "We'll make you a to-go plate when you leave."

"I'm down for that. Now. Hair and makeup." Abby rummaged through her satchel again and found a zebra striped makeup case.

"This part won't take too long. I don't wear a lot."

Abby fished through the makeup. "But it's evening and a date."

Penn chewed on her cheek. "I don't want to look like a clown."

"I promise. You won't." Abby drew out eye shadow pallets.

"Or a floozy."

"Not that either. A floozy. Who uses that term, anyway? But you do need a little enhancement." She found tubes.

"Thanks a lot." Penn grinned. "And Jancie and Winnie use that term."

Abby added brushes to the mix. "When I said, 'you,' I meant that in the plural sense. Makeup helps everybody."

"Uh huh."

"I'm going to pluck your eyebrows first—just a bit. Don't worry." She stilled Penn's hand and waved a pair of tweezers. "It'll open up your eyes."

Pluck. Pluck. Pluck. Sneeze.

Pluck. Pluck. Pluck. Sneeze.

"Seriously, Penn? I've never heard of anybody being allergic to plucking eyebrows before."

Penn snatched a tissue and blew her nose. "Can we be done yet?"

"Yeah, yeah." Abby dabbed around Penn's eyes and opened a bottle of foundation. Her movements were swift and certain.

Abby. She'd pushed her way back into her life. Didn't cower when Penn puffed and roared a little bit in the coffee shop. She held onto the tenuous cord of friendship, and here she was helping her, teasing her, eating cookies with her.

Thank you, God.

"I flew in a plane."

The hand holding a small, tapered brush froze in mid-stroke. Blue eyes met brown.

"What?"

Penn broke eye contact, studied the top of the dresser. "John flew me to Oxford when Jancie had her heart attack."

Abby lowered the brush. "You're serious."

Penn loosened the scarf. "As a—well, you know what they say."

Abby nudged her hand away and fluffed the scarf again. "Do you want to talk about it?"

"There's nothing to talk about, counselor person." *Back off, Abby.*

"I disagree. There's a heck of a lot to talk about. You don't have to talk with me, but—"

Penn shrugged. "I had to get to my aunts. John offered. I accepted. Whole story in a nutshell." She fingered a lipstick tube.

"If you don't want to talk about it, why'd you bring it up?"

Penn dropped her chin into the scarf. "I don't know."

Abby raised the brush. "Well, if you—"

"It was hard, OK? The hardest thing I've ever done." She picked up an eye pencil, removed the top, recapped it, removed the top again. "It's hard to talk about, too."

Abby rescued the eye pencil and laid it on the dresser. "Sure it is. How did you feel?"

Penn rolled her eyes.

"I'm not asking as a therapist, Penny. I'm asking as a friend who loves you. I can't imagine what you must have gone through on that plane. How do you feel now?"

"John helped. He was...he was a rock, but gentle and kind. He prayed before we left, and *Bible* verses kept flooding my mind. The entire two hours. I had a barf bag on my lap, but I didn't use it."

Abby snorted. "Thank goodness, right? Throwing up in front of the man you love isn't exactly the romantic way to go."

Penn threw her head back. "What?"

"Sorry." She held Penn's gaze with her own. "I may have been premature, but you do care for him. I've seen the way you look at him." She laid her hand on top of Penn's. "And now you're going out with him. What do you think?"

She rubbed her arms. "I don't know what to think."

"How do you feel?"

"I don't know. Nervous, like I can't catch my

breath. Excited, like I can't wait for him to get here. Scared because I don't know what all this means or how it can end." She hid her face in her hands, but Abby transferred them to her lap.

"It means you're going out with a really great guy. It means you could have a really great time tonight and discover you'd like to spend more time together." She raised the brush again and surveyed her early work. "Or not. One date doesn't have to mean anything, Penn."

"I know." A date could mean nothing or everything. But on a scale from everything to nothing, this date might fall closer to everything for her.

What might it mean to John?

~*~

"Why did you let us sleep so long?" The aunts buzzed around the kitchen frantic to create a bag of their goodies for John. "We're behind. He'll be here before too long. We haven't sliced the bread yet."

"You were exhausted by your efforts to out shine the bakers down at the grocery store deli." Penn twisted the ends of Abby's scarf over and under her knuckles. "You needed the rest."

"Pish posh. We're fine. Do we have any of that colored cellophane left over from Easter?" Winnie's backside stuck out as she hunted for a box of plastic wrap in a low cabinet.

"I'm sure regular will work. John won't care what the food's wrapped in." Penn frowned. "Are you sure you ought to be on your knees like that?"

"Don't worry about me. Jackpot." Winnie emerged from the cabinet holding a roll of green cellophane.

"Way to go, sister. Bring it here. The stuff's laid out, ready to wrap." Jancie laid a final slice of banana chocolate chip bread on a cardboard container. "Let's put the pie slices in first." She flounced out a gift bag.

Jancie ripped off a long tail of plastic wrap and folded it over the pie slices resting on a plastic plate. "You know, it's a good thing Abby stopped by. Besides the fact that you look beautiful, Penny—"

Winnie slid the cinnamon rolls toward the bag. "She always does."

"True, of course. And I'm grateful she took some goodies with her. We've got food for days here."

Penn released the scarf and smoothed the ends. "This is where I'm supposed to refrain from saying, 'I told you so.'"

Jancie swatted at her. "Don't be sassy. We can make a bag for the preacher, too. Take it to him in the morning."

The doorbell pealed.

Panic set in the sisters in motion. "He's here. The bag's not finished. Open the door and let him in, Penn. We'll come with the bag in a minute."

Penn's thumb found her ring. "Settle down, for Pete's sake." Heeding her own advice, she inhaled slowly before taking a step. She glanced in the mirror hanging above the bookcase, and the image startled her.

She'd forgotten Abby swept a few curls back from her face and clipped a barrette to hold them in place.

"We emphasize your gorgeous eyes this way," Abby had said.

Penn's heart thumped a frantic rhythm. She smiled. She'd flown in a plane. She could go out with a man she liked.

Liked a lot.

She flexed her trembling fingers and opened the door. Her breath hitched.

John.

"Hi, Penn."

He wore dark jeans, a buttoned down shirt the color of storm clouds and a huge smile.

Joy unfurled in her chest and stretched all the way to curl her toes. "Come in. The aunts want to see you."

"You look beautiful, by the way." His voice, low, for her ears alone, ramped her pulse.

"Thanks. So do you." Her voice sounded breathless.

"A compliment. I'll take it although I admit I was hoping for 'handsome.'" His eyes skimmed up to the barrette. "You're hair looks nice like that."

She grazed the barrette. "Abby suggested it." Insisted had been more like it.

Jancie strode from the kitchen. "John. It's wonderful to see you."

He met her halfway and kissed her cheek. "It's good to see you up and around, Jancie. You look wonderful."

"I feel wonderful."

John sniffed. "Mmm. It smells like—"

"A bakery?"

"I was going to say, my grandmother's house."

Winnie appeared in the doorway with the laden gift bag in both hands. "Hooray. You're here. We've a present for you."

John arched both brows.

Winnie raised the bag. "We promised you baked good weeks ago, and we've been slow in fulfilling it."

He peeked inside. "You've had a lot going on

lately."

Penn rested a hand on her hip. "They baked today. All day. So that you'd have options."

John shifted the contents. "I see some chocolate chip bread and celebration cookies." He pulled them out of the bag. "That leaves cinnamon rolls. Yes." He high-fived Winnie. "And slices of pie. Is that pecan pie?"

"You know it." Winnie's grin wrinkled her whole face. "You can leave the bag here and get it on your way home so it won't be a bother on your bike. We just wanted to give it to you now since we'll likely be sleeping later."

"Thanks so much. I love all of these treats, but I can take the bag now. I traded my bike for a car."

Penn whirled toward him. No bike? She bit her lip. "You don't have your motorcycle anymore?"

He shrugged. "People kept telling me about these western Pennsylvania winters. I figured I'd need a car."

A knot clogged her throat. He traded his motorcycle?

No wrapping her arms around his waist?

And no snuggling up against him.

31

John smiled as he rounded the car after settling Penn into her seat. Was that disappointment clouding her face when she'd realized he'd sold his bike? Interesting.

He slid in beside her and pushed the key into the ignition.

"Nice car. It smells good in here." She stretched the seat belt to clasp the catch.

"Oh, yeah. That."

Nerves clenched his stomach. What if she hated his idea?

He'd racked his brain for something different, something special like her, but now when she questioned him with those big brown eyes...was his idea crazy? He rubbed his hand over his chin and faced her. John stretched his arm across the back of the seat. "Here's the deal. The Mars Astronomy club is hosting a star gazing event at Camp Trees tonight. I thought it might be fun to check it out."

Her eyes widened, but she didn't grimace or protest. So far so good.

"I picked up some food from Pines Tavern—is that a good gasp or an I-hate-that-place gasp?"

She grinned. "It's an I-love-that-place gasp."

He wiped his forehead. "Whew. I can breathe again. Anyway, I thought we could take it over to the camp and eat there while we wait for the stars to come

313

out."

"Sounds perfect."

He grabbed the steering wheel and turned the key. "Let's do it then."

~*~

Penn scooped a forkful of lemon risotto and let the creamy goodness slide down her throat.

John had chosen a secluded picnic table near the edge of the open field. He thought of everything including a checkered tablecloth. A thick candle flickered from a glass jar.

She surveyed the table crowded with cardboard boxes of culinary delights. A nationally recognized restaurant, Pines Tavern boasted chefs who regularly won awards and changed its menu every season to use the vegetables and herbs grown in their back-of-the-restaurant garden.

She spread her hands over the table. "The Pines is one of my favorite restaurants. I love it. Thanks for doing all this."

"Glad you like it. So you go a lot?" John speared another shrimp from the mixed seafood grill.

She laughed. "Hardly ever."

"But it's your favorite?"

"We'd go once a year when I was a little girl. Pines Tavern and the Northern Tier Library over in Gibsonia used to team up together and host a Christmas at the Pines children's breakfast the first Saturday in December. Tickets were a premium, not because of the cost but because of the limited number of seats. Every second Saturday in November, the aunts and I would wake up at what I thought must be the crack of dawn, drive over, stand in line, and buy our tickets."

A breeze threatened the candle.

John cupped his hand around the rim and saved the flame. "Must have been a special breakfast to go to all that trouble."

"Truly magical. The food was usually kid-friendly—waffles, scrambled eggs, maybe a fruit cup—but my favorite part was the entertainer. For a few years a professional storyteller told great stories." Leaning on her elbows, she clasped her hands. "One year a children's librarian read stories and then played her guitar while we sang Christmas carols. The second year we went, I won a door prize, a book I'd wanted for Christmas."

"Cool. Good for you." He rested his chin on his hand, his fork dangling loose in his fingers.

"I was thrilled." She pushed aside her plate. "The whole place was decorated like some beautiful Christmas village with two or three gorgeous trees packed with ornaments—for sale, of course. The aunts always bought one for me, as a surprise, and I opened it on Christmas Eve."

The silhouettes of the trees along the back of the field caught her attention. "Even the pictures hanging on the walls depicted Christmas scenes, cross stitched by the owner's wife or mother. I can't remember which." She scanned the open field, memories of the special times warming her. "It was such a beautiful place."

"Great memories."

She swung her focus to him. "The best. I hadn't thought of those breakfasts in a long time. Thanks for reminding me."

He held her gaze until the intensity tripped her

heart.

Penn glanced away.

"More people are arriving."

John dragged a box closer to her plate. "It's getting darker. We'd better eat up."

She arched backwards. "I can't eat another bite. I can't believe all this food—lobster bisque, two different salads, the seafood plate, and the steak dinner, not to mention the delicious sides. You must think I eat like a horse."

He waved his hands over the table. "We got choices. If we'd eaten at the restaurant, we'd have ordered this much."

"Maybe it looks like more when it comes in boxes."

"Last bite of the crab cake. You want it?"

She fanned her fingers over her stomach. "I'm stuffed."

"You didn't save room for dessert?" He popped the seafood morsel into his mouth.

"Dessert, too?"

He jutted his chin. "Of course."

"Maybe later?"

"Whatever you want."

She tilted her head. "What are the desserts?"

"Ah. Your stomach says, 'no,' but your sweet tooth is curious, huh?"

She crossed her arms. "I can wait. I don't have—"

"Heirloom Fudge Cake and Vanilla Bean Cheesecake."

"Two desserts?"

He stacked the trash and re-covered the leftovers. "Two people. Two desserts. I'll put these in the cooler, and we can settle in for the star show." He stowed the food and retrieved two chairs from the trunk.

Setting them up perpendicular to the picnic table, he eased himself beside her. "Comfortable?"

"Hmm. Thanks."

"I brought blankets if you get chilly." He tugged on her sleeve. "That little jacket might not be enough in a while."

Penn snuggled into her chair.

John took care of all the details. From the cooler for the leftovers to the chairs and blankets, to the flashlight he'd placed on the table when he blew out the candle. John oozed dependability, capability, and plain old, hard-to-resist charm.

He pointed to the crowd growing around a huge black tube. "The club's supposed to have a high-powered telescope here tonight. I guess that's it. We can walk over there if you want. I picked this spot so that we could talk without bothering the star gazers."

"I'm good here." Any other time, looking through the telescope, trying to find the rings around Saturn, finding Jupiter's moons would have been interesting, but tonight being part of a crowd oohing and aahing over the beauty of the heavens wasn't tempting. Tonight, being with John...

"Me, too. I have to tell you. I don't know anything about astronomy. I can sometimes find the Big Dipper. That's about it."

"There it is." She pointed left. "See the four stars that make up the bowl?"

"Where?' He leaned so close that she could smell the familiar spicy scent of his aftershave. Concentrate on the stars, not on his smell. "Right there. Beside the—"

"Cluster of little white dots?"

"No, silly—" Her dipper explanation evaporated.

His face hovered inches from hers, but his gaze was pointed to somewhere in the stars.

He pivoted.

If she'd moved an inch, her nose would have touched his, but he moved first, tilting his head and brushing her lips with his. "I've wanted to do that since you opened the door tonight."

Should she answer him? Maybe say, "me, too?" Maybe she did.

He grinned and palmed her cheek. His lips teased the base of her throat, explored the side of her neck, and claimed hers with a lazy, lingering kiss.

Thank goodness for her chair. Dizzy waves rippled through her brain.

She slid her hands up his chest to wrap around his neck, straining against him, wanting him closer. With her encouragement, he scooted nearer and deepened the kiss, tangling his fingers in her curls.

Excited voices carried from the crowd. He broke away, resting his forehead against hers, breathless. He pressed her hand against his chest. "Penny. Feel what you do to my crazy heart."

She kept her eyes closed. The reality of the cool night under the stars settled on her body. She shivered.

He kissed her cheek, then left to fetch a blanket from the backseat of the car. When he returned, he positioned his chair closer to hers and retracted the arms between them. "There. That's better." He tucked the tartan blanket around her and fit her under his arm. He threaded his fingers through hers.

"Warm now?" His breath ticked the top of her head.

"Toasty."

Very warm, in fact. The heat from his body pressed beside hers sent tingles in every direction. She scrunched in her seat, dropped her head back to take in the celestial view.

"Good idea." He copied her position. "I think we've missed some of the shooting stars, although I think we created some of our own."

She giggled.

He rolled his head toward her. "Corny, huh?"

"Just a tad."

"Sorry. You make me feel…"

"Like you have to say corny things?"

He snorted. "Cute. Like I don't know what to say. Like I'm tongue-tied."

Familiar feeling for her, but him? "I find that hard to believe."

"It's true, though."

His thumb's slow track over her wrist played with her concentration. Silence descended and lingered for several minutes.

"Like now. I want to ask you about the CPA exam, but I'm not sure if you want to talk about it."

She plucked at the wool blanket. "I'll talk about it."

"How was it? Have you heard your score?"

"I felt pretty good about it. Better than last time. A couple more weeks, and I should hear."

His thumb stilled against her wrist. "So you'll pass, get a fancy job, and move to the city?"

She shrugged. "I don't know."

"You don't know? What does that mean?"

"I've been thinking over the past few weeks. I love my life here. My aunts. My students. I'm reconnecting with Abby." She met his eyes. "You've been a part of my change in attitude, John." She traced the scar above his cheekbone. "You helped me see the value in my life here."

He glided his fingers through her curls and over her ear, cradling the back of her neck. "That sounds good." He kissed the corner of her eye. "Brings me to my next question. Does this new look at your life include me maybe?" He kissed the bridge of her nose.

She worked to concentrate on the conversation and not on his lips. "I hope so."

"Good." He kissed the corner of her other eye. "But, Penn, you remember that I'm a pilot." He sat back and left her blinking at his retreat.

"I remember. It's kind of hard to forget something like that." She leaned toward him.

He withdrew and loosened his hold on her shoulder. "You remember, too, it's the primary way I make a living, right?"

"Yes." How could she forget?

"Do you...think we could spend time together?" His eyes pinned hers. "See where this...attraction between us goes?" His bouncing leg wiggled the blanket.

"Yes."

He rubbed the back of his neck. "You don't think it'll be a problem?"

"I don't know. I don't want it to be." She tugged at his sleeve, wanted him to move closer again.

John drew in a breath and blew it out slowly. "Honest. I told you I like that." He gathered her hand with his, held it between his knees. "I get that you flying the other week was an extraordinary event. I won't ask you to fly somewhere just because you flew once. I saw how difficult it was for you." He kissed the back of her hand, flipped it over and left a matching kiss on her palm.

His caresses rendered her breathless. How could she answer him? "Thank you for saying that."

If he didn't let go of her hand, she'd have to snatch it away or lose her mind.

He caught her chin in his fingers, lifted her eyes to meet his. "I'm not just saying it, Penn. I know it." His thumb swiped her lips. "And even though my goal is to make a living writing, I still love flying. I love being up there."

"I know. I'm not asking you to stop." *But please stop talking and kiss me again.*

"So. You think we've got something interesting to pursue?" He kissed the corner of her mouth.

"Mmm. Most definitely." Her fingers found the silky hair at the nape of his neck, reveled in the softness and pushed him to her.

"Good." He tightened his arm around her again, stopped teasing her with kisses on her cheek, beside her eye, near her mouth, and finally covered her lips with his.

Epilogue

"Rabbit. Rabbit!" Winnie greeted Penn as she entered the kitchen and glanced out the window over the sink.

Jancie repeated the silly words.

Penn joined the game. "Rabbit. Rabbit."

Ever since Winnie heard a newscaster mention her family's unusual first-day-of-the-month greeting, she'd adopted it as their own.

Winnie poured Penn a cup of coffee. "Good morning, dear. I hope you slept well." Her gaze darted to the kitchen door. She wore a bright smile, a tad too bright before eight o'clock on a Saturday morning. "Remind me what you plan to do today?" She shot a look to the window.

Jancie dropped a dollop of rhubarb jam onto her slice of toast. "Oh, that reminds me. Andy left a message on the machine. Wants to know a good time to pick up his taxes."

Tax forms. Would her heart ever not thrill at the sound of her name associated with tax forms? Penn Davenport, Certified Public Accountant slash teacher. Penn Davenport, teacher slash Certified Public Accountant. It didn't matter which came first. She answered to both. *Thank You again for helping me pass the exam.*

She'd acquired four clients, not including her aunts, for her on-the-side tax business.

And as it so often did when happy thoughts filled her brain, her mind snapped to John. John. He'd been as patient as a rock with her over the past six months. Calling before taking off. Calling as soon as he landed.

She still prayed throughout his flights and sometimes was a little agitated, but panic didn't control her as it had before her own flight. She traced the rim of her mug with her fingertip.

"Penny, dear." Winnie knocked the table with her knuckles. "Hey, where'd you go, honey?"

Jancie dawdled at the sink, peering out the window.

"Sorry. Just thinking." Penn drained her coffee. "What is the deal with the window?"

Jancie grabbed the refrigerator door and stuck her head inside.

Winnie scratched her nose. "Ahmm. It may be April on the calendar, but the station is forecasting snow by the middle of next week. It's a little gray out this morning. You never told us your plans for today."

"Well, after I check on Peri—"

"Good plan." Winnie bobbed her head. "Checking on Peri."

Penn narrowed her eyes. "It's not good or bad. It's the normal plan. I check on him every day, remember?"

"Of course, we do." Jancie raised an eyebrow at Winnie. "What then, sweetie?"

Penn pointed a finger at both of them. "You two are up to something." What were they planning? "Or you wouldn't be so interested in my boring plans for today."

Jancie buttoned her navy cardigan. "We're going to run up to Wagner's Market and just wanted to know if you'd be here for lunch or not."

"Is that all?" She raked her nails across her chin. "Really?"

Jancie unbuttoned her cardigan. "Really. Would you like anything special?"

Their angelic faces revealed nothing. They didn't even blink. "You're planning something. I know it, but I'll let it go for now." She pushed her chair from the table. "I'll be here today. Al Martin and Mr. Blanton are picking up their taxes. I'll call and see if Andy wants to drop by, too." She stretched and yawned. "I better get out to Peri. He'll be wondering where I am."

Her garnet-colored barn jacket hung on a hook by the back door. She shrugged it over her shoulders. As she reached for a hat, a shriek froze her hand midway to the other hook.

"Oh, no. Don't wear that old cap." Winnie snatched the black and gold tassel cap off before Penn could grab it.

"What?"

"The pom-pom is about to fall off." Winnie stuffed it under her arm. "Here's a nice dark blue beret instead." She plopped it on top of Penn's head and fluffed curls around her face.

Penn shuffled away from Winnie's ministrations. "Will you stop already? I'm checking on Peri, not having my picture taken."

"You're right. Silly me." Winnie reached up again to tug the beret more to one side.

Penn batted Winnie's hand from the hat and kissed her on her cheek. "It's good. Thank you."

Winnie fidgeted with the cap. "All righty, then. We'll be shoving off, too."

Jancie plucked her jacket off a hook. "Come on,

sister." She handed Winnie hers. "Bundle up. It's still cold out there."

Penn trudged to the stable and enveloped her neck with her collar. The overcast sky blew a chilly breeze that ruffled curls peeking out of her beret. Snow might be forecasted for next week, but signs pointed to the possibility of earlier flakes.

Buds on the forsythia bushes along the side of the yard already showed a faint yellow tint. Maybe the snow wouldn't zap those fragile bits of color.

She raised the latch on the rough-hewn door. The hinges creaked, and Peri neighed an answer from his stall.

"Good morning, buddy. Did you think I wasn't coming? Huh?" She moved to her friend who hung his large head over the railing in greeting. "You might want to get your pasture time in early today. Looks like snow could happen. Smells like it outside, too."

She grabbed his face with both hands and snuggled her nose against his. "Although in here it smells like you and hay and," she wrinkled her nose, "other stuff."

Peri stomped his hooves.

"Hey, don't get me wrong. I like the way it smells in here." She opened the gate to the stall.

Peri shook his head and backed up.

"What? You don't want to go out? You love to go out. What's up?" She entered the stall with him, hey crackling under her feet. "Are you hurt?"

Concern knitted her countenance as she examined the front hooves.

Peri shook his head again.

She trained her eyes on his head and stepped to his rear. She ran her hands over the gaskin and down the cannon of each leg. Perfect.

"Peri? Come on. Don't you want to get out of here?"

The horse rocked his head, neighed for emphasis.

With his head movement, something glinted from the side of his neck. She inched toward his neck. Something was entwined in his mane. She inspected the thick black hair. A blue ribbon twisted within the coarse tresses. A periwinkle blue ribbon.

The ribbon was new, definitely not tangled in Peri's mane yesterday afternoon when she'd groomed him. She tugged on the ribbon and gasped.

Attached to the end was a ring. A platinum diamond ring. A beautiful, platinum, brilliant cut diamond ring with baguettes on each side. She drew the ring closer to her face, and the end of the ribbon, still tied to Peri's mane, lifted a hank of hair.

"I hope that's a good gasp."

Penn whirled toward John. Her heart flew to her throat.

A tentative smile hovered on his mouth.

She swallowed and grabbed a handful of the black mane to support her wobbling legs.

Acutely handsome in a vest, a green plaid shirt, and a tan Henley peeking out from underneath, he leaned against the door frame, his hands in his pockets.

"John."

He'd been gone all week, returning last night. They had plans for dinner tonight, but here he stood in her stable this morning.

"Do you like it?" He hadn't moved, his eyes glued to her movements.

"It's beautiful." She twirled the ring with trembling fingers.

He pushed away from the door jam and padded toward her. "I've had it for a while. I know you have your mom's ring, but I wanted to give you a ring. I wanted you to have your own."

John entered the stall, and Peri sidestepped, allowing him room. He loosened the knot. "I've planned a whole fancy night out on Mt. Washington for tonight. I made the reservations two weeks ago, but I can't wait any longer."

John freed the ribbon and dropped to one knee.

"Independence Jane Davenport. I love you. I love your courage and determination. I love how you love your aunts and your students. I'm so proud that you passed your CPA exam and have six clients already."

He clasped the hand holding the ring. "If you want to change your mind and move to the big city, I'm down with that. But I'm glad you decided to stay in Mars." He caressed her fingers. The ribbon dangled. "I know that being friends with a pilot was a big deal for you, and that was good. Right? Dating one has been even a bigger deal. But we've done that pretty successfully, wouldn't you say?" He raised his brows.

She nodded.

He licked his lips. "Then what about the next level? Marry me, Penn."

A marriage proposal. In her stable. To the man she loved.

Her heart squeezed and flipped and swelled till it stole every word from her throat. She found the tiny scar on his cheek and watched emotions play across his face. Pictures of him darted through her mind, winning her confidence as a friend, wooing her with slow, gentle steps over the past few months, entrusting her with secrets, forgiven and forgotten.

She kissed his scar. His skin, soft and warm, freshly shaved, smelled like spice and...a future. She lingered there, inhaling his scent, trailed her mouth down his strong jaw and pressed her lips against his.

He hauled her onto his knee, gathering her into his arms.

A squeak announced someone else wanted to join their party. They drew apart. Two heads peeking in the doorway, Jancie in her bright purple parka and Winnie in her hot pink one. Fake fur framed their shining faces.

"She said, 'yes!' She said, 'yes!'" Both of them clapped and skipped into the barn.

John loosened his arms around Penn. "Nope." He shook his head. "She didn't."

Both mouths dropped open, jostling the fur at their chins. "What? Penny? You didn't say 'yes?'"

Penn tightened her arms around him, digging her fingers into the black hair skimming the top of his jacket collar. "Didn't I say, 'yes?'"

"No. You left me hanging. You've left me here hanging, kneeling in humiliation—"

"Yes. Of course, yes." She spread her left hand in front of his chest to accept the ring. He obliged, slipping it over her finger, and clamped his mouth on hers again.

"She said, 'yes'." The aunts jumped up and down, and Peri stomped his feet behind them. "Oh, we've got a wedding to plan."

"And babies!"

Penn jerked her head toward the aunts. "What?"

John laughed. "We'll take it slow. A level at a time. Sound good?"

"Sounds great." And somewhere around the

region of her heart something shifted and settled and swelled so that she could barely breathe. She had Abby again. She had her aunts back. She had John.

Gifts from God.

She should contemplate those gifts right now, but she had other things to do like watching her ring sparkle and kissing John.

Yes, definitely. Kissing John.

Recipes

Celebration Cookies

1 cup butter
1 teaspoon vanilla
¾ cup packed brown sugar
2 cups plain flour
¾ cup white sugar
1 teaspoon salt
2 large eggs
2 cups old fashioned oatmeal
1 teaspoon baking soda, dissolved in 1 teaspoon water
12 ounces semisweet, mini chocolate chips

Cream butter and sugars with electric mixer. Add eggs one at a time. Beat well. Add dissolved baking soda and vanilla. Mix well. Add flour and salt. Stir in oatmeal and chocolate chips.

Drop dough by teaspoon onto ungreased cookie sheet or baking stone. Bake at 375 degrees for 8 to 12 minutes. Cool on wire racks.

Yield: Approximately 6-7 dozen cookies

Cinnamon Rolls

Dough
2 pints milk
4 ½ cups plain flour
½ olive oil
½ teaspoon baking powder
½ cup sugar
½ teaspoon baking soda
1 package dry yeast
2 teaspoons salt

Filling
1 cup melted butter
1 cup sugar
1/8 cup cinnamon
Icing
1 cup powdered sugar
½ teaspoon vanilla
1-2 tablespoons *milk
(more or less to make icing consistency)
*try using coffee, orange juice, or other liquids to change the flavor of the icing

Heat the milk, oil, and sugar in saucepan over medium heat. Do not boil. Allow to cool to lukewarm. Dissolve yeast in milk for 1 minute. Stir in 4 cups of flour until just combined. Cover and set aside in warm place for 1 hour.

To the mixture, add baking powder, baking soda, salt, and remaining flour. Combine thoroughly. Refrigerate dough for at least 1 hour.

Remove half the dough from bowl. On a floured baking surface, roll the dough into a large rectangle.

Pour 1/2 cup of melted butter on top of the dough. Spread butter evenly.

Sprinkle ½ cup of sugar and half of the cinnamon over the butter.

Starting with the short edge, roll the dough slowly and tightly. Pinch the end to seam together. Cut 1-inch slices with a sharp knife. Place the slices onto sprayed pans. Repeat with remaining dough.

Cover slices and let rise for 20 minutes.

Bake at 375 degrees for 13 to 17 minutes or until golden brown.

Mix the icing ingredients until desired consistency. Pour icing over hot rolls.

Yield: approximately 30 rolls

Yeast Rolls

2 cups warm water
¼ cup olive oil
2 packages dry yeast
1 egg, beaten
½ cup sugar
3 cups whole wheat flour
2 teaspoons salt
3 ½ to 4 cups plain flour

Dissolve yeast in warm water for five minutes in large mixing bowl. Add sugar, salt, olive oil, and egg. Mix well. Add about half the flour and mix well. Gradually add remaining flour and knead until dough is smooth and elastic (about 8 minutes).*

Cover and allow to rise till doubled in size. Punch down and form into rolls. Place into muffin tins. Allow to rise again.

Bake at 375 degrees for 12-15 minutes or until rolls are golden brown.

*At this point, the dough can be covered and refrigerated overnight to rise. Let come to room temperature and punch down before shaping into rolls.

Yield: at least 30 rolls

Chocolate Cake

12 ounces semi-sweet chocolate chips, divided
1 cup light sour cream
1 package chocolate cake mix
½ cup applesauce
¾ cup chocolate milk mix (like Ovaltine)
½ cup water
4 eggs
1 8-ounce tub frozen whipped topping

Mix cake mix, chocolate milk mix, eggs, sour cream, applesauce, and water with electric mixer until well blended. Stir in 1/3 cup chocolate chips. Pour batter into 2 9-inch round pans prepared with cooking spray.

Bake at 350 degrees 30 to 35 minutes until center springs when touched. Cool in pan for 10 minutes. Cool completely on wire racks.

Microwave frozen whipped topping and remaining chocolate chips for 1 minute. Stir, then microwave in 30-second increments and stir in between until chocolate is melted. Blend well. Let stand 15 minutes to thicken.

Frost layers with chocolate mixture. Store in refrigerator.

Scrolls

1 can refrigerated crescent rolls
Shredded sharp cheddar cheese
Italian seasoning or assorted spices and garlic (basil, rosemary, thyme, oregano)

Separate rolls into four rectangles. (If perforations to make the triangles separate, seal them back together with a fork.) Generously sprinkle cheese on top of the rectangles. Generously sprinkle the seasoning or spices on top of the cheese.

Roll up the rectangles beginning with the short side. With a sharp knife, cut the rectangle rolls into four spiral pieces. Lay the spirals, cut side up, on a greased, baking sheet or a baking stone.

Bake at 400 degrees for 10 or 12 minutes or until the tops are golden brown.

Red-Ribbon Pecan Pie

½ cup butter, softened
1 teaspoon vanilla
1 cup white sugar3 eggs
1 cup dark corn syrup
2 cups chopped pecans
½ teaspoon salt
1 pie shell

Mix butter, sugar, syrup, salt and vanilla. Beat in eggs. Fold in pecans. Pour into either 2 regular pie shells or 1 deep dish pie shell.

Bake at 350 degrees for 30-40 minutes or until the center is almost set.

This recipe won second place at the St. Richard's church picnic in Gibsonia, Pennsylvania, in 2001. Thank you to Auline Toler for this recipe.

Thank you

We appreciate you reading this White Rose Publishing title. For other inspirational stories, please visit our on-line bookstore at www.pelicanbookgroup.com.

For questions or more information, contact us at customer@pelicanbookgroup.com.

White Rose Publishing
Where Faith is the Cornerstone of Love™
an imprint of Pelican Ventures Book Group
www.PelicanBookGroup.com

Connect with Us
www.facebook.com/Pelicanbookgroup
www.twitter.com/pelicanbookgrp

To receive news and specials, subscribe to our bulletin
http://pelink.us/bulletin_

May God's glory shine through
this inspirational work of fiction.

AMDG

Free Book Offer

We're looking for booklovers like you to partner with us! Join our team of influencers today and receive at least one free eBook per month. Maybe more!

For more information
Visit http://pelicanbookgroup.com/booklovers
or e-mail
booklovers@pelicanbookgroup.com

CPSIA information can be obtained at www.ICGtesting.com
Printed in the USA
LVOW07s0328070915

453096LV00003BA/104/P

9 781611 164985